THE DANGEROUS DESCENT

Tennington glanced at his watch. "Almost noon." He looked down to a broad shelf of rock many yards below—separated from them by a sheer drop of wall. "If we can reach that shelf, we'll have it. Then we can stop and have a bite to eat."

They picked their ropes from the packs.

"Wait," said Fallon. "I think one rope will do it." He dropped one end of his rope over the edge of the ledge, lowering it to its full length. It landed only a foot from the shelf. "Good!" he exclaimed, and knotted the uppermost end about a round rock formation almost a foot in diameter. "It might slip," he observed. "Tenny, keep an eye on it. I'll slide down the rope first and see how safe it is."

Fallon descended in safety to the shelf. Then he steadied the rope for Ramón's careful descent. Marcelina followed, then Valera, and finally Sir Wilbur. But without the Englishman there to steady the round rock to which the rope was secured, Sir Wilbur had only halfway completed his descent when Fallon shouted: "Look out, Tenny! The rope's slipping!"

Other *Leisure* books by T. V. Olsen:
LONE HAND
RATTLESNAKE
A KILLER IS WAITING
BLOOD RAGE
DEADLY PURSUIT
LONESOME GUN
EYE OF THE WOLF
TRACK THE MAN DOWN
KENO
STARBUCK'S BRAND
MISSION TO THE WEST
BONNER'S STALLION
BREAK THE YOUNG LAND
THE STALKING MOON
BLOOD OF THE BREED
LAZLO'S STRIKE
WESTWARD THEY RODE
ARROW IN THE SUN
RED IS THE RIVER
THERE WAS A SEASON

TREASURES

OF THE

SUN

T.V. OLSEN

LEISURE BOOKS   NEW YORK CITY

A LEISURE BOOK®

August 2001

Published by special arrangement with Golden West
Literary Agency.

Dorchester Publishing Co., Inc.
276 Fifth Avenue
New York, NY 10001

If you purchased this book without a cover you should be aware that
this book is stolen property. It was reported as "unsold and
destroyed" to the publisher and neither the author nor the publisher
has received any payment for this "stripped book."

Copyright © 1998 by Beverly Butler Olsen and Golden West
Literary Agency

This story is a work of fiction and any resemblance to incidents or
persons living or dead is purely coincidental.

The author wishes to acknowledge the technical assistance of Pedro
Castaneda concerned with the Peruvian aspects of this story.

All rights reserved. No part of this book may be reproduced or
transmitted in any form or by any electronic or mechanical means,
including photocopying, recording or by any information storage
and retrieval system, without the written permission of the
publisher, except where permitted by law.

ISBN 0-8439-4904-X

The name "Leisure Books" and the stylized "L" with design are
trademarks of Dorchester Publishing Co., Inc.

Printed in the United States of America.

Visit us on the web at www.dorchesterpub.com.

Your children are not your children.

They are the sons and daughters of Life's longing for itself.

. . . You may give them your love but not your thoughts,

. . . for their souls dwell in the house of tomorrow,

which you cannot visit, not even in your dreams.

—Kahlil Gibran, *The Prophet*

Chapter One

"Tell me, Chris," said Sir Wilbur Tennington, thoughtfully fingering his pipe, "have you ever heard of the lost city of Haucha deep in the heart of Peru?"

Christopher Fallon regarded him quietly for a moment. He was tall, dark, and lanky, having just arrived in San Francisco after having acted as field guide and trouble-shooter on an expedition to the upper Amazon in search of rare species of tropical fish sponsored by Rudolf Stamm of New York, a wealthy piscatologist and aquarist. He had last worked together with Sir Wilbur during an excursion to Egypt in quest of archeological artifacts with Dr. Mindrum W. C. Bliss of the Bliss Museum of Egyptian Antiquities. Sir Wilbur had cabled Fallon while still aboard ship, sailing back to San Francisco from South America. Since already for several months in 1922 Fallon had had his share of strange adventures in the Brazilian wilderness, he longed for nothing so much now as a little time to rest before returning to the small family ranch in Arizona, but here in his hotel room Sir Wilbur Tennington was finally getting around to his purpose in having sent that cable.

"I don't think so, Tenny," Chris Fallon said cautiously.

"A most fascinating tale," explained Sir Wilbur, reclining lazily in the chair where he sat. "Perhaps, however, you've heard the legend of the Inca who . . . ?"

"Possibly," interrupted Fallon, "but I really know very little about the Incas."

Tennington's ruddy, stoical Celtic features now registered a trace of annoyance. But Fallon remained silent with an attentive expression, as Sir Wilbur launched into his narrative.

"In the Sixteenth Century," he continued, "the Incas were the great ruling tribe of the vast Empire of the Sun in what now is Peru. They considered themselves the People of the Sun. *Pirua,* in fact, was their word for the planet Jupiter, and to this day it has remained the name of the country. Prior to the Spanish invasion, the Incas had attained a degree of culture and government probably unparalleled in all of what was to become New Spain. Their ancestors dated back to the time of Christ, though they made their first substantial gains in culture beginning in the Twelfth Century.

"They were expert farmers, knew irrigation, were great builders of roads throughout their empire. They built houses of granite or sun-dried adobe, but so wealthy were they that they ornately and lavishly embellished their palaces and temples with gold and silver. They were excellent weavers and skilled workers in metal. They actually had decorative gardens made up of tropical flowers and plants designed entirely from gold and silver.

"The emperor of the ruling family was called the Inca. You see, this was not a hereditary title, but one filled by selection. In Fourteen Ninety-Three the empire attained the very apex of splendor under the rule of Huayna Capac, the last Inca before the invasion. Upon Huayna Capac's death, probably in Fifteen Twenty-Seven, there were two claimants to the throne of the Incas. One was Atahuallpa, king of the province of Quito. The other was his brother Huascar, the legionnaire sovereign who ruled over the rest of the Empire of the Sun.

"In a bloody war, Atahuallpa conquered and imprisoned Huascar and assumed the throne of the Incas. But the powerful empire had been severely weakened by this civil war, and it was in this weakened condition that Francisco Pizarro, the cruel, unscrupulous Spanish adventurer, found the country when he landed at Tumbes in Fifteen Thirty-One.

"At this time the war between Atahuallpa and Huascar was in its final stage of termination. Pizarro seized his opportunity. Realizing the danger of advancing far into Peru with a following of only a hundred men or so, Pizarro by means of a ruse of friendship was able to capture Atahuallpa.

"Atahuallpa, in an effort to gain his liberty, offered to fill a room in which he stood with as much gold as the height of his upstretched arm. Having obtained the ransomed gold, the treacherous Pizarro, instead of releasing Atahuallpa, put the Inca to death by strangling. Thus commenced the beginning of the end for the great empire of the Incas. Weakened by internal strife, it became prey to the conquering Spaniards. The empire was dissolved. The Spaniards began their own administration. The Incas were reduced to slavery to sate their conquerors' thirst for gold, but the race was not exterminated. Eventually they became respected inhabitants of Peru. Doctor Luis Valera, professor in archeology at the University of California in Berkeley and attached to the San Franscio Museum which is co-sponsoring this expedition, believes there may be Incan blood in his own family. He will accompany us, if you agree to join me on this journey.

"At any rate, to get back to what I was saying. Many of the great Inca cities, centers of culture, were occupied or fell into ruin and decay. Some of them were lost to the memory of man. Others became mere legends of antiquity. In Nineteen Eleven Hiram Bingham discovered the lost Incan city of Machu Picchu. There is one more that is believed to have existed, perhaps the most ancient of all, Haucha, named for the planet Saturn, an almost mythical place, and it was from here, presumably, that the Incas were supposed to have come originally before they founded their mighty kingdom with its capital at Cuzco. Haucha has been presumed to contain a tremendous store of wealth. But all this is history.

9

"Until now, it has been generally assumed that Machu Picchu was actually Haucha, but a certain finding of mine recently has borne out . . . to my satisfaction, at least . . . that this is not the case."

Chris frowned. "What sort of a finding, Tenny?"

"I'll show you," smiled the Englishman with pride. "I made this discovery while browsing in a small, musty antique shop in Gibraltar when, at the bottom of a back shelf littered with the accumulated manuscript miscellany of years, I came across . . . *this*."

He rose, drew from his coat pocket a carefully coiled scroll of paper, and unrolled it in the light of the table lamp, producing from within the roll an ancient, yellowed, frayed bit of parchment paper. Fallon was suddenly very interested and crowded close to examine the missive.

It was apparently a partial map, with all the lettering written in a fine, close hand in a language that appeared to be Spanish. There were symbols indicative of a mountain range and plateau region and certain lines evidently representing routes and trails.

Sir Wilbur Tennington carefully turned over the parchment, and on the other side was a long, closely written narrative in the same language.

"Spanish," said Fallon. "But what is it?"

Sir Wilbur nodded excitedly. "It's Spanish, all right . . . I had a time deciphering it, Chris . . . but Professor Valera has authenticated it, and, if the story recorded here is genuine, then this map is our key to the lost city of Haucha."

"But who wrote it?" asked Chris. "And how did it get into an old curiosity shop in Gibraltar?"

"Well, according to the story on the back, the writer of this document was a soldier in Pizarro's army . . . a man named Fernando García. By his own account, García was a scholar who joined the army because of the persecution he had experienced in Spain due to certain of his religious beliefs. He was in the party that came from Spain to supplement Pizarro's force as he launched a full-scale offensive to what turned out to be the Incan empire.

"One party of the Incas, however, containing some rich and influential men of high office escaped the clutches of Pizarro in Cuzco, the Incan capital city, and fled toward the east, into the Andean wilderness beyond. Pizarro feared that these men might return some day and cause trouble. He tortured some of the Incas into divulging the direction taken by those who had escaped and learned also that they were fleeing to the refuge of a mountain stronghold . . . called Haucha . . . many days' march to the east.

"Pizarro forthwith sent a force of soldiers after these Incas with one of the natives as a guide. There was also to be considered, Pizarro thought, the fabulous wealth of this fabled city of which he had heard . . . a wealth by no means to be dismissed as fancy.

"For weeks the Spaniards, with their Indian guide, followed the fleeing Incas across desert and mountain and jungle. Fernando García was in this little party of pursuing Spaniards, and he relates the hardships and terrors that beset them. They were in unfamiliar country and could trust only to their guide, who might well be misleading them. Their heavy armor and weapons and the strain of unaccustomed travel on foot coupled with wild beasts, savage tribesmen, and fever together with the fact that they were not inured to the tropical heat finished many of them and severely impeded their progress. At one time, García relates, they were traveling over a mountain when they were attacked by giant birds that pecked one man to death.

"Eventually, however, a mere handful of the *conquistadores* came at last to the hidden plateau above which, their guide informed them, lay the city of Haucha. The entire plateau con-

11

sisted of a barrier cliff that even the nimblest mountain goat could not scale. The only entrance by which one could gain access to the top of this plateau was by a sharp, deep cleft, or cañon, that cut right through the surrounding cliff. For centuries, apparently, it had been the only means of ingress or egress to the city of Haucha.

"But the Incas had seen the Spaniards coming from afar, for they had had a guard posted at the top of the plateau to warn them of any pursuit. Therefore, when the Spaniards started to enter the plateau and crossed over to a gorge that bounded the fortress city, the Incas from the cliff on which the city stood rolled boulders down and started an avalanche that buried the pursuing Spaniards beneath tons of rock and, later, closed up access to the great plateau forever, so that no one could ever again enter or depart from it. Hence, they had destroyed their pursuers, but they had done it at the price of trapping themselves forever in the fortress city.

"Only one Spaniard escaped and lived long enough to tell the story . . . Fernando García. He was a little behind his companions as they entered the gorge when the landslide was loosed upon them by the Incas from above. Once the first rocks descended, García turned and ran for his life. Great boulders thundered and bounded all about him, but by a miracle he emerged from the gorge unharmed before the main slide of rock hit.

"Now he was safe, but he had no food, and the Lord knew how many miles lay between him and his fellows back at Cuzco. Suppose that he could traverse that savage wilderness of feverish swamp and rugged mountains? . . . how would he ever find his way back? He knew no more than that he must travel in a general westerly direction. And yet, somehow, by the grace of Providence, García did make it!

"He made his way alone and inadequately armed, eating

12

only what he killed on the way, through as savage a country as existed in the world. He evaded beasts of prey and hostile native tribes, and staved off hunger and weariness long enough to stagger into Cuzco and fall at the feet of Pizarro, saying . . . '*Señor*, the mission is done. These Incas will trouble you no more, for they are held forever by a trap of their own making.'

"But García was a dying man. The jungle and swamp had done their work. He was expiring of malnutrition brought on by lack of food, and he was attacked also by a fever he had contracted while on his journey . . . possibly malaria which, then, was deadly.

"His last act was to pen his adventure down on the ancient sheet of parchment you see here, together with a map of the way to Haucha, for he had made notes of the route on the return journey. Whose hands this parchment passed into afterwards, there is no way to ascertain, and, of course, we cannot know how it . . . a treasure, priceless beyond belief . . . finally found its way to an obscure antique shop there in Gibraltar where it had been rolled up for heaven knows how many generations. It is surprising to me personally that Doctor Robertson, the collector of Peruvian antiquities who assembled so many manuscripts and documents associated with the Peruvian conquest which he eventually donated to the British Museum for safekeeping, did not locate it. If he had, I'm sure he would have paid a higher price for it than I did. The dealer from whom I bought it said that he hadn't looked closely at the document before, and that it might well have been there when he purchased the shop many years ago."

Sir Wilbur Tennington could tell a story. His graphic, vivid narrative had held Chris Fallon entranced. But now Fallon inquired skeptically: "How can you . . . and Professor Valera . . . be sure this parchment isn't a fake?"

"Its tremendous age, for one thing . . . also its obviously archaic style. I realize it may be only a 'plant,' as you Americans put it, to snare unwary suckers like myself, and there are processes for lending a bit of paper an aged aspect. In fact, I might almost believe this might have been the case, except for one thing."

"What?"

"It wouldn't have been worth the trouble unless that dealer were trying to put his hooks into me for a big amount of cash . . . and I only paid two pounds for it."

"It might still be the trick of some practical joker," Fallon observed pragmatically. "Even if it is authentic, the old gent who you say wrote it might have been out of his head with fever. The map's also very probably inaccurate."

"I don't think so," Tennington shook his head, "nor does Professor Valera, and he has been able to convince the curator and other museum officials of its authenticity. Remember, García was an intelligent and educated man . . . not just any common soldier. He'd have a penchant for accuracy in description. The document itself bears that out. I'd be willing to bet on that. As for the map, Valera has worked diligently to elaborate its details from what is now known of Peruvian topography."

"So?" queried Fallon teasingly, "I suppose you and the professor want to go off after treasure?"

"Not so much for the sake of treasure," Sir Wilbur assured him. "I have about all of that I require . . . as you know, my father left me a considerable inheritance that covers not only my estate in Devonshire but also a fund from which I receive a sum of money every year. It comes to an annuity of some thirty thousand pounds, and that enables me to pursue any exploration I may choose. After all, I helped finance Doctor Bliss's Egyptian excavations in Ethiopia, didn't I? God's truth, Chris, is I can't abide staying in one spot very long. Indeed, I most re-

14

cently concluded a journey to Afghanistan, and after three weeks I'm already growing weary of San Francisco."

Fallon smiled. "I'd be lying to you if I didn't say it is the thought of an ancient city that attracts me. I've had my fill of a life of danger lately just to bring back some rare varieties of tropical fish."

Sir Wilbur grinned. "I doubt in any event we'll get much gold. The Peruvian government has its claim on lost treasures. However, if you care to go along as our field guide, it should certainly prove rewarding for us both. And while I would agree that the thrill of finding the fabulous seven cities of Cibola once inspired the *conquistadores* four hundred years ago primarily because of their gold, in the monetary terms of today I'm only able to stake you to two hundred a week . . . pounds, not dollars."

"Three months in South America with Rudolf Stamm, and now again for at least as long," Fallon reflected. "We might fly, you know."

"Not into this wilderness, Chris," cautioned Tennington. "Besides, unless we're on foot, we cannot follow the landmarks. I have already booked reservations for us on the *Sea Queen*." He was obviously as excited as he ever permitted himself to become by anything. "In fact . . . ," he added a little sheepishly, "I hope you don't mind terribly, but I've already booked passage for you."

Fallon laughed. "You've got it all figured out, haven't you, Tenny? When are we to leave?"

"Tomorrow. Can you get packed and ready to leave by then?"

"No rush, eh?" Fallon asked in amusement.

Tenny protested mildly. "It's been a long time already for me, and I'd like to be on the move. Oh . . . I forgot to tell you . . . there will be a young, attractive lady coming with us."

"What . . . ?" Chris began when the telephone rang in the room.

The Englishman got up from the table at which they were sitting and answered it. "Hello?"

"This is the room clerk, sir. There are two gentlemen here in the lobby who wish to see you. They are quite insistent."

"I told you I cannot be disturbed," Tennington replied impatiently. "Please convey my regrets to them."

"I did, sir, but. . . ."

Tennington hung up. "These confounded newspaper men!" he said irritably. "Heavens, but I'm tired of them."

"The price of fame," said Chris Fallon.

"On the other hand, did you see that picture of Valera and myself in the *Chronicle*, and the little story about the expedition?" the Englishman inquired.

"No. Tenny, I just got here, and came almost at once to this hotel."

"Well, all that to one side, I get bloody well tired of it." Sir Wilbur sighed. "It was the same way after that trip of ours to Egypt and Ethiopia. Of course, that one was of tremendous historical and ethnological importance. Heavens, I believe I've received a thousand telegrams or letters of inquiry and congratulations from Egyptologists. I still find it a bit difficult to believe . . . a real portion of ancient Egypt in the heart of Ethiopia, where the people live just as did their ancestors on the Nile countless generations ago."

"You'll be on the heels of another discovery," said Fallon, "if you can really locate this lost ruin of Haucha."

"Well, I don't mind confessing I'll be pleased to have you along, if you bring me the same kind of luck you did on our last expedition," said Sir Wilbur. "You're an exceedingly capable fellow in a pinch."

"Why, that's a right nice thing for you to say, Tenny,"

drawled Chris. "But what's this about a girl going along? That will be nothing but trouble."

There was a knock on the door. Sir Wilbur, who was still on his feet, scowled. "These news hawks don't seem to realize that when one of His Majesty's subjects says, no, he means *no!*"

But the two men who confronted the Englishman's startled gaze as he opened the door were quite obviously not newspaper reporters. The first was lean and of diminutive stature. His face was thin and bronzed with a long nose and tightly compressed, almost bloodless lips. His eyes were black and piercing and glittered with a dark inner intelligence. A distinguished cast was lent to him by a small black mustache and short goatee, but his black suit and black felt hat, pulled low, gave him the appearance of a villain in a stage melodrama.

The older man who stood a little to his rear was a giant Negro, similarly attired except for a red fez. He was close to seven feet in height. His face was thick and flat, and he regarded the occupants of the room with a dull, unblinking gaze.

"Have I the honor of addressing Sir Wilbur Tennington?" asked the lean man in a gentle guttural voice that bore a markedly foreign accent. "My card, sir."

Tennington read aloud: "Don Estaban de Ferrar." He looked up, flustered, and said: "Pardon me, sir. I had the notion that you were a pair of newsmen. Come in . . . sit down, won't you?"

"Thank you, sir," replied Ferrar as he stepped inside, removing his hat to expose black, sleekly combed hair.

The giant Negro followed and stood by Ferrar's chair when he sat down, making no move to seat himself.

"My associate, Abdullah Simbel."

"And this is my friend and often field guide, Chris Fallon."

Ferrar nodded politely to the American.

"Sit down," Sir Wilbur said to the Negro.

The man made no reply, but remained standing by Ferrar's chair. Only when Ferrar looked up at him insistently did Abdullah seat himself, shifting his great bulk into the chair that had been indicated by Sir Wilbur. Once seated, he again surveyed them with unblinking eyes.

"Abdullah forgot momentarily that we are now in America where all men are equal," murmured Ferrar in apparent humor, as he removed an Egyptian cigarette from a jewel-encrusted gold case and tapped it. "Years ago, in Tunis, I encountered Abdullah who belonged to a Turk who had threatened to cut his tongue out for vilifying his master. I bore that Turk a grudge for cheating me in a bargain. Later, when I had opportunity to kill that Turk, I also freed his slaves. Since then, Abdullah has been my associate."

"By choice," boomed the giant black man.

"Thank you," Ferrar said as Tennington leaned forward with his pipe lighter and lit Ferrar's cigarette for him with the long flame. Then Sir Wilbur sat back, picked up his bulldog pipe, and began lighting it.

Ferrar blew a cloud of tobacco smoke and fixed the Englishman with a piercing gaze. Fallon, having risen when they entered, had not resumed his chair — Ferrar had taken it — and was now leaning unobtrusively with folded arms against the wall near the door. He stirred uneasily. There was a suggestion of something he didn't like in Ferrar's manner.

"I will get right to the point, Sir Wilbur," Ferrar said quietly. "I wish to buy from you the document you purchased at that little curio shop in Gibraltar." At the astonishment registered on the face of the Englishman, Ferrar smiled. "Certainly you are surprised. However, permit me to enlighten you. I am a Spaniard, directly of the line on my grandmother's side descended from Francisco Pizarro."

It was possible, upon a moment's consideration on Fallon's

part as well as Sir Wilbur's, to give credence to these words and perhaps even to believe that this man might conceivably be a reincarnation of the dark-faced, large-eyed, black-bearded man who had done to the Incas of Peru what his fellow conqueror, Hernando Cortés, had done to the Aztecs of Mexico.

"My ancestor," continued Ferrar, "possessed a parchment map written by Fernando García, one of his soldiers who had been to the lost Incan stronghold of Haucha, a map showing the location of a fabulous treasure. He never used it, however, and the family eventually lost it. For nearly ten years now I have been searching for that ancient *pergemina*. I have spent many thousands. I have followed vague clues all over Europe . . . always false clues . . . and I was discouraged when, at last, I attained a little information that convinced me the map had never been taken to Europe at all. I was born in Peru and still own property there. I went back to Peru and eventually traced the map to Gibraltar. When my inquiries still turned up nothing, I was practically ready to consider my quest hopeless, when I came to this one shop. But at my inquiry, the dealer informed me he had sold just such a document to an English gentleman minutes before.

"I ran frantically outside and hailed you just as you entered a cab, but it was too late. The cab drove off, although I caught a clear glimpse of your profile disappearing around a corner before I could obtain the license number of the taxi, and there was no other nearby cab in which I could pursue you.

"I returned, however, and questioned the antique dealer. He knew absolutely nothing about you. For an hour I roamed the streets, despairing. I knew your face and your nationality, but nothing more, and you were probably a traveler who would be leaving Gibraltar soon. Then I found a newspaper . . . the London *Times*, I believe . . . and there was an article in it about certain antiquities acquired by the British Museum as the result of an African expedition to Egypt and Ethiopia which you had headed some time before the war. Fortunately, there was a photo of you accompanying this article. Upon my arrival in San Francisco, still in pursuit of you, I saw the article about you and Professor Luis Valera in the San Francisco *Chronicle*. The article indicated you were staying at the Sir Francis Drake. What could be simpler? It was pure serendipity that you came across this document, for the dealer assured me he had had no knowledge of it . . . that you had found it and shown it to him for the first time . . . and had I come in only a few minutes sooner, he would have informed me that there was no such document in his shop."

"And now," said Sir Wilbur, fixing the Spaniard with his bleak blue eyes, "you wish to buy the map?"

"Exactly."

"I deplore disappointing you after your long and discouraging search," replied the Englishman slowly, "but I fear I sha'n't sell it at any price."

"Not for . . . ten thousand American dollars?"

Tennington raised his eyebrows. "No."

"Twenty thousand!"

"I'm sorry."

"Fifty thousand . . . my final offer, sir."

Tennington's cherubic face reddened to the roots of his immaculate blond hair. He rose to his feet impatiently. "*Señor* Ferrar," he said deliberately, "money is not the issue. I have about all I need, and apparently you likewise have all you require from the nature of your extravagant offer. I am an explorer, as you know. I like to mix archeology with my explorations. It's for that purpose that I intend to undertake an expedition to Peru with Professor Luis Valera and Chris Fallon on a quest for the lost city of Haucha. Our passages are already booked on the *Sea Queen*. She sails tomorrow . . . and most of the treasure, if any, should it really be found, would rightly be claimed by the Peruvian government. The San Francisco Museum has agreed to help finance this excursion in exchange for what artifacts we may be able to bring back, preferably some dating back to the single dynasty of Incan rule that may have been preserved. I am very sorry, sir, but effectually all of this does rather leave you out, whatever your familial claims."

"There is more than archeology at stake here," Ferrar pressed quietly. "A manuscript I examined in the British Museum . . . *Inscripciones, medallas, templos, edificios, antigüedades, y monumentos del Peru,* dating from about the time of Charles the Third, approximately Fifteen Eighty-Five . . . indicates that there was a secret hall in the fortress of Cuzco where an immense treasure was concealed, consisting of full-scale statues of each of the Incas wrought in pure gold. Doña Maria de Esquivel, the wife of the last Inca, confirmed to the anonymous chronicler of this document that she actually saw these statues, and also many vessels of silver and gold. There is every reason to believe, since they were not found by my ancestor, Francisco Pizarro, or any of his followers, that these *tesoros del sol* . . . these treasures of the Sun were possibly among those transported overland to the fortress city of Haucha. Do you know what that name means in ancient Incan? Haucha was the Incan name for the planet Mars."

Sir Wilbur gravely shook his head. "You may be right about what was transported," he conceded, "but you are most likely wrong, as you are about the meaning of Haucha. It was the Incan name for the planet Saturn. As for any treasure, we sha'n't know until we get there, shall we?"

He put down his pipe and rose, indicating that the meeting was at an end.

The Spaniard smiled slowly — a pleasant smile, perhaps, but also suggestive of dark menace. "You are foolish, my

21

English friend," he said softly. "That *pergemina* is rightfully mine."

Perhaps the Celtic strain in Sir Wilbur's ancestry prompted the stubborn anger that now kindled in his eyes like a blue flame. "Are you threatening me?" he demanded.

"You leave me no choice," rejoined Ferrar.

Just from where he produced it, no one saw, but they all abruptly caught the steel gleam of a .38 Enfield in Ferrar's hand.

Chapter Two

Luis Valera and his wife, Francisca, lived in a bungalow in San Francisco on Laguna Street, between Vallejo and Post. By streetcar he had only to transfer once to reach the small cubbyhole of an office he maintained at the San Francisco Museum. The family Ford, parked now in the narrow driveway adjacent to the bungalow, was used when he had to go to the university where he lectured in the anthropology, history, and archeology of native American civilizations in South America. Both he and Francisca were Peruvians by birth, although Valera had been lecturing at the University of California in Berkeley since before the Great War.

The master bedroom on the second floor of the Valera bungalow had served for several years now as the professor's study and map room. Since his youth in Lima, Valera had been fascinated by the Incan civilization, and he had visited the ruins at Cuzco and Quito several times before coming to the United States. In the center of his study was a rectangular table on which he had constructed by means of plaster of paris, meshing, and water colors an elaborate topographical small-scale map of the Incan empire as it had existed prior to the Spanish conquest. The topography of that empire from its center in the Andes up and down the western coastline of South America encompassed more land than even had the Roman Empire and was perhaps only equaled by the far-flung, discontinuous British Empire of the present day. Valera's table-top map had necessarily to be on a very small scale in order to accommodate such a vast land surface, and there were a series of tiny flags mounted on pins to mark the remains of temples, palaces, fortresses, terraced mountains, military roads (also indicated by narrow, hand-painted lines), and aqueducts. Even more remarkable were the broader white lines that indicated the great roads whose broken remains Valera had personally seen and traced. What had survived all the centuries since was still sufficiently imposing to attest to their former magnificence.

There had been several of these great roads, but most impressive were the two that extended from Quito to Cuzco and, diverging from the ancient capital, continued in a southern direction toward Chile. Based on the fragments that remained, Valera estimated their geophysical length had once been nearly two thousand miles. Stone pillars, in the manner of European milestones, had been erected at intervals of somewhat more than a league all along these routes, and many of them still could be seen, although buried in many cases by accretion or vegetation that had reclaimed the ancient byways. One of these roads passed over the grand plateau, and the other along the lowlands on the border of the ocean. The road over the grand plateau was perhaps the greatest engineering achievement because of the rugged character of the country. It had been laid over pathless sierras buried in snow. Galleries had been cut for leagues through living rock. Rivers were crossed by means of bridges suspended in the air. Valera had constructed his small-scale models from balsa wood and thread, although the originals had been made from the tough fibers of maguey, the osier of the Incas, woven into cables of the thickness of a man's body. These huge ropes were stretched across the channels above the water, strung through rings or holes cut in immense buttresses of stone raised on the opposite banks of the plunging mountain rivers, and there secured to heavy pieces of timber. Several of these enormous cables, bound together, formed the bridge itself, covered with well-secured planks and defended by railings also made of woven maguey that afforded safe passage.

Some of these aerial bridges had exceeded two-hundred feet, causing them, confined as they were by the extremities, to dip with an alarming inclination toward the center. There was no doubt in the professor's mind that what he loved most about San Francisco was that it, too, was bound to opposing masses of land by gigantic suspension bridges, and he could never pass over them, on the way to the university or driving elsewhere beyond the city, without marveling at how wondrous must have been these Incan bridges, and how awesome it must have been for a passenger afoot to experience the oscillation of their suspension as his eye would wander over the dark waters that foamed and tumbled many a fathom beneath him.

Valera had been able, by means of studying the account of Haucha in Sir Wilbur Tennington's possession, to locate its probable whereabouts in the vastness of the Andean mountains, and true to form the ancient citadel had been joined to its only access road by means of a great suspension bridge that had finally, for reasons of self-protection from the invading Spaniards, been severed, plunging into the gorge far below it.

"May I trouble you for a match?" asked a low, melodious voice at the professor's elbow, disturbing his reveries.

Valera, from where he was sitting, studying his topographical map, turned to find himself looking into the blue-gray eyes of Marcelina O'Day. Her reddish-brown, lustrous hair was attractively arranged in a marcel. She had high cheekbones, a straight and slender nose upturned slightly at the round tip, and she was shyly smiling. She was wearing a pair of white jodhpur breeches with highly polished black jodhpur boots. She seemed somehow very young, although the cigarette in her mouth made her appear older. She appeared to sparkle with the joy of living.

He turned, mumbled something, and pulled out a box of matches.

As he lighted her cigarette, she acknowledged the courtesy with a polite: "Thank you, *Tío* Luis."

Valera rose and walked over toward the rolltop desk at a right angle to the three curtained windows through which shone the late-afternoon sun. He selected a small, hand-rolled cigar from a tin and lit it before putting away the matches.

"Women should not smoke," he stated bluntly.

Marcelina smiled at him in a friendly manner, her eyes bright with anticipation. "What do you think of my outfit?" she asked, stepping back slightly and turning in a circle.

"I think she looks very much the rôle, Luis," Francisca Valera said. She had entered the study behind Marcelina. She had very black hair, dark eyes, and a smile flashed, revealing bright, perfect teeth. She wore a print dress that Luis thought very becoming. Francisca was more sober than Marcelina, a quality Luis regarded as most becoming in a woman.

"What rôle is that?" Valera snapped, but only his tone was stern, not his eyes as they remained on Francisca.

"Of an explorer," supplied Marcelina.

"You know, I am still uncertain of the prudence of this, Marcie," Valera remarked.

"Her father gave his permission," Francisca reminded. "Of what use is this education she has been receiving if it hasn't prepared her . . . ?"

"I have showed both of you the probable location of Haucha," said Valera, waving a hand toward the topographical table map. "It will be very dangerous. Even I have had second thoughts about going, Marcie, and, as much as I love Francisca and will miss her, I would not ask her to make this trip."

"Nor would I go," Francisca responded, "even if you asked me. But that is not to say Marcie shouldn't. You thought it a good idea for her to study archeology, not exactly a traditional subject for young women."

"I agree," said Valera.

"I might have gone to Mills College," interjected Marcelina.

"God forbid," said Valera, puffing at his small cigar. "But the world is changing," he observed then, and his glance fell on the topographical map and the gorge that had once united Haucha with the high plateau.

"You will admit it is exciting, Luis," Francisca insisted, "and you will be there, and Sir Wilbur, and Sir Wilbur's guide . . . all of you to look out for her."

"Even so," he said, "there will be danger. I have no idea what it is that we will find."

"But just think of it, *Tío* Luis," said Marcelina, vibrant with excitement. She was not really a niece to the Valeras, but their families had been close in bygone times in Lima. Thomas O'Day, who had married into a Spanish family years ago, and his wife, Isabella, had entrusted Luis and Francisca Valera with being, at least figuratively, *el señor y la señora que acompañaran a su hija cuando esté sola* once they had sent her abroad for an American university education. "We may find Incas there who have had no contact whatsoever with the modern world for four hundred years! What will they be like? How much of the Incan way of life have they been able to preserve?"

Those were questions Luis Valera hoped to answer as much as Marcelina. Of course, he had his suspicions. From their mountain fastness for four centuries now these Incas had probably kept their eyes on the heavens, studying the stars as they moved with each equinox and each solstice, rising and falling slowly over all that time with the gentle rhythm of a celestial *balsa,* the native raft to which the ancestors of this ancient people had attached a sail and navigated up and down the coast of their once-great empire. Perhaps here was the most important answer of all to what, for Luis Valera, remained the essential enigma of the Incas. How had it been that a people so great,

27

who had spanned a sub-continent with their highways, should have been unable to withstand the invasion of little over a hundred Spaniards, but have collapsed as suddenly and as irretrievably as that mighty suspension bridge that had once united Haucha to its access from an Andean plateau? By degrees and with only restrained violence there had arisen the great fabric of the Incan Empire, composed of numerous independent and even hostile tribes, yet, under the influence of a common religion, common language, and common government, united as one nation, animated by a love for the Incan institutions and a loyalty to the Inca sovereign. Gold, in the figurative language of the Incas, had been tears wept by the Sun, and it was the Sun these people had worshipped. The gold that adorned their temples everywhere, that had been used to personify the deity of the Sun in massive plates of enormous dimensions thickly powdered with emeralds and other precious stones on the western walls so that the rays of the Sun should be reflected as innumerable shimmerings of light — it had been this that had attracted the Spaniards. Luis Valera hoped, at last, to see through the great eastern portals of one of those temples, toward a sun rising as this one was setting — shining through a gathering fog into the windows and into the study — to see first-hand what had been at once so stupendous and at the same time so infinitely fragile about these — until now — vanished worshipers of the light.

"Coffee?" Francisca asked.

"Yes," agreed Luis Valera.

"Let me help," Marcelina proposed.

Together the two women left the room.

What did her age matter, Valera reflected to himself. At any age, he would have given anything to have gone on such an expedition.

Chapter Three

It had grown dark outside the hotel. Below lay the alternate glare and gloom of the city, while far in the distance the lights of the ferry boats plodded across the harbor like sluggish fireflies. Clearly audible was the fog bell over at Belvedere, which meant that there was a sea mist drifting in through the Golden Gate. By midnight, perhaps, it would whirl and eddy about this lofty hotel, shutting out the world like the veil of a filmy tulle. Chris Fallon loved the San Francisco fogs best. Leaning now against the wall near the door, he was somewhat in shadow, and Ferrar was paying little attention to him.

Sir Wilbur Tennington, red-faced, said with cold fury: "You sha'n't get away with this, Ferrar."

"My good man, I assure you the map is mine, by proprietary right. It was given to my forebear, Pizarro, by Fernando García himself."

"Pizarro enslaved, murdered, and robbed the Incas to whom the treasure belonged."

"Please," Ferrar said gently, "let us not bandy words. Are you going to give me that map, Sir Wilbur, or must I give you lead?"

Fallon now caught Tennington's eyes, and a look of tacit understanding passed between them. The Englishman gave a barely perceptible nod and remarked in a loud voice: "It's over there on the table, old boy."

"Thank you," said Ferrar and moved carefully past Tennington toward the table, still keeping his gun on the Englishman.

The big Negro was watching both Fallon and Tennington,

29

but he was unarmed, and Fallon knew he could easily complete his maneuver before Abdullah could rise to interfere. A single swift movement of Fallon's arm snapped off the light switch by the door, and even the table lamp was extinguished as the room was plunged into darkness.

"Take him, Tenny," shouted Fallon and made a wild lunge in the blackness for the table beside which Ferrar now stood. He hit a wiry body in the fashion of a gridiron tackle, and he felt Tenny's charge beside him. Between the two of them, they bore Ferrar to the floor as the table crashed over. There was a roar as the Spaniard's Enfield went off in the darkness with a lurid gleam of flame.

A second later Fallon felt himself plucked from Ferrar as though he were a baby, and he knew that Abdullah had stepped in. In an instant he fell with a crash against the wall where the giant's mighty hand had hurled him, and there was a duplicate thump at his side as Sir Wilbur was thrown after him.

Through a hundred stars Fallon saw the giant rear up against the dim light emanating from the two outside windows, Ferrar tucked under one huge arm. One of the windows was open, and Fallon could distinguish the silhouette of the two against the lesser darkness outside. He saw Abdullah clamber through the window with his burden and drop onto the fire escape outside, then disappear from view.

A second later the light snapped on. Tenny was standing by the light switch, his hair rumpled, while Fallon leaned somewhat dazedly against the wall. The table had been overturned.

"My word!" exclaimed the Englishman. "I tried to intercept that Negro, and he threw me aside like a matchstick."

"Did they get the map?" Fallon asked ruefully.

"No . . . here it is . . . it fell under the table when it overturned. Thank goodness! I fear for what may remain of the treasure of the Incas in the hands of a man like Ferrar."

Fallon had left the wall now and moved over to the open window, looking downward. "I don't see them," he said. "But, if you still have the map, you can be sure they'll make another try."

Tennington nodded agreement. "Still, we sha'n't trouble the police. Luis Valera has made a far more detailed map than this one, so even if Ferrar had been able to make off with the original, it would not interfere with our expedition, except that we would probably either be following him, or he would be following us. As it stands, he may follow us anyway. There has been no end of public comment about our planned trip in the newspapers. You know, the San Francisco Museum is partially financing the trip, at least as concerns Luis Valera's part and that of his student, Marcelina O'Day."

"Is she the woman you mentioned?" Fallon asked, as Tenny straightened a chair. "Even without Ferrar this expedition would be no place for a woman."

"Originally, I quite agreed with you Chris, and I've been over all that with Valera. However, it seems that this young woman, who's been studying archeology in this country, comes from a well-to-do family in Lima, and she goes with the permission and approval of her parents."

"I'll grant," responded Fallon, "that hiking in the Andes may not be the same as the jungles of the Amazon, but we have to go through jungle to get where we're going, I'm sure, and I still insist it is no place for a woman."

The Englishman was in the process of restoring the table to its upright position. "I rather think," he said, "that Valera's wife, Francisca, is more sensible when it comes to the trip. She is more than happy to remain here in San Francisco, but I've met this Marcelina O'Day, and she seems to have absorbed more than archeology while studying in this country. I should

31

also tell you, incidentally, although you did not ask, that she has unusually high spirits and apparently is game for anything." He bent now and was picking up the scattered papers that had fallen to the floor, including the map. "Yes, everything is definitely here, I'm pleased to say."

Fallon had joined in, fetching up several writing instruments, a magnifying glass, and an ashtray.

"I say," Tennington commented, as he stood surveying the room, "I could stand a spot of grog. How about you?"

"Did you manage to bring some with you?" Fallon asked, smiling. "You know, the Puritans have had their way again in this country, and in addition to banning the sale or imbibing of any spirits whatsoever, in some states they have even banned tobacco."

"Yes, I know," Sir Wilbur conceded. "Somehow that didn't greatly surprise me when it happened. American lawmakers singularly believe they can legislate the behavior of their citizens, notwithstanding all the talk about life, liberty, and what have you." While speaking, he walked over to his valise which had been placed on a luggage stand at the foot of the bed. "I couldn't bring my favorite Scotch with me into this country. It was seized by customs in New York. But I was able to acquire a quart from a local bootlegger shortly after I registered. The hotel management was most co-operative in that regard. Right after I signed the register, I was told the procedure for obtaining just about any sort of alcoholic beverage I wanted, provided I had no objection. Of course, I didn't have any objection. And here it is."

He held up a clear bottle about seven-eighths full from the look of it.

"Fetch us a couple of glasses from the buffet there, Chris, like a good chap. You'll notice the hotel furnishes the seltzer with the room!"

"Certainly," Fallon said, now grinning openly. He brought the glasses and the seltzer dispenser over to the table. He continued: "I understand why you wouldn't want to have the police in this matter, since it might delay our departure. Still, don't you think you ought to take some sort of precautions about the original map? . . . Ferrar and his henchman are likely to make another attempt."

"Chris, I definitely intend to do just that. After we've had our spot, I plan to take the map with García's narrative down to the desk and have it deposited overnight in the hotel safe. I imagine it should be quite secure there, although, as I say, Valera has a copy of this document in his possession and a much better map. It was a precaution I thought advisable as soon as I received the commitment from the museum to help finance the expedition."

Sir Wilbur began pouring a small quantity of the pale Scotch into the glasses, and Fallon followed with a shot of seltzer water in each, although less in his glass than that intended for the Englishman. They had traveled together before and so knew each other's preferences in many things.

"Here's how," said Sir Wilbur, proffering his glass.

Fallon joined him in the salute, and each drank slowly and silently. Then the Englishman put down his glass and looked around on the floor briefly, until he spotted his pipe, where it had fallen, and picked it up. Very little of the tobacco had spilled from the bowl.

"Do you think," Fallon asked, "should we actually reach Haucha, that the Peruvian government will allow enough of what we find there to leave the country so it can be brought back here to San Francisco?"

"Why, Chris, that is precisely what was so attractive about having Luis Valera throw in with me on this venture. He personally knows the minister of culture in Lima, and this

Marcelina O'Day's family is well connected. I do not anticipate much of a squabble, really. After all, if the current Peruvian government has any interest whatsoever, I rather imagine it will be no less troublesome than the British and Egyptian officials we dealt with on that Bliss expedition, and there, you will recall, we also had the complications of the government of Ethiopia. There was a lot of wrangling, but in the end Doctor Bliss got his share of the artifacts. He was satisfied, and so was everyone else, including the British Museum which also managed to claim a few of the more valuable pieces."

Fallon had sat down on one of the chairs beside the table now and brought out a cigarette that he proceeded to light, as the Englishman, also sitting now, was stoking his pipe.

"You'd think these national governments would make more of a fuss," Fallon observed, exhaling tobacco smoke. "I'll grant you, there wasn't much to create a stir in catching rare species of tropical fish in the Amazon, but it was another matter altogether when it came to locating a buried Egyptian city."

"Listen, dear fellow, I haven't been idle in this matter," Tennington assured him. "While waiting your return to the States, Valera was able with a relative degree of certainty to locate the approximate longitude and latitude of Haucha by means of a topographical map he has of the entire region once ruled by the Incas. We have been able to secure through the minister of the interior in Peru a concession for this approximate area. Neither the Peruvians nor anybody else has had any reason to believe, before this, that such a place as Haucha even existed, although I see from what Ferrar had to say that, at least, he has been more than vaguely aware of it. To be perfectly frank, the request for a concession was met with some skepticism, since the Peruvians seem convinced that no such place, no matter how cleverly hidden all these centuries in the Andes, could possibly exist. While they were perfectly willing to negotiate a fee for a concession and reserved the right to claim the major portion of any treasure in gold, silver, or other precious metals or jewels we may find, I fear our entire mission has been met with only disbelief and even amusement. I would jolly well like to see the reaction some of these Peruvian government officials would have to Ferrar's claim, which he was willing to make to me at gunpoint."

Fallon again sipped his drink. "I'm sure you don't believe we've seen the last of those two."

"Assuredly not," Tennington agreed, also taking his drink in hand. "But I rather suspect they were so easily sent scrambling because the last thing Ferrar would want is to create an international incident shooting a British subject in a foreign country where he might very well find himself detained and charged. I'm willing to let him off precisely because no real damage was done, and, in fact, should he pursue us to Peru, I don't expect any real trouble out of him since we quite definitely have the concession, and I seriously doubt his spurious claim of a proprietary right to what treasure may be located in Haucha would stand up against the Peruvian government's intervention. Forgive me, Chris, but I regard his visit here as little more than the nuisance I can expect from newspaper reporters."

"I would agree with you," said Fallon, "insofar as what he would do in this country, or even in one of the cities in Peru, but you've got to remember that we'll be in the mountain wilderness for much of this trip, and, where there's no law, I figure he might be less inclined to restraint."

"That's what I'm paying you for," the Englishman remarked, with a small humorless smile. "To see that we are not bothered precisely by Ferrar or any other treasure-seeker who might become aware of our mission."

Putting out his cigarette, Fallon rose and walked over to the open window. The fog he had noticed coming in earlier had increased even as they had been talking, and he thought he could detect the salt of the Pacific on its breath as well as the scent of distant gardens.

Chapter Four

The next morning Sir Wilbur Tennington with Chris Fallon did a paper check of the supplies and gear needed for the excursion. These had been sent ahead to the dock and probably had already been loaded when the two checked out of the St. Francis in the lobby and had their most personal luggage carried by a porter down the Post Street corridor where their taxicab was waiting. The suitcases were placed on the luggage rack at the rear of the taxi and secured, while the Englishman tipped the porter.

"We're early," Tennington remarked to Chris Fallon, looking very smart in his English tweeds, "and that's good. Our ship doesn't leave for four hours yet, but we have to pick up Professor Valera and Miss O'Day on our way."

Fallon, dressed more casually, remained quiet as he followed the Englishman into the tonneau. He still had difficulty in accepting the notion of any woman, and a young one at that, accompanying them on what was likely to be a dangerous undertaking.

Sir Wilbur gave the cabby Luis Valera's address, which meant pretty much a straight passage down Post Street to Laguna Street.

The driver grinned broadly, turning from where he now sat behind the wheel. "Sure t'ing, buddy. Nuttin' I like better than cruisin' troo the suburbs . . . especially when there's two payin' passengers in the back wit' me."

The taxi had pulled out into traffic and was proceeding along Post Street.

"Say, Tenny, doesn't it seem to you that black coupé is following us?" inquired Fallon, frowning as he peered out the rear window.

"Why, I hadn't noticed . . . ," replied Sir Wilbur. "How long has it been with us, Chris?"

"Ever since we left the hotel. It was parked by the curb a way down the street. As soon as we pulled out, it pulled out. It's been keeping a ways behind us ever since."

"Say, my good man, perhaps you might pour on the petrol . . . the gas," Sir Wilbur admonished the driver. "We think that black coupé may be following us."

It presently became evident, however, that the black coupé had no intention of being shaken. It clung tenaciously to their wake, even when their cab pulled into a less crowded street and increased its speed.

"Say, buddy . . . you on the lam?" queried their driver.

"Not at all, my dear fellow. Those gentlemen behind us are attempting to . . . er . . . put us on the spot, as you might say."

"You kin count on me, pal," the hack informed them, and proceeded even more to increase their speed despite city traffic.

The taxi took a corner on two wheels. For a moment it careened wildly before righting itself. The brakes shrieked.

"Put 'em on a little late there," remarked the driver with stoical calm, ignoring the consternation of his passengers.

The chase proceeded, however. In fact, the coupé seemed intent on overtaking them.

"Can't you go any faster?" asked Tennington.

"Buddy, this old crate ain't what it used to be . . . and it ain't mine, either. That jived-up heap behind us has got power."

"That's so," conceded Fallon, looking out the rear window, but he couldn't see it.

The black coupé was now drawing up alongside them.

"Slow down!" exclaimed Sir Wilbur. "The fools are trying to ram us."

"They're tryin' to run us right off the street," muttered the driver, as he slowed abruptly. "Well, two can play that game."

The coupé had pulled in sharply toward them now, but the driver's swift action in slowing his cab thwarted the purpose. The coupé, expecting to collide with a solid car, instead shot on past, carried by its great momentum completely over to the other side of the street where the car braked frantically and swerved back into the right lane, trying to avoid a head-on collision with an oncoming car. The cabby's strategy had worked. Now it was the taxi's turn. The driver again applied his foot to the accelerator and shot ahead, coming up behind the coupé.

"Wid my compliments," murmured the driver, just as his front bumper crashed into the rear bumper of the coupé, giving it a final bit of impetus needed to send it lunging forward directly toward the curb. The driver then plunged the cab ahead down the street. The coupé was seen to have come to a stop, its impetus gone, as street traffic intervened.

When they arrived at the Valera house, the Englishman got out of the cab and examined the front bumper. Then he slipped their driver, who had also got out of the vehicle, twenty dollars.

"That ought to cover the damage."

"Say, that's O K, buddy," said the driver. "That bumper ain't even badly dented, and it sticks out too far for the radiator to have been touched."

"Nonetheless, you've earned it."

Marcelina O'Day had preceded Luis and Francisca Valera out of the house and down the porch steps. A number of suitcases were lined up on the porch, and, as the cab driver surveyed them, he shook his head.

"I'm Marcelina O'Day," the girl introduced herself to Chris Fallon who had just got out of the taxi. She was wearing a white traveling dress, her blue-gray eyes shining brightly. She was only three inches above five feet, making Fallon almost a foot taller.

"Chris Fallon," he said, gently shaking her outstretched hand.

"Yes," she replied. "*Tío* Luis has told me about how you were with Sir Wilbur in Egypt and Ethiopia."

Valera came up, nodding and smiling at Sir Wilbur. Francisca was behind him on the front sidewalk. The Englishman bowed slightly to her.

"I'm sorry you have chosen not to accompany us," he said.

Francisca smiled. "Luis and Marcie have both promised to keep me posted by mail. I have no great inclination to venture into jungles or to climb mountains."

"Nor have I particularly," Valera put in, "but, if we want to find things out, sometimes it is a necessity."

"Missus Valera, Luis," Sir Wilbur said, "this is Chris Fallon. He shall be acting as our field guide."

Fallon nodded at Francisca and then shook hands with Valera. "Guide, I'm afraid," he confessed, looking at Francisca, "is a little exalted, especially in view of the fact that I have never been in this part of the Andes before."

"Say, buddy," the cab driver interrupted, addressing Tennington, "there ain't room on the luggage rack for all that stuff up there on the porch."

"Much of that baggage, I fear, is Marcelina's," said Valera, chuckling.

"Only two of them are mine," Marcelina corrected him.

Fallon liked the gentle precision with which Marcelina enunciated her words when she spoke, and the clear, melodious tone of her voice that bordered on being, if it was not quite, a contralto. "I'll be glad to help you load that stuff," he told the driver.

The cabby was shaking his head as he started up the walk.

40

"I'm afraid you're gonna have tuh stow some of that baggage on the floor. Also, if two more are goin', one of you is gonna have to ride up front wid me."

"Be happy to," Sir Wilbur said.

While Fallon and the cab driver worked, arranging what luggage they could on the rack in back, and leaving two suitcases out to be placed on the floor of the passenger compartment, Sir Wilbur chatted with Luis and Francisca Valera. Marcelina insisted on carrying the smaller of her two suitcases to the cab herself.

"You oughtn't've troubled yourself, miss," the cabby remarked.

"I'm going to be roughing it on this trip," she explained. "I might as well get used to looking after my own things at the very beginning."

"Have you ever been to Peru before?" Fallon asked, as he carried the heavier of her two suitcases to the luggage rack.

"I was born and raised there, Mister Fallon."

"Yes, Tenny did mention that, I recall. But with a name like O'Day?"

She smiled. "My father came from Ireland. He is in the import-export business. My mother and father knew the Valeras years ago in Lima, and, when it came time for an university education, and I wanted to study archeology and pre-Columbian civilization, they entrusted me to the Valeras."

Fallon set Marcelina's heavier suitcase down on the luggage rack and set about securing it. Marcelina held onto her smaller bag.

"Where did you study?" she asked.

"On the job, mostly," he confided. "Doctor Bliss in New York got me together with Tenny when he got a concession in Egypt and northern Ethiopia. In my work I find I've got to know a little bit about a lot of things, but chiefly how to overcome obstacles and just plain see to it that everyone survives. My last excursion was leading a party in search of tropical fish . . . and I don't mean fish to eat."

He paused and smiled. Marcelina smiled back.

"You don't really approve, do you?" she asked.

"Not really," he admitted. "In addition to the natural problems we're likely to encounter just with terrain and the hardships of this kind of excursion, I'm afraid there's another party that is trying to make a claim on Haucha. They tried to run us off the street . . . or at least get us to miss the boat . . . on our way here."

Marcelina's brow was knitted by a slight frown.

"Do you know who they were?"

"I've got a good idea. A fellow came to see Tenny yesterday and wanted to buy his map. I think he was in that black coupé that tried to force us off the street today."

"Does Sir Wilbur recognize this man's claim?"

"Miss, Tenny isn't that stupid. He sent him packing. But the fellow did pull a gun, and I rather think he means to press his claim. If you need another reason for changing your mind about coming, that fellow would make a good one."

"Now, Chris, don't try to alarm Miss O'Day," Sir Wilbur said, coming toward them. "I couldn't help overhearing what you were saying. Really, I think we've seen the last of those fellows . . . even if they were in that coupé, which somehow I find hard to believe. In any event, I'll not be put off by any such crude attempt at intimidation. Come, let's get underway. Soon we'll be aboard the *Sea Queen*."

"My father took me to the Cuzco ruins when I was younger," Marcelina put in, not ignoring Sir Wilbur but concerned with making herself understood by Chris Fallon. "That trip only fired my interest in Incan civilization. A chance like this does not really come very often, if ever, and I think, whatever the ardors of it, that I couldn't possibly stay behind. After all, Peru is my homeland. Perhaps I know what to expect . . . even more than you do, Mister Fallon."

"My dear," Sir Wilbur assured her, "there is no question about your coming, and both Luis and I shall be happy to look to your welfare. Chris is just being a fuddy-duddy about it."

Fallon found himself regretting having said anything, particularly since his reservation seemed to have produced in Marcelina a certain archness toward him.

Luis Valera embraced Francisca, and then Marcelina hugged her. To have seen them off at the dock would have required her to drive there herself, and she preferred it this way. Fallon got into the back seat first, taking Marcelina's smaller suitcase with him, followed by Marcelina, and then Luis Valera. Sir Wilbur took the front passenger seat next to the driver.

The tonneau of the taxicab was not overly accommodating, and Fallon could not help but be aware of Marcelina's slim thigh and hip beside him, although she spoke very little to him during the remainder of the drive to the docks. He did not know if she were greatly interested in athletics, but she did seem to have what would be regarded as an athletic body. He supposed, with her very small breasts and animation, she was what in popular parlance would be called a flapper, a word that had come about because of the fashion in which modern young women flapped their arms like an unfledged bird when dancing the Charleston. Yet, somehow, Marcelina also seemed more serious than that. There was about her a high degree of self-possession, more than he would have expected in a girl who could not be much more than in her very early twenties. She was conversing readily with Valera, however, about how Francisca would probably regret not having gone in the long run, and how she was looking forward to seeing her parents in

Lima. The way she talked about the lost city made it seem that she knew far more than Fallon did about what they might expect to find there.

"One thing still puzzles me," Fallon broke in on their conversation. "How could it be that this city might have existed for four hundred years without anyone before us having heard about it? After all, the world these days is a much smaller place, I'm sorry to say, and, if a part of Incan civilization should actually have survived all this time, why wouldn't the Peruvian government itself know about Haucha?"

"To understand that, Mister Fallon," replied Luis Valera, "you have to realize that virtually all of the centers of Incan civilization long ago were subjected to the Spanish crown, first by Pizarro and his mercenaries, and then by the Church, which followed in the wake of the *conquistadores,* as was the case also here in California among the native Indian peoples. Haucha was, as nearly as we can tell, an outpost of the Incas in the high mountains. It was scarcely a center for commerce, and it cannot have had an extremely large or wealthy population at the time of the conquest . . . very little is known about it, and certainly nothing to invite treasure-hunters. For what reason would anyone set out to find such an isolated mountain village? I doubt that there would be much reason to send modern census takers or tax collectors in quest of it, especially when there was actually no record prior to this that there was such a city as Haucha."

"I can tell you this much, Professor," Fallon said. "This man . . . Ferrar is his name . . . who called on Tenny yesterday and may have tried to force us off the street on the way to your house today . . . is convinced that there is a wealth of Incan gold to be had at Haucha, just for the taking."

"Anyone who thinks that is obviously delusional," Valera said in a dismissive tone. "As I said before, if there was some fabled treasure city in the Andes, as fabled let us say as the so-called gold cities of Cibola, Haucha would have been raided long before this. What treasures did you and Sir Wilbur discover in Ethiopia?"

"If you mean gold," said Fallon, "nothing to speak of, although Doctor Bliss seemed well satisfied with the artifacts he was able to bring back to his museum in New York, among them some extraordinarily elaborate cartouches and a statue of the Egyptian god, Set. I have read that Lord Carnovan has a concession now in the Valley of the Kings, and I know that he expects to find a good deal of treasure should he and Howard Carter be successful in their effort to locate the tomb of the last pharaoh of the Eighteenth Dynasty. But, then, they've just started their search, and I would imagine they'll be some years at it."

"But this is so different, Mister Fallon," Marcelina said, turning her head to face him sideways. "Artifacts there might be, perhaps even gold, but what is really exciting is the prospect of learning more about the Incas, from what might have survived and hasn't been destroyed through Spanish and now cosmopolitan contamination."

"That's a bit lofty for me, Miss O'Day," Fallon said, smiling. "I fear I am more concerned about practical matters. For example, just how we might be able to bridge the gorge that supposedly has cut this city off for all these centuries. You know, it is entirely possible that you and Professor Valera may be mistaken. Once that bridge to the outside world was destroyed, everyone left in Haucha might very well have perished from simple starvation. At such an altitude, how easy would it be to raise food crops to feed a city population? We might encounter the same thing Tenny and I found in Ethiopia . . . the remains of a once-thriving city, buried in the dust of the ages, and not a living soul."

45

Sir Wilbur, who had been looking out his side window as they had been going along, now leaned backward in his car seat and craned his head around slightly to address those in the tonneau. "I agree with you, Chris. I haven't the vaguest idea of what it is that we actually will find, or, once we've found it, if it will excite even as much of an article in the *Chronicle* as our intention of finding it was able to create. The excitement, after all, is in the adventure of it, of going some place no one has been for hundreds of years, and seeing what we will find."

"There is one possibility I do not think has been mentioned," Luis Valera interjected. "The Incas were far more advanced in the mummification of bodies than were the Egyptians. We have eyewitness accounts at the time of the conquest that the preserved bodies of most, if not all, of the previously deceased Incan emperors were brought from their mausoleums during the festival of Capac Raimi . . . the festival of the dead . . . which occurred for three days during the December solstice. The *huacas* . . . the monuments detailing lineage for each of the many separate peoples in the empire . . . were also brought forth from their shrines and placed in the main plaza at Cuzco. The celebrants ate and drank with the bodies of the dead, as if they were still alive, and newly initiated knights in the fraternal orders could ask their ancestors at this time to make them as valiant as they had once been. It was only during the time of the December solstice, a day before it, the day during it, and one day after it, when the sun appeared to be stationary in the sky at its southernmost point of rise on the eastern horizon, that the *río debajo de la tierra* . . . the river that flows beneath the earth . . . was bridged, allowing the souls of those who had departed and crossed over into the world below to cross back over and commune with their descendants."

"Whatever happened to those mummies after the conquest?" Fallon asked, his interest piqued.

Valera shook his head sadly. "Unfortunately, once the intentions of the Spaniards became obvious to the Incas at Cuzco, the mummies of the dead emperors were hidden away. The Spaniards believed the festival was a fiendish form of devil worship. Finally, in Fifteen Seventy-One, the Viceroy Toledo found the mummies and burned all of them. Lost with them, perhaps for all time, were the secrets of the embalming process the Incas used. It was said by eyewitnesses that the remains of Huayna Capac, the last Incan emperor before the conquest, were so well preserved that he appeared to be truly life-like, except that the tip of his nose was missing."

"How did Huayna Capac come to die?" Marcelina queried.

"It is said," replied Valera, "of smallpox."

"Pizarro's curse?" suggested Sir Wilbur.

"Actually, no," replied Valera. "The emperor was celebrating in Quito when a messenger arrived from the coast. He told of the coming of strangers, arriving in floating houses, men so fierce that they frightened the jaguars in the royal zoological gardens. Huayna Capac was sobered by this report. The messenger then kissed the Inca with reverence and gave him a closed box with a tiny key. Huayna Capac ordered the messenger to open the box, but he declined, insisting that the god Viracocha, the Creator, had ordered that only the Inca himself should open it. Huayna Capac did so. When he had opened the little box, small butterflies fluttered upward from where they had been kept imprisoned within it. The emperor retired at once from his revels to undertake a fast in which he hoped to receive a spirit vision. After some time, it is said, the emperor did, indeed, have a vision. In this vision three dwarfs came to him, announcing that they had arrived for the purpose of summoning him to the *río debajo de la tierra*. He knew the dwarfs were announcing his own death. It is believed that the infiltration of smallpox came not from the invading Spaniards, but by

47

way of the Caribbean through what is now Colombia. In any event, the prophecy soon proved true. Within days the general of the army and many of the captains died of smallpox, their faces covered with hideous scabs. Although Huayna Capac was sealed away behind walls of stone while on his vision quest, within eight days he, too, died. It is said that, at the hour of his passing, he repeated the meaning of the prophetic vision and that, as it was with him, so it would be in the future for all the Incas and their empire. His half-rotted corpse was embalmed and taken from Quito to Cuzco. Apparently, except for the loss of a fragment from his nose, Huayna Capac was preserved to appear more life-like than he had been during his final days or in the short period following his death before he was embalmed."

"Preservin' this crate of a taxicab is excitin' enough for me," muttered their driver, pulling at the visor of the cap he wore. "We're predanear where you're wantin' to go at the waterfront docks."

Chapter Five

In the stateroom which Luis Valera shared with Chris Fallon, Valera lay down to take a nap. Sir Wilbur Tennington, who had his own stateroom, came across the hall to see how they were doing. Marcelina O'Day also had a stateroom to herself and would be joining them later.

"I say . . . it sounds like we're weighing anchor," Sir Wilbur commented to Chris Fallon. "Care to go up on deck?"

"No, thanks," said Fallon, nodding in the direction of the professor who was reclining in the upper bunk, his eyes closed. "I think Luis has the right idea. I could stand a little *siesta* myself."

"Dear me! I seem to recall you as being a bit more of a red-blooded American than that, you know."

"Maybe, but I've been traveling a mite lately, and I figure on sleeping when I can. There may be little enough of it later on."

Valera and Fallon slept all afternoon and barely roused themselves in time for the evening meal. Afterward, Fallon strolled out onto the deck. Marcelina, who had changed to a becoming evening gown for the occasion, remained behind with the others in the dining salon.

Fallon leaned against a rail, not feeling much like promenading. The deck was largely deserted, except for a few people at intervals farther along the rail. The black velvet of the sky was studded with stars, and on the horizon at water level the moon had risen to cut a swath of sparkling silver across the sea. Fallon, in a posture of dreary languor and cognizant only of the sound of distant voices and music now in the dining salon and the waves that lapped gently away from the sides of the ship, felt his mind surrendering gradually to romantic wanderings. It was pleasant to lean here with a cigarette and consider the venture that lay ahead. Danger? Yes. There would be countless savage dangers, and perhaps not least of all further interference from Ferrar. But contemplation of none of these troubled Fallon. He had preferred a hard, rigorous life and had faced whatever fate threw across his path with a cool courage. To the corners of the globe he had traveled, from the frozen tundra of the Far North to the equatorial veldts of Central Africa. He could look forward toward whatever lay ahead with a pulse-quickening excitement that had nothing to do with fear.

He thoughtfully removed his cigarette from his mouth as he wondered whether Ferrar had also boarded this ship. It was very possible he had, unless he had been unable to secure reservations. He remembered that it had been mentioned that they would be sailing on the *Sea Queen*. Yes, Ferrar would surely follow them, one way or another, until he secured the map — and they had had an indication that morning that he was nothing if not determined.

"May I trouble you for a match?" asked a voice behind him.

Fallon turned to find himself looking down into the blue-gray eyes of Marcelina O'Day. Her evening gown hugged her slim body, accenting her small breasts, her sculpted, nubile figure. She seemed, somehow, very young. She was smiling, and her face, even in this poor light, was irradiated by a puckish sense of humor.

Fallon pulled out his lighter and lit her cigarette. She shielded her face with her hands as she leaned forward, for there was a breeze off the water.

"Thank you," she said, tossing her head backward slightly. "I've heard something more about your exploits from *Tío* Luis, and Sir Wilbur was talking about you after you left us."

"I suppose your uncle was the one who persuaded you to

take this journey," Fallon said, drawing again on his own cigarette and then throwing it overboard.

"In a manner of speaking my uncle did, but Luis Valera is not really my uncle. It is just that he and Papa have been friends since before Luis and Francisca left Peru for the States. *Tío* Luis and *Tía* Francisca, you might say, have been my chaperónes. You must remember I grew up in Peru, Mister Fallon."

"Not in the part where we're going, I'm sure." Fallon smiled. "Do you live with the Valeras? I ask . . . because that's where you were today . . . when we came to pick you up."

"No, I have my apartment room in a boarding house near campus." She took a puff on her cigarette and moved closer to the railing.

"Have you ever gone on a date without them?" Fallon asked.

"Why, most certainly . . . to dances and to the movies." There was a somewhat surprised expression on her face. "After all, I am twenty-one years old, and I have been studying anthropology and archeology in the United States. Besides the tremendous opportunity, most probably, of finding actual descendants of the original Incas relatively isolated from Spanish and Peruvian culture since the Sixteenth Century . . . I will benefit greatly from the experience of working in the field."

"Tenny and I have been on expeditions before, and I can honestly tell you that there have never been women along. The going, ahead of us in Peru, is likely to be very rough, from the ardors of the jungle to the fastnesses of the mountains. I have no idea of what we're going to encounter, and I'm sure neither your parents nor Luis Valera could imagine it. If all that weren't enough, there is another threat against the whole expedition. I mentioned it before, and, unquestionably, the personal danger for us is great, and it will be just as great for you."

Marcelina had been listening to Fallon with rapt attention, but with no little defiance in her eyes and posture. Rather than attempting to argue with him, she looked about, saw an ashtray on a round table clamped to the deck between two deck chairs, and went over there to extinguish her cigarette. When she walked back toward where he still stood at the railing, she was smiling that puckish smile again.

"Mister Fallon," she said, standing before him, "I shall tell you a story. One day when King Midas was in Macedonia an ancient satyr was caught drinking at a spring. The king had earlier mixed wine in the water of the spring in the hope of just such an occurrence. Since the old satyr was unaccustomed to the intoxicating effect of wine, he soon became drunk, and in this state he was placed in bonds and brought before the king. Unwilling to speak at all when sober, now that he was drunk, the satyr did reluctantly answer the question King Midas put to him. The king asked the satyr what was the best fate that could befall a human being, and the satyr replied that the best fate that could befall any human being was not to be born at all."

"And was there no alternative?" Fallon asked, his attention arrested.

"Yes," replied Marcelina. "King Midas responded just as you have. The old satyr thought for a moment and then conceded that there was at least one next best fate to the one he had already provided."

"And what was that?"

Marcelina's smile broadened, and mischief glistened in her blue-gray eyes. "The next best fate any human being could experience, the old satyr said, was to die as soon as possible after birth." Even though her evening gown did have sleeves, she then gave forth with a little shudder. "But I have no wrap with me. As it is getting a little chilly, I think I had best go below now. Thank you again, Mister Fallon, for lighting my cigarette."

From his position at the railing, Fallon watched Marcelina as she retreated down the deck toward the door leading to the staterooms. She had, he reflected, an exquisite figure, and he chided himself now because he wished she would have stayed longer talking with him. He realized that, more than ever, he was looking forward to seeing her again, that the prospect of seeing her every day indefinitely in the future pleased him, and that his voicing reservations about her ability to cope with the excursion would only alienate her from him. Henceforth, he had best keep his mouth shut about what dangers might lie ahead, because he found, now, he wanted her along.

Fallon looked down toward the sea, toward the small, swirling whitecaps that rolled away from the ship as the bow cut the mostly placid surface, illuminated by the moonlight and star shine as well as by lamps on the *Sea Queen*. Some way, despite the ease with which the passenger ship moved, almost, it seemed, riding the surface of the sea, being buoyed aloft, the receding ripples murmured indistinctly a melody he could not quite apprehend. Marcelina had said she had grown cold being on deck, and so it was with some curiosity that Fallon became aware now that the night abroad was actually somewhat tepid, an iron-like gray where the moon was not reflected on the water, and the railing itself was slightly damp, as if it were itself exuding a saline dew.

He could not put his finger on what made him think of it, but for a moment he felt — if he did not really think it — how Pizarro and his men must have felt aboard their much smaller ships, as they sailed down the coast from what now was Central America. He felt how just such a deep and persistent murmur from the sea must have penetrated an otherwise profound silence, even a sense of peace, as if something had happened to the world itself, as if for this time reality had shimmered and faded through some strange magic into a dream; as if the human soul had become by some bewildering process transformed, turned upside down; as if sailing from the north in a southerly direction was like descending, indeed, into a netherworld of spirits that could be reached by no other route than this. Instead of riding a crest, he had the illusion that the *Sea Queen* was in the throes of a rapture generated by the sea, that under its sway the ship was but wandering on a very long journey.

This feeling was only increased when he noted that the dimly luminous moon was making the dark water so clear in such a way that it seemed that all the light in the world was, in fact, radiating from the depths of the sea and only being reflected by the soft vacuum of the sky. By this view the gentle, great outward undulations of the sea appeared to have become so solid that he felt he might — were he to try — actually be able to walk safely outward, away from the *Sea Queen*, following the radiant light from the depths, coming closer, somehow, to its source; while it was the sky itself that seemed it might sink, even fall, downward into that netherworld, here brightly the color of gleaming silver, there of dull, tarnished, white gold, the most precious kind of gold of all, reflected forever within a silvery world, moving, changing, massive, and yet weightless, towering up, only gracefully to recede again.

Fallon suddenly found himself wondering if that old satyr had been right, after all, if the next best fate for any human being, other than not being born at all, was to die as soon as possible after birth. If such had, indeed, been his own fate, what would he really have missed? In a strange inversion of his life — for the world did now seem to be upside down — he acknowledged that he would actually have forsaken nothing at all; that what he most stood to lose was what had not yet happened, for it might be down there somewhere in the depths of the ocean, softly illumined by the distant source of light that only vaguely broke the surface of the great, rolling, whispering sea.

Don Estaban de Ferrar, in sports clothing, paced back and forth the length of his stateroom, puffing impatiently on his Egyptian cigarette. Abdullah stood unobtrusively with folded arms in one corner of the room. He was wearing a white suit and the red fez. The open porthole was a blind eye looking out onto the dark ocean.

Ferrar regretted the near accident that had resulted from his effort earlier in the day to run Sir Wilbur Tennington's taxicab off the road. Even had he succeeded in delaying the Englishman, it would actually have bought him very little. The whole incident had been the consequence of almost insuperable frustration. What right had the English explorer to claim any part, much less all, of the treasure of Haucha? It had been merely a matter of serendipity that the Englishman should have come upon the location of the lost city of the Incas a matter of a few hours, actually only a few minutes, before the authentic claimant to the fortune!

Ferrar was scarcely a poor man. He had an estate in Tetuán in Spanish Morocco and apartments in Madrid and Lima. His sister had married well, and she was hardly in need of more money. Indeed, it was the principle of the thing. The Spanish monarchy, centuries ago, had squandered the fabulous wealth they had taken from the Incas, financing a ridiculous war. Francisco Pizarro by virtue of the right of discovery should have been able to lay claim to *all* the wealth of the Incan Empire. Instead, he had been forced to satisfy himself with only a fraction of the treasure due to a conqueror. Don Estaban recalled a fragment from Lope De Vega's play, EL NUEVO MUNDO:

> **So color de religión**
> **Van a buscar plata y oro**
> **Del encubierto tesoro**

It was true enough for what had happened to the fabulous hidden treasures of the Incas. Under the guise of religion, the Spanish government had annexed the greatest land empire in the New World, arrogantly seeking possession of all silver and gold. And now, how many generations later, he was confronted by a similarly hideous reversal of personal fortune. An arrogant Englishman, with no legitimate right to anything at all in South America, had the effrontery to push forward in his quest for what didn't belong to him, using, instead of the hypocritical claim of religious conversion, the pretense of an archeologist interested in artifacts of antiquity. What transparent nonsense it all was!

There were three loud knocks at the door. Ferrar turned, dousing his cigarette in an ashtray. "Come in," he called.

Marcelina O'Day entered.

"¡Marcelina, querida mía!" He spoke to her in Spanish. "And with what success have your efforts with that damnable Tennington progressed?"

The girl's face was pale and cold. "Everything has gone well so far, *tío mío*," she replied in a level voice in which her elocution was quite as poised and precise as it was in English. "I shall accompany the expedition into the interior all the way to the lost city of Haucha."

"Ah, then you have succeeded in gaining his confidence?" Ferrar rubbed his hands together. "He suspects nothing?"

"Everything has gone as planned," she repeated warily.

"Excellent." Ferrar scowled abruptly. "But what is wrong

with you? You are not yourself this evening, Marcelina."

The girl's lips trembled. "It is because I am very uncomfortable deceiving Luis Valera and his wife, Francisca, as well as the others."

Ferrar's eyes grew narrow and smoldered. "Do you mean that you're turning to water over this crude Englishman?"

"No," she returned in the same toneless voice. "You need not fear that. You have taken pains to erase any such softening thoughts or emotions from my nature, *tío mío,* and I have learned my lesson well. It is also as my mother would wish it."

Ferrar's expression softened. "Then what can you possibly mean?"

"I mean simply that I have grown very attached to Luis and Francisca Valera during my time in San Francisco, and that I find difficulty in keeping up this hard, self-assured shell of deceit that I have had to build about me for the occasion." The girl's voice now held a faint suggestion of bitterness. "I stood there tonight, talking with Chris Fallon, who is to be our field guide into the Andes, with a false smile on my lips, faced and lied to him when I felt like turning my back on him and running away to be alone with my shame."

Ferrar glanced at her with great gentleness in his eyes and held his breath for an instant. *This is not the way it is to be done,* he told himself. When there was so much feeling, it could not be done effectively at all. If it were to be done, it must be done lightly, almost as in jest. "Gracefully, *niña mía,*" he murmured, "is how it is done. Imagine that you are bounding aloft, executing a flawless pirouette perfectly, without even thinking about it. At such a moment, believe me, *tesoro mío,* it is really possible to doubt the fall of man. And, therefore, do not worry about it. The thing is you haven't run away from it, and Tennington suspects nothing. He . . . *¡pobre hombre!* . . . imagines you to be, as, indeed, you are, a sweet innocent who has set him up as a hero, an ideal."

"I do not believe he thinks about me at all," disagreed the girl with an edge of sarcasm.

Her uncle chuckled softly. He seated himself at the table and placed his hands on the top of it, gazing at them abstractedly. "First," he said softly, "Abdullah and I made a personal attempt to gain the map. I think Abdullah could have snatched it up before we escaped, but his one thought was for my safety. I cannot really blame him for that. Next we tried to waylay Tennington, and . . . and failed." He mused broodingly for a moment. "These English and Americans are crude, barbaric creatures . . . but they do have a certain measure of cautious intrepidness in warding off mere open attacks. However, our present approach is not violent. It is far less obvious, and, I think, will prove a thousand times more effective, because it will raise no alarm."

He glanced up at Marcelina who remained standing uncomfortably before him. "It is your duty either to secure the map for us or find its hiding place, even if you must become deeply involved with Tennington to do so. You are very beautiful, my dear Marcelina, and, if I judge correctly, this Tennington is a lonely man. Continue doing just what you have been doing. When I came to you in San Francisco and urged you to join this expedition, I was already preparing for just such a situation as has arisen."

He arose slowly and walked forward to face her, speaking softly. "I am no fool, *querida*. Do not attempt to deceive me. Deceive these interlopers. Beneath this hard surface you say you have thrown up around yourself, you have foolish, romantic ideas like any young *niña*. Is Tennington looking forward to seeing you again?"

She replied in a flat, hopeless voice. "I cannot very well avoid him. Thanks to Professor Valera's intercession, I am a member of the expedition. But I have scarcely spoken with Sir Wilbur."

"Excellent, though! Already you have made admirable headway. I have faith in you, as does your mother. By what right could this Englishman and this American lay claim to the treasure of the Incas?"

"They have, I suppose, as much right to it as anyone else . . . which is no right at all. If treasure of the Incas has been kept in this lost city all of these centuries, I am sure the people there today, as descendants of the Incas, have the only legitimate claim to it. Professor Valera is not the least interested in gold or wealth, but rather with what can be learned from these people about ancient Incan civilization. If I am in sympathy with anyone, it is with him."

"Nor do I have any objection at all to such sympathy," interposed Ferrar. "My concern, always, has been, if the city is in ruins and all the people who once lived there are now long dead, any claim to their treasure belongs to our family by right of conquest, and, perhaps secondly, to the modern Peruvian government. Certainly no Englishman has any right to claim anything. I am asking you to steal nothing. All I wish is a copy of the map the Englishman has devised based on what he found in the memoir he acquired. Not the map itself, *querida mía,* but only a copy of it. At least, then, we shall begin at the same point, and may the better man win."

Marcelina, looking far from confident, nodded, bid her uncle and Abdullah *buenas noches,* turned, and departed slowly. As the stateroom door closed behind her, a deep growl rumbled up from the cavernous chest of Abdullah. Ferrar turned with a smile toward the giant who still stood in the same corner of the stateroom, regarding him with unblinking eyes.

"You do not trust her, do you, Abdullah?" said Ferrar. "I fear you are right. Despite her upbringing, she is weak. Her father did not whip her often enough or thoroughly enough. Still," he added broodingly, "perhaps I have also myself to blame. She has no compelling reason to love me, and possibly to betray me might cause her no qualms. Nevertheless, it is a chance we must take. Surely, she loves my sister, Isabella, and by extension has a certain loyalty to her family."

Abdullah said nothing. He knew that Ferrar had named Marcelina O'Day in his last will and testament as his heir, having no children of his own, and that, except for the house in Spanish Morocco and its furnishings, all his worldly wealth, including the encumbered lands he still retained in Peru, would go to his niece in the event of his death. He hated Marcelina O'Day for the place she occupied in Ferrar's heart, and nothing she could or would do for her uncle was likely to temper that feeling.

Chapter Six

The next day Chris Fallon spent the morning on deck, acquainting himself with other passengers. Sir Wilbur, Luis Valera, and Marcelina O'Day had spent some time on deck, but then had retired to the Englishman's stateroom to go over the map that had been elaborated by the professor, showing now in some detail the way through the Andes to the lost city of Haucha.

Fallon was strolling on deck past the ship's club room — the American prohibition of alcohol had not reached the high seas as yet and perhaps never would. It was here that he encountered Don Esteban de Ferrar as he was leaving the club room with Abdullah.

"*Señor* Fallon . . . greetings," Ferrar said, smiling cordially.

Fallon returned the smile. "Sir Wilbur and I suspected you were probably aboard the *Sea Queen*, but somehow we missed seeing you last night at dinner or this morning at breakfast."

"I fear I was not feeling well last night, and so stayed in my stateroom. I came out for the first time about a half hour ago. May I buy you a drink?"

"It's a little early, perhaps, but I have nothing pressing . . . so, why not?"

Ferrar turned and led the way back into the club room. Abdullah followed Fallon. They found a table with comfortable wicker chairs set under a porthole. Ferrar sat on the southern side of the porthole, Fallon on the northern, and Abdullah sat between them, facing the porthole. The steward came and took their drink orders. Ferrar selected a Burgundy wine, Fallon a gin fizz with lemon, and Abdullah a pilsner beer.

"I am sure Sir Wilbur will be pleased to learn," Ferrar said, once the steward had left their table, "that I intend to make no further overtures to obtain the manuscript he acquired concerning Haucha."

"You must have changed your mind, then," said Fallon, "since yesterday morning when you tried to run us off the street."

"Actually," Ferrar returned blandly, "what happened was purely unintentional, brought about by our unfamiliarity with San Francisco traffic. Abdullah and I merely wished to follow your taxi to see where you went."

"I think the article in the *Chronicle* indicated Sir Wilbur would be sailing on the *Sea Queen*."

"As a matter of fact, it did," Ferrar confessed, producing his jewel-encrusted gold cigarette case from which he took an Egyptian oval-shaped cigarette. "However, it was purely coincidence that Abdullah and I should have been booked on the same steamship. I have friends and relatives in Lima whom I intend to visit. I maintain an apartment in Lima, and still have my family's land." He lit the cigarette with a gold-plated lighter.

"I imagine it must have been something like that," Fallon said. "On the other hand, I would not suggest you follow us into the Peruvian interior. You'll find it much more difficult to navigate in the mountains than in the relatively tame streets of San Francisco."

"I dare say," Ferrar said, exhaling smoke, "but certainly the traffic will be much less."

"Certainly," Fallon agreed. "But without a map, you are liable to get lost . . . a potentially dangerous predicament in the wilderness."

"*Señor* Fallon, as Abdullah would tell you, were you to inquire of him, I am, above all, a gracious loser. Your party has the map. We do not. Any poor sportsmanship I may have displayed in San Francisco is now a thing of the past. I am a realist. There is nothing I can do to induce Sir Wilbur to surrender the manuscript of Fernando García. Oh, yes, I know the man's name, and actually quite a bit about his parchment record . . . more, to be sure, than was contained in the newspaper account. After all, I was on the track of that document before Sir Wilbur even knew that it existed."

The steward came with the drinks, and Ferrar tipped him generously.

"Do you know what the Incas meant by Haucha?" Abdullah asked, his deep bass voice rumbling.

"You've studied the language?" Fallon asked skeptically, lifting his drink.

"The culture . . . for some time now, *Señor* Fallon," Abdullah replied. "Haucha is the name of a planet."

"Yes, I believe *Señor* Ferrar told Sir Wilbur that it was Mars, before Sir Wilbur corrected him."

"Don Esteban was certainly excited, which is how the confusion came about," Abdullah said slowly. "The correct planet, of course, is Saturn. To the ancient Greeks, it was known as Kronos. The Romans called it Saturn. And it is Saturn who gave human beings their sense of time, their sense of the passing of the ages, the ability to weigh and measure, and it is Saturn who now sits on a throne in the Land of the Blessed. It is to him that the ancients attributed the idea of justice . . . and *Señor* Fallon . . . of retribution."

"And what in all that makes you believe that Haucha meant the same thing to the Incas?" Fallon asked.

"Because Haucha is the name the Incas . . . who from their mountain cities studied the skies so diligently . . . gave to the most distant of the five planets that are visible to the naked eye in the nocturnal sky . . . the planet that takes thirty years to revolve once around the sun . . . Haucha . . . the bringer of old age . . . and death."

"Is it any wonder," Ferrar interrupted, "that, when the Incas were fleeing the Spaniards led by my illustrious ancestor, they should have sought to hide their most fabulous wealth in a city named for Saturn? They thought, doubtless, that they would find protection beneath its mantle, as, indeed, they did."

"Since the two of you appear to know so much about the subject," Fallon conceded, "I suppose it is unfortunate that you cannot accompany us."

"Unfortunate . . . *Señor* Fallon?" Ferrar asked sharply. "It never occurred to me . . . as you say . . . to accompany *anyone* to Haucha, but rather to be the first after four centuries to lead the way there, to penetrate behind the curtain of time. As it is, Abdullah and I shall have to be satisfied, as all others, to remain behind and await the news of your conquest."

"I do not think *conquest* is really the right word," Fallon objected. "We will in all probability find the city in ruins and vacant of any life at all. It is something to which I have become accustomed on expeditions with Tenny . . . Sir Wilbur." He paused for a moment to sip from his drink. "The Egyptian city we found in Ethiopia was twenty-five hundred years old and buried under twelve feet of sand, the dust of the ages, you might say."

"Haucha is scarcely that old, *Señor* Fallon," Ferrar insisted quietly. "It could be at most six hundred years old."

"Cut off from all contact with the outside world for four hundred years?" Fallon scoffed. "I cannot imagine any people, no matter how ingenious, capable of being totally self-sufficient for that length of time . . . and in all the centuries since the conquest to have remained undiscovered, even unsuspected! It staggers belief."

"You speak as a man who does not believe in the existence

of Haucha," Abdullah said. "Yet, you of all people, having access to Fernando García's record . . . a record so clear that the way to Haucha lays mapped before you . . . such skepticism makes one wonder why you have joined in the Englishman's expedition."

"Oh," Fallon said, "I believe there was such a place as Haucha during the time of the conquest. It is just that I reckon it has long ceased to exist as a place that is habitable, cut off the way it was so long ago. I imagine what we'll find will be similar to our experience in Ethiopia . . . the ruins will have to be excavated . . . and at great expense. Far from enriching anybody, this discovery in the end will only cost money . . . Tenny's money, the museum's, perhaps in time it will cost the Peruvian government some money, should they actually be all that concerned about ancient Incan ruins in a country where there are a wealth of them already.

"But it is rather interesting, Abdullah, that you should have brought up Saturn. In that buried Egyptian city in Ethiopia the centerpiece of the find was the temple. It was obviously erected by followers of a sect that worshipped Kronos, as there were temples devoted to the worship of Kronos at Thebes, Rhodes, and later Athens. The members of this sect had an annual harvest festival they called the Kronia."

"Yes, I am very familiar with the teachings of the sect of Saturn," Abdullah said. "The harvest festival was a memorial to what the Romans called *Saturnia regna*, the Golden Age when Saturn ruled the world and all men lived long and virtuous lives, when there was no labor, no strife, and men shared everything freely, dwelling in safety amid a great abundance of all manner of produce that the earth had brought forth."

"It sounds rather similar to the Garden of Eden in Genesis," put in Ferrar, extinguishing his cigarette. "And what, pray, led to the destruction of this Golden Age? Was it somehow, again, a matter of a woman disobeying a divine law?"

"In a way," answered Abdullah. "Terra and Uranos, the parents of Saturn, warned him that he was destined to be overthrown by one of his own children. Therefore, he swallowed his children as soon as they were born of his sister and consort, Rhea. But it was Rhea who hid from Saturn his youngest child, Jupiter, and surrendered to Saturn, instead, a stone wrapped in the clothes of the newly born infant. When Jupiter reached his maturity, he rose up against his father. Rhea deceived Saturn into vomiting up his elder children, and these, too, joined forces with Jupiter. The battle on Mount Olympus raged for ten years, before Saturn was defeated and relegated to his position as lord of the Land of the Blessed."

"And this harvest festival?" Ferrar asked. "Of what was it in memory? Surely not Saturn's consumption of his own children . . . or his vomiting up of them again?"

"That is something that may come to you as a bit of surprise, Señor Ferrar," Fallon said, leaning back in his wicker chair, "although I rather suspect Abdullah knows it better than I do. For the time of the Kronia men recalled the Golden Age, as things had been before the war waged by Jupiter. They recalled the time of innocent happiness before there was slavery. All social distinctions were abolished, and master and man feasted together as equals in the eyes of Saturn. It was quite apt, really, since it is death that does make equals of us all."

"I could not agree with you more, Señor Fallon," Abdullah said. "For me, Saturn is still the king of kings, the most blessed of the blessed ones, the most perfect among the perfect."

"Excuse me, if I take exception," Ferrar objected in an arched tone.

"And excuse me," said Fallon, "but I take my Greek volume of Æschylus with me wherever I go, and I believe that he said that of Jupiter, and that he added the word *blissful*."

"My, my, you are rather accomplished for a brash American, aren't you?" Ferrar said with a touch of hauteur.

"You will pardon me for leaving that word out, *Señor* Fallon," Abdullah said. "It seems inappropriate, somehow, since the only bliss death can bring is that among the living. Bliss has little place in Saturn's distant kingdom."

"Abdullah is absolutely right, *Señor* Fallon," Ferrar added. "After all, we are sailing south, are we not? . . . away from the upper sphere to the north? The time is approaching the winter solstice, and the winter solstice is when, the Incas believed, for possibly three days the souls of those who are departed can cross over from the netherworld to this middle sphere where we live. It would be fitting, would it not, that the period of the winter solstice should occur when you enter the lost city of Haucha? Perhaps all of its legions, whom you believe to have been long extinct, will be there, waiting for your arrival, to take you and your party back with them."

Marcelina O'Day was dressed in white jodhpurs (she had two pairs of them) with a white blouse and bright blue scarf tied at her throat. With her Luis Valera had been again going over the map he had elaborated from his knowledge of the topography of Peru and the directions provided by the parchment of Fernando García. He had then excused himself from their session to visit the head. Marcelina, while fixing firmly in her memory the markings of the proposed route that would be followed to Haucha, now paced about the narrow stateroom Valera shared with Chris Fallon. She saw a small group of books that had been set out on the little shelf above the bunk occupied by Fallon, and she paused to look over the titles. There were a thick worn black volume of Æschylus's plays in the original Greek, two volumes of Homer also in Greek, a three-volume set of Shakespeare's plays, and a two-volume set of Prescott's THE CONQUEST OF PERU. It was the first volume of this last title that she took from its place on the shelf and opened.

Fallon must be reading it, because there was a leather book mark on the page at Book III, subtitled "Conquest of Peru." Flipping back to the title page, she saw that this edition had been published in New York in 1898. Opposite the title page was a *frontispiece* illustration of Francisco Pizarro. Certain facial characteristics had been inherited, she could see, by her uncle, the long, prominent nose and the very large eyes. The ears with their rather wide lobes were similar to those of her mother and, she had to admit, of she herself. She noticed that missing from the title page, but familiar to her because it was to be found in her edition of the book, was that Latin interrogatory: *quem colorem habet sapientia?* What color, indeed, is wisdom? She ventured to conjecture that for Francisco Pizarro, as for Don Esteban de Ferrar, it would be the same color as the corona of the sun, a radiant aureola.

It was then that she snapped the red volume shut, overwhelmed suddenly by a wrenching turmoil, an inner feeling of self-repugnance and shame at betraying Luis Valera, Francisca, Sir Wilbur Tennington, and even Chris Fallon, although until this time she had felt him to be merely an adventurer without any depth of soul. If Fallon read at all, she had surmised, it would probably be the sports pages in a newspaper or perhaps a pulp magazine with a garish cover illustration. All that time with Sir Wilbur in Egypt and Ethiopia must have had some affect on him . . . yet, no, she had studied Greek and Latin herself, and they were not languages easily or superficially mastered. Ancient Greek, in fact, was a language far more inflected and complicated than English, which now she could speak so well, but also a language as rich in color and nuance as her native Spanish.

Luis Valera came back into the stateroom. He saw Marcelina holding the red volume of Prescott.

"Chris is reading up on the conquest, as I see you've noticed," he said, smiling. "He's quite a fellow, actually. Been so many places I've only read about. He was recently in Brazil, you know, on a different kind of expedition . . . searching for rare species of tropical fish in the rain forests of the Amazon."

"I believe I've heard about that," Marcelina said, replacing the book on the little shelf. "I hope you won't tell Mister Fallon that I've been snooping in his library."

"Not at all," Valera said. "He told me that he takes that little library of his wherever he goes. It is readily transportable, and, although it may seem exciting to be up and doing, there is actually a lot of idle time in what he does . . . usually at night on the way and, of course, once he has arrived at a destination, since the goal of these various quests is usually on behalf of someone else who wants very much to be where they get, far more, apparently, than he does."

"Why does he do it, then?"

"I haven't asked him, but I have learned he grew up on a ranch in Arizona but came to dislike ranching. An interest in Homer led him to learn to read Greek, and probably an interest in antiquity and zoology generally got him involved in field work. I know he did post-graduate study for a year at Harvard. During the summer of Nineteen Twelve he actually worked for the British Museum as a field collector in Baja California and parts of northern Mexico. He's been at it ever since. Tenny swears by him. They are both men whose experience of archeology has been more active than academic."

"You mean, like you . . . and now me?"

"Well, yes, Marcie, if you put it that way . . . and certainly it is so in the case of Haucha." A look of concern crossed the professor's face. "I truly hope your parents will not change their minds about your accompanying the expedition . . . especially now that you are familiar with the difficulties of the route we must take."

"I'm sure not, *Tío* Luis. We will all be visiting Papa and Mama once we reach Lima, and I'm sure they will be even more excited for me, the more they hear about it."

"If I know your father," confided Valera, "I suspect he might want to come along himself."

It was not a remark intended to create fear in Marcelina, but it did in a way, as she wondered how much of Don Esteban's intentions were known to her parents. She was certain Isabella knew of his prior claim to the García parchment, but she did not know how much of the whole affair would be familiar to her father. Once Thomas O'Day did know Ferrar's objective — which she would be only furthering through her betrayal of the trust Luis Valera and the others had placed in her — he might forbid her to go at all.

Concealing as best she could her tremendous agitation, she excused herself, saying she felt the need to repair to her stateroom. Her effort at dissimulation must have been successful, since Valera was gracious and encouraging as he bid her farewell until they would see each other later at dinner.

Don Esteban de Ferrar and Abdullah Simbel had gone to the stateroom they shared where, sitting across from each other at the table in the center, they discussed what, if anything, they had learned from their conversation with Chris Fallon. Ferrar's view of the American was that he was of negligible significance and could be discounted entirely. He was confident that Marcelina O'Day would not fail him.

"You are fond of stories of antiquity, Abdullah," Ferrar said, calmly lighting another of his oval Egyptian cigarettes.

"Are you familiar with how the blind seer, Teirésias, who has such a central rôle in Sophocles's Theban plays, came to be blind?"

"I believe," Abdullah replied, "that the legend has it that he once came upon the goddess Athena, when she was bathing in the nude, and that in anger at his effrontery she destroyed his sight, but in compensation gave him the gift of foreseeing the future."

"Precisely," agreed Ferrar. "But it has always seemed to me that the legend, as you have stated it, was somehow incomplete. Athena was not really outraged that Teirésias should have looked upon the incredible beauty of her nakedness. Rather, she was outraged that he should have desired to peer behind the veil of mystery that envelopes a woman. The image of Athena's nakedness is tempting and charming at the same time, for there she was, believed to be keeping the world in order, preserving the rhythm and balance of it, yet wishing all the time to preserve the mystery of her sex while knowing herself that there was no mystery at all. I have even heard the comment made that Athena lacked, above all, a sense of humor . . . to have so punished Teirésias. But that is because we respond to the legend as men, and as men it is we whose sense of humor is rather flat and colorless compared with hers. The blinding of Teirésias managed to sustain the sense of mystery about a woman's nakedness, keeping men, however impudent or curious, if you will, so frightened that they have preferred to worship at the temple, but never to penetrate behind the tabernacle and learn, as did Teirésias, that there really is no mystery about it. The concealment, that is the mystery in itself, and, really, as we have learned now from anatomy what Athena sought so cleverly to veil was a biped that micturates once a day, defecates once a week, menstruates once a month, and propagates at every available opportunity!"

71

The giant Negro's broad mouth spread into a smile, almost a grin, but he said nothing, as happened when he was most profoundly amused.

They were both still sitting at the table, conversing, some time later when Marcelina came to the door of the stateroom and knocked softly. Abdullah rose and opened the door, closing it after her.

She walked over to the table and placed on it a copy of the map of the route to Haucha that she had made back in her own stateroom after leaving Valera. Ferrar's solemn black eyes swiftly scrutinized the map.

"¡De perlas!" he murmured in Spanish, glancing up at Abdullah who stood with an expressionless face behind the girl who had seated herself across from Ferrar in the chair Abdullah had been occupying upon her arrival. Then Ferrar glanced toward Marcelina. Her blue-gray eyes, perhaps a little sullen, perhaps a little fearful, were fixed on him. "Yes, you have done well," he said approvingly. "But, *niña mía*, your evident reluctance troubles me."

She shrugged. "The map is yours, *tío mío* . . . is that not what you wanted?"

"It is, but your attitude of mind troubles me. Perhaps I understand you better than you think I do."

"Then why do you not respect *my* feelings?" she asked with dignity.

"Dear child," he replied patiently, "think what this wealth will mean . . . you will have rich clothes, luxuries, servants, money, ease . . . all that a girl could desire."

"You know my family is relatively well off," she replied tonelessly, "and you certainly are not wanting. What wealth may come from this venture . . . I want no part of it. There are some things that wealth cannot buy, and I feel that, in a way, when you asked me to give you that map, it was like abandoning my very soul . . . for all eternity."

"Why, in God's name?"

"Devotion . . . respect . . . decency. I have lied and have robbed to get you this map. The wealth you may obtain can bring only unhappiness."

"Bah! You're a fool."

"You are correct, *tío mío*. I am a fool, and I wish from this time forward to have nothing to do with you. Do not acknowledge me, please, on board ship should we meet in public."

"And in Lima?" Ferrar asked softly.

"Do you intend to visit Papa and Mama?"

"As a matter of fact, I do not," Ferrar admitted, "at least not when we arrive. For this map to do us any good we have to be on our way in advance of the infernal Englishman and the rest of your company. But I am certain your parents will agree that you did the right thing. There is no greater loyalty we can have than to our family."

"I think there is one," Marcelina said quietly, rising, trembling now, tears in her eyes, "and I believe it is *that* one I have betrayed."

Then she fled the stateroom.

Abdullah emitted a low rumbling sound. "Have we not seen the exquisite Marcelina O'Day stand naked before us this day?" he asked. "What will be our punishment? What hers?" He twisted both hands in opposite directions in an efficient gesture.

Ferrar rose and smiled wanly. "Perhaps we may yet have to do that very thing to protect what is ours . . . and hers, even though she denies it . . . but let us wait and see."

Chapter Seven

Days passed, long, sunny days, and the *Sea Queen* forged ever closer to its goal — Lima. Chris Fallon had told Sir Wilbur Tennington of his encounter with Ferrar and Abdullah in the club room the same day it happened, only to learn that Sir Wilbur had already confirmed the Spaniard's presence on board after a visit with the captain. The Englishman listened with equanimity to Fallon's quoting Ferrar that there was now a truce and that he had resigned himself to the fact that his claim to the Fernando García parchment was regarded as spurious. Although Ferrar and Abdullah could be seen in the dining room, they made no effort to speak with Sir Wilbur. Occasionally, Fallon would encounter Ferrar and Abdullah walking along the deck and would receive an acknowledgment, but no overtures for further conversation were made by any of them.

Marcelina spent a good deal of time in her stateroom or reading on deck. Fallon found himself drawn to the girl, and they would dance together in the evenings or stroll about on deck. It was Fallon's impression, however, that something was preying upon her mind, that there was a reticence, even a sadness, about her that she was unwilling to share with him. Luis Valera had noticed it as well and, when approached on the subject casually by Fallon in the stateroom they shared, attributed it to worry that, perhaps, her parents would have second thoughts about allowing her to accompany them on a journey likely to be so dangerous.

One night, after dinner, Marcelina did not feel like dancing or going to the club room. She was willing, however, to stroll on deck. Fallon led the way to the stern where they paused at the railing, looking out over the wake left by the ship, white foam curling outward to each side, appearing incandescent in the moonlight.

"You know, Marcelina," Fallon said, "in the beginning, I was cautious about your coming along on this expedition. You've seemed a bit preoccupied lately, and Luis commented that you might be fearful that your parents will object to your accompanying us once they learn the particulars of where we will have to go to find Haucha. I want you to know that I haven't felt that way for some time, now that we've come to know each other. I believe you should come. The experience, no matter what we find, will be worth it."

"It's been . . . I've seemed that obvious . . . ?" she responded hesitantly. "I mean . . . no, I'm not worried about what will my parents will say. I am sure, if I still wish to go, they won't withdraw their permission. It is just . . . well, maybe I'm the one who's no longer so certain."

"You mean you might not want to go?" Fallon asked with some surprise.

"Would that be so terrible, Chris?"

"But why . . . why change your mind now? I'm sure you know about Ferrar's actions in San Francisco and about his being on board, and you also know that he told me he has no interest in competing with us in getting to Haucha."

"There is much that you do not understand, Chris."

"Maybe not, but the dangers I had in mind in the beginning had to do with the rigors of the terrain and those that you encounter whenever you venture into a relative wilderness."

"I am not afraid of those things."

"But you are afraid?"

"I did not say that."

"Well, what is it, then, Marcelina?"

She did not answer, but, instead, opened her small handbag

75

and brought out a cigarette. Fallon produced his lighter, and this time it was he who shielded the flame from the breeze, while she bent forward. She inhaled and expelled smoke.

"You know," she said then, "I saw your little library when I was in the stateroom you share with *Tío* Luis. He said you told him that you take your Æschylus with you wherever you go."

"That's true."

"Why?"

"I love his plays. They never age for me. If I took a magazine story or a modern novel, I would read it once, and that would be it. It may sound strange, but as many times as I've read his plays . . . you know, he wrote at least seventy plays, but only seven have survived. How often I've wished there were more. But even as it is, every time I read one of them, I find something new, something I had not realized before, or hadn't lived enough to recognize before. His plays are about human nature, really . . . about life, about meaning."

Her face was partly in shadow and partly illumined from a nearby ship's lamp. She was smiling. He could see her smile, but there was still that wistfulness.

"I was reading AGAMEMNON last night, late," he continued, a bit ill at ease now. "Early in that play there is a passage given to the Chorus that speaks of how there is a sinful sense of daring which can lead to a man's dark action and bring him to disaster . . . that this same sinful daring can stay in certain families for generations. I've also been reading Prescott's history of the conquest of Peru. Now that I have almost completed it, the notion struck me of the disaster that overtook Pizarro, the other members of his family, and it made me wonder if there might be some truth in the belief that such a destiny can befall a family generation after generation."

Marcelina had begun trembling. In her anxiety, she dropped her cigarette, caught it with a swift movement of her right shoe, and snuffed it out on the deck.

"I didn't mean to upset you," Fallon said, and stopped talking.

"It's nothing you said, Chris," Marcelina responded. Her voice seemed somewhat distant. "It is just that reality met me, such a short time ago, and it came in such a hideous form that I thought there might be some way to escape from it. There came in me such a dark fear, as if threatening to seize me, to possess me altogether, that I wanted to find refuge in something fantastic. I play the piano . . . perhaps *Tío* Luis told you."

Fallon shook his head negatively.

"Well, it is something I do every day, but I cannot readily do it here on the *Sea Queen*. Music for me is like that, something fantastic, in which I can lose myself. When life makes a very nasty face at me, there is no recourse, it seems, no way I can make a worse face back at life, except when I play. Right now I have a distrust of the future. It is as if I were asking myself . . . am I to pay for this? What am I to pay? One hopes, Chris . . . even if amid all the miseries of the past . . . to die in a state of simple happiness." As she spoke now, Marcelina's face seemed to be transformed, lit from within by an heroic gentleness, although her tone and inflection were scarcely heroic.

"Do you recall the story you told me about the old satyr when asked about a man's best fate?" Fallon asked.

"Yes," she answered, but so very quietly he scarcely heard her.

"You make it sound now as if that old satyr were right, that the only hope to die in simple happiness would be to die as soon as possible after birth. Agamemnon probably said it better . . . 'call blest only that man who has in sweet tranquillity brought his life to a close.' It is an achievement that, perhaps, only the most fortunate among us ever might attain." He paused to laugh before continuing. "Not that I think like that at all times. While I was up the Amazon on that field trip for tropical fish . . . when onshore we had to sleep on cots with their legs set in cans filled with kerosene because the centipedes grow to a foot long there, and one bite can kill you, or make you delirious. Where we're going this time, we don't know what we're going to run into, except that part of the route . . . which, I know, Luis has gone over with you . . . is through wilderness and part of it is in the mountains. Even if you're prepared for it, there is no way of telling what might happen. Although it is unlikely that Haucha is still inhabited by Incas, it might be, or their fierce and war-like descendants. The impression I've had reading Prescott is that the Incas were, in their way, superior to the Spaniards in both social and cultural civilization. They were not the avaricious fanatics the Spaniards were, although they were probably more profoundly religious than the invaders. The Spaniards, after all, garroted the Inca to death, after compelling him either to be baptized or burned at the stake."

"I know," Marcelina admitted. "The prospect that some part, if not all, of Inca culture should have survived, untarnished over time, that is what so excited *Tio* Luis. It is what excites me. It is why I so much desired to be part of the journey. Perhaps, though, that was only girlish and silly. It may be that Sir Wilbur . . . although he will not admit it . . . is interested only in being the first since the conquest to claim more fabulous Incan treasure."

"If you think that, Marcelina, you don't know Tenny as I do. He's only happy when he's on that road in which lies so much of the happiness of the true traveler . . . when he is sure of his direction. I am certain, at least in the beginning, we'll pass any number of wayfarers in all manner of vehicles, on horseback and afoot, and they will all seem to have a destination. But so many having a destination is not the same thing as a direction. I don't know how to say it, perhaps, but for Tenny a jour-

78

ney like this isn't merely through space. That is only the most obvious part of it. For him . . . and, I imagine, for Luis . . . it is really a journey through time, into a part of the past that we can no longer touch, except in books or artifacts in some museum. It is like a journey into another dimension."

"And," said Marcelina, her blue-gray eyes, even if they were in shadow, transfixing Fallon, "what of betrayal?"

"I'm not quite sure I understand you."

"I'm . . . I'm not sure I completely understand myself. It is like being torn apart, loving someone you should love but hating that person, too, because it is as if a part of yourself were an enemy. Not an enemy outside. When an enemy is outside, there are ways we can defend ourselves. But what happens when the enemy is within?"

Fallon was struck by the image of the undefiled Artemis, driven to anger and pity at the fleet hounds of her father's eating the unborn young in the shivering mother hare. "I suppose," he said slowly, "that we die a little, or, at least, a part of ourselves will die. In the end it may be that our lives and all that we do is like a legend or a tale, where it is not really such a bad thing if you understand only half of it. And, if you understand only half of it, or even a smaller part of it than that, you best not judge, for you are likely to be too harsh. Does anything ultimately happen without God's blessing? That old satyr may have been right, as far as he went. But, as it is, no one of us knows whether his or her life will be long or short. It used to be believed that a person died when he was destined by God to die. Now it is believed, somehow, that death can be delayed, by following a certain regimen. Some imagine it as a game, and, if you follow certain rules, you can somehow determine the outcome, or delay it. Only in all truth, you can't. There is your person with all his defenses turned toward the enemies outside, but there are also accidents. I might fall from a cliff in the Andes. If you accompany us, you might fall heir to some catastrophe. You could not possibly know what was coming, no matter what precautions you might take. At some point, whether it is supernatural, or genetic, or fate, the body begins to shut down. Probably we'll never know enough about all the factors to understand it completely. That's why I say, life is a tale where we understand only part of it. Perhaps, like I told you about camping on the Amazon, we place all the legs of our cots in cans filled with kerosene, but, as happened to me, there can be the unexpected that cannot be prevented. One night one of those foot-long centipedes entered my tent and hid under my cot. It did not try to climb up over the cans and so fall into the kerosene. Instead, it climbed up the wall of the tent, and, when it was overhead, it would have dropped down onto me."

"Were you bitten?"

"No," Fallon replied. "Something else unexpected had happened. I still hadn't fallen asleep that night when I saw the shadow of the centipede, moving up the canvas wall of the tent. There was a fire outside in camp, and my tent was near enough to the fire that I could see the centipede's shadow as it moved along the canvas wall. I jumped off my cot and then could kill it."

"But . . . ?" began Marcelina softly.

However, Fallon was now lighting a cigarette and was disinclined to say any more about it. Instead, he asked: "What has happened since we boarded the *Sea Queen* to make you want to change your mind? About going, I mean? I would have sworn when I first met you that day at Luis's home you were totally committed to the venture. Why, if you were so unsure, are you here now? If it's not concern that your parents might change their minds and withdraw their support of your going, what can it be?"

"Oh, but I do want to go," Marcelina said, a vibrant urgency

80

in her voice. "It is just . . . well, perhaps it will not be possible. Chris, I can't tell you why." In her anxiety she reached out and touched his arm. "And do not tell the others that I've even said such a thing. It has nothing to do with the journey itself, and for any number of reasons it is the direction in which I wish more than anything to go. It is only . . . that part of me has. . . ." She dropped her hand and turned away from him, toward the railing and the churning wake of the ship, vaguely visible far below them. "It is better we do not speak more of it," she said then.

Fallon suspected tears had come to her eyes. He cast his cigarette overboard and sought to turn her toward him. She resisted.

"Let me be," she said sharply. "There's nothing wrong. I'll be all right."

"Please, Marcelina, won't you tell me what it is? . . . what is troubling you? Is it Ferrar? Has he threatened you? It certainly wouldn't be out of character from what little I've seen of the man."

"Why do you say that?" she demanded, turning on him swiftly. "What do you know of anything? I have never even mentioned his name?"

"But you certainly know about him," Fallon insisted, "the way he threatened Tenny, and tried to run us down on the way to pick up you and Luis. I've met and talked with him in the club room. He claims he's given up . . . as far as trying to compel us to surrender the map we have."

"And why did Sir Wilbur refuse to co-operate with him?" Marcelina asked somewhat coldly. "Can you be so sure that Sir Wilbur isn't simply interested in what treasure he may find . . . in spite of what you say about his having some exalted direction? Couldn't it just be a matter of one man's greed against another's?"

"Now you are talking nonsense, Marcelina. I'll admit I

81

don't really know Ferrar, and I won't try to judge the legitimacy of his claim. But I do know Tenny, and you surely know Luis Valera. Neither one of them is in this for any treasure, no matter how much there is or . . . as is more likely . . . none at all. Even if they do find treasure, do you imagine either will try to keep it, or that I will? Has finding treasures that the Incas sought to conceal from the invading Spaniards been your reason for wanting to come?"

She did not answer.

"Was that ever your reason?"

"Do you know me so little?"

"I only asked you because you insist on attributing motives to Tenny and the rest of us that we've never felt."

"I don't know."

There were tears in her eyes. Fallon could see them glisten. He shook his head in bewilderment. "Do you want to know something, Marcelina? I'm not sure what we're talking about. Not really sure. Are you?"

"I believe you answered that yourself when you said that all we ever understand is part of the tale . . . never the whole thing. And that's why we so often make mistakes. But I would not worry about Don Esteban de Ferrar. He shall never find Haucha."

"How can you be so certain?"

"Because he cannot go in the right direction."

"Of course, he can't. He doesn't have the parchment, and he doesn't have the map."

"That's so," she agreed. She leaned forward and up, and took Fallon by the arms, and kissed him gently. "Good night, Chris," she said. She was smiling when she turned and walked quickly away, leaning a little toward port because the ship had slanted slightly upon encountering a momentary turbulence in its passage.

82

Chapter Eight

When, at last, the *Sea Queen* docked in Lima, Marcelina's parents were on hand to meet them. Thomas O'Day was a man in his fifties, with a broad but angular face, a somewhat wide mouth, pale blue eyes, and hair beneath his Panama hat that once had been red but now was shot with an iron gray. Fallon could see whence the reddish tint had come to Marcelina's brown hair. Her father was of medium height, but Isabella O'Day was closer to five feet, with a darker complexion than Marcelina's, a petite woman with her daughter's high forehead and cheekbones, a straight nose with a slight flair at the nostrils, and rather large but perfect teeth visible because she smiled frequently. Where Marcelina had exuberance and a sense of humor and seemed often to be secretly amused, her mother was more withdrawn although there was about her a graceful gentleness.

Marcelina embraced her father and then her mother. Luis Valera then came forward, and he embraced Thomas O'Day heartily, the Irishman obviously joyful at seeing his old friend again. Luis then took Isabella's hand affectionately into his, and told her that Francisca missed her and would have come had it been a social visit. Marcelina introduced Sir Wilbur to her father and mother, and then Chris Fallon.

Thomas O'Day had a touring car, and it was determined that Chris Fallon would drive Isabella and Marcelina back to the O'Day home. Sir Wilbur had made reservations at a hotel for himself, the professor, and Fallon, and Thomas O'Day insisted on seeing that Tennington and Valera and the luggage were safely conveyed there in a taxicab. He was more than willing to put all of them up, but the Englishman insisted he did not wish to be an imposition. Arrangements had to be made to travel overland across the Cordillera Occidental into the Andes in the general direction of the Cerros de Canchyuaya. He deliberately was not more specific than that about their destination.

Thomas O'Day gave Chris Fallon the keys to the touring car and, after passing through customs, Fallon left the dock area with the two women. O'Day accompanied Sir Wilbur and Luis Valera through customs and saw that they had assistance with the luggage, much of which would have to be sent on to the hotel for separate delivery after they had registered. At the hotel, Sir Wilbur proposed O'Day join them for a drink before they went up to their rooms. It was a sunny tropical day, with a very blue sky and puffy white clouds, and the three men went out onto the hotel's verandah where drinks were served to them at an awning table with wicker chairs painted white. O'Day was keenly interested in details of the expedition and was excited that his daughter was to have the opportunity to accompany them.

Valera was very solemn once they were seated and broached a subject that had obviously been troubling him.

"Tomás," he said, "you must forgive me for bringing up something unpleasant, but I have waited this long before saying anything . . . even to Sir Wilbur . . . because I wanted you to be present." He looked across at the Englishman, who had taken out the bulldog pipe and his tobacco pouch. "And you, Sir Wilbur, I hope, will forgive me for having remained silent about it until now. I wanted first to see what, if anything, should happen when we disembarked."

"Pray, Luis," said Sir Wilbur, "what are you getting at?"

"Just this," Valera continued. "Tomás, are you aware that Don Esteban de Ferrar was our fellow passenger on the *Sea Queen*?"

"No," admitted O'Day, struck with some embarrassment.

84

"Certainly Marcelina didn't mention anything about it when we were at the dock."

"I beg your pardon, Luis," interrupted the Englishman, "but I wasn't aware in the least you knew anything at all about Ferrar personally except what Chris Fallon or I may have told you."

"Of course, I learned that you had trouble with him on the way to my home in San Francisco and before that, and I spoke further with Chris about him in our stateroom. We all were certainly aware of his presence on board ship and in the dining room."

"Agreed," said the Englishman, "but I gather he's decided to be amicable, now that he knows he isn't going to get anywhere trying to intimidate us. He told Fallon as much aboard the *Sea Queen*."

"Ferrar," put in O'Day, "is a very wealthy and powerful man, Sir Wilbur. He also happens to be my wife's brother . . . and so, although I won't defend him, he is a member of my family."

"If that is so," said Sir Wilbur, "then I am surprised that he made no effort to converse with Marcelina, or she with him."

"That, I fear, was entirely Marcelina's doing," conceded Valera. "I do not know from her if he approached her concerning the García parchment or the course we are to follow, but I did ask her about him shortly after we boarded the *Sea Queen*, based on what you and Chris told us in the taxicab on the way to the boarding dock in San Francisco. This was before, of course, I learned that he was on board himself. She asked me to say nothing about her being his niece, and she would take care to see that he no longer endangered any of us or our enterprise."

"I find this very disturbing, indeed," O'Day said emphatically. "Don Esteban has often been a guest in our home. True, more in years past than recently, and I have always been cordial to him because he is part of the family. He seemed fond of Marcelina when she was younger, but I would never permit him to have her visit him at his estate in Spanish Morroco, and I will tell you frankly I do not trust him or that so-called associate of his, Abdullah Simbel. I had no knowledge, before you brought him up, Luis, that he was on the *Sea Queen*, much less that he has had any dealings with Marcelina. Believe me, when I get home, I will talk to her and get to the bottom of it."

Sir Wilbur, in his reserved way, appeared somewhat agitated. "Luis, tell me . . . you don't think it possible, even likely, that Marcelina has told her uncle anything about the route we plan to take?"

"I assure you, Sir Wilbur," O'Day said forcefully, "my daughter may have her faults, but dishonesty or betrayal would not be among them."

"I wasn't accusing the girl," Sir Wilbur conciliated, "but, after all, this Ferrar is her uncle, and who knows what kind of pressure he may have brought on her for information." He abruptly put his pipe down on the table. "I thought there was something wrong . . . that after pulling a gun on us in my hotel room in San Francisco, and then trying to run us off the street on the way to your home, Luis, he should suddenly declare that he had lost all interest in Haucha. Fair play does not seem to be part of that man's make-up."

"He pulled a gun on you?" O'Day asked in astonishment. "That does seem somewhat out of character."

"I assure you, sir," said the Englishman coldly, "that is, indeed, what he did. Fortunately, Chris was able to diffuse the situation."

"I promise you this, Sir Wilbur," O'Day said, "I will find out what, if anything, has gone on between Don Esteban and my daughter, and, further, you can lay to it that she will be staying at home, and not going on with you!"

"Please, Tomás," interceded Valera, "that is precisely what I do not wish to happen, and why I have hesitated until now to say anything to Sir Wilbur. Marcelina, as you know, is an excellent student and has the interest and ability to excel in the field of archeology, even though she is young. . . ."

"And a girl!" O'Day interrupted emphatically.

"Her gender ought have nothing to do with it!" Sir Wilbur said. "Fallon had some misgivings about Marcelina and the dangers we might encounter, but he has since changed his mind, and I never was concerned about her in that way in the least. The young woman is bright, energetic, and, I am convinced, will be an asset on the expedition." He held out a hand toward the Irishman. "You yourself say that the girl is not deceitful. I am inclined to agree with you. If her uncle has, indeed, brought pressure on her, I am sure she will tell you about it. In fact, her closeness to Luis has been such that, I am sure, were there anything on that order, she would not have dissembled to him about it."

"My brother-in-law can be a most persuasive man at times," O'Day replied. "I confess I would not have expected him to be violent, but he does take great pride in the descent of his lineage from Francisco Pizarro. Do not forget, Pizarro was able to defeat the Incas . . . thousands upon thousands of armed troops fresh from a battle over succession . . . with less than two hundred Spaniards."

"But *how* did he do it?" Valera asked. "Not by military might, or by numbers, but by guile and deceit!"

"Let us not get into that, Luis," O'Day insisted. "His men had armor, rode horses, had gunpowder and crossbows, and seemed altogether miraculous to the Incas who had never seen anything like them before."

"Yes, Tomás," put in Valera, "but how far would any of that

have gotten him, had he not been able to kidnap the Inca and hold him as a captive?"

"About as far as the Irish have gotten in trying to drive the English out of Ireland," O'Day shot back.

"I beg your pardon," responded Sir Wilbur, somewhat testily.

"Gentlemen, please," said Valera, almost laughing. "I was feeling badly for having kept quiet about Ferrar as long as I have. Apparently it was a mistake to bring him up at all."

"All right . . . all right," O'Day said placatingly. "Before we go any further, perhaps you can explain to me just why Don Estaban has involved himself in what I thought was basically an old bones and pottery expedition to some lost Inca city."

"Ferrar is of the opinion," explained Sir Wilbur, picking up his pipe again, "that there is a vast Incan treasure located at Haucha."

"And you don't?" asked O'Day.

"There are indications in the García parchment which I acquired that would give credence to that belief," Sir Wilbur admitted, "but it has been centuries, now, and who knows what may have happened to any treasure that was there originally."

"And if there is treasure," inquired O'Day, "just how much of it do you plan to claim on behalf of the British crown?"

"Not a farthing, sir," the Englishman replied emphatically. "This expedition is being co-sponsored by the San Francisco Museum, with which Luis is associated, and myself. Chris Fallon is our field guide. Frankly, other than the ardors of the trek itself, which will take us high into the Andes, I did not even foresee any special dangers."

"You took Marcelina to Cuzco when she was younger," Valera reminded O'Day.

"Well, why not? It's a Peruvian city now, and has been since the Spaniards came, and before that it was the Incan capital.

Since she was a young girl, Marcelina has been interested in ancient civilizations, and the Incas in particular. After all, it is part of her heritage. I might not want to have any business dealings with Don Esteban . . . and he did once approach me concerning one . . . but I do not doubt for a moment that he would be the last person to cause Marcelina any harm. After all, she is his niece. I also believe . . . in his way . . . that he loves his sister, Isabella, my wife. The more I think about it, the less inclined I am to believe that Don Esteban would have asked Marcelina to pry into your affairs, or that she would have done so, if he'd had the gall to ask it. He is an estimable man . . . and I do not fault him for daring. He was involved in some way dealing in munitions both with the Allies and the Central Powers in the recent war. While it is true that he inherited money, he has also added a good deal to his personal fortune . . . although do not ask me just how, because I have refused to have any commercial dealings with him. He is family, and I accept him as such, as I am sure Marcelina does."

"Now this is so much more sensible," said Valera. "I know Sir Wilbur will be going to see the minister of the interior before we actually depart on our way to Haucha, and, so far, our expedition has had the acquiescence of the Peruvian government. My interest and the interest of the museum is the same . . . to add what we can to the knowledge of Incan civilization . . . and, of course, should we discover artifacts of historical or cultural value, I am sure that it will be possible to claim some of the specimens for the museum's permanent collection. I think the view has been expressed before . . . and I can only repeat it . . . that Don Esteban de Ferrar is acting under some kind of delusion that there is a vast quantity of gold hidden at Haucha."

"And just how does he claim an interest in such treasure, if there is any?" O'Day inquired.

"According to him," Sir Wilbur said, somewhat contemptuously, "on the basis of his descent from Pizarro."

This statement incited the Irishman to laughter. "That," he said, "is not only ridiculous, but . . . you are serious now? . . . he tried to force you to divulge your route to him at gunpoint?"

"It may amuse you, sir," said Sir Wilbur, "but, I can assure you, the man was very much in earnest."

"If he threatened your life at gunpoint," asked O'Day, "why didn't you simply have him arrested?"

"Because it might have caused an incident," admitted the Englishman. "After all, neither he nor I is a citizen of the United States, and I could only see further complications arising from any attempt to involve the San Francisco authorities, without anything more being resolved."

"And then, you say, he tried to run you off the street in a car?"

"He claimed to Chris Fallon that it was all an error, due to his being unfamiliar with city traffic," said the Englishman.

"Now that I can believe," O'Day said, his good humor having returned. "I've never known the man to drive any kind of a vehicle. When he's been here, he's always hired transportation, horse-drawn, I believe, before automobiles became more common."

Luis Valera lifted his drink and sipped at it. "Please, Tomás, do not punish Marcelina because of anything her uncle may have done, or tried to do. Also do not distrust her. She is a good girl. Francisca and I know you have every reason to be proud of her, and to trust her. She has blossomed into a modern young woman."

"She was something of a tomboy growing up," her father stated.

"The old Spanish ways of sheltering girls have passed," Valera said.

"I never thought much of 'em myself," O'Day rejoined. "I had a hell of a time when I was courting Isabella . . . and, don't forget, I was considered a foreigner here . . . still am by some."

"Very well, Tomás, then do not destroy young Marcelina's hope of accompanying us to Haucha . . . whatever may be Don Esteban's attitude about it. After all, you are quite right that she is his niece and I, too, am certain he would see no harm came to her."

"I am inclined to agree with Luis when it comes to Ferrar," Sir Wilbur said, lifting his drink. "By all means, let us talk to the young lady, but let us not hold her responsible for her uncle's incivility or his brutishness in San Francisco. After all, the affair really ends here in Lima for him, unless he actually plans to follow us like a shadow into the interior. Even if he does, he'll get there behind us."

Thomas O'Day smiled, as did Luis Valera.

The O'Day home was in an upper-class residential neighborhood. It was a hacienda in the Spanish style with thick adobe walls painted a brilliant white and with red-tile roofs. It was surrounded by a iron grille fence, painted black, with white adobe columns at the gate and intersecting the fence at fifteen-foot intervals. There was a circular drive paved with crushed stone and a majestic double front door of inlaid wood, highly varnished. There was a sunroom off to one side with an adjoining verandah that extended along one whole side of the house.

Thomas O'Day didn't have a chauffeur, but there were servants, a *majordomo,* whom Chris Fallon did see, and two maids and a *cuisinière* whom he did not. There was also a gardener who maintained the elaborate tropical flower gardens around the house. Fallon parked the Pierce Arrow touring car in the front drive and helped Isabella O'Day from the front passenger seat, and then, although she was smiling with amusement as he did it, he also opened the rear door for Marcelina. The *major-domo* who was at the front door appeared to be a native Peruvian, dressed in livery, somewhat formal in demeanor. He welcomed the *señorita* home and then went to the car to bring in the suitcase Marcelina had brought with her as well as Chris Fallon's bag.

Fallon accompanied the women to the drawing room. It was elegantly furnished, with a stone fireplace before which there were two chairs across from each other on either side and a divan beyond them facing it. Isabella commented that the room had recently been redecorated. The walls had once been painted white with ornaments of stucco. Now they were covered with wallpaper in the form of scenic mosaics of a pastoral character. There were fields of Indian corn shown in various stages, from the green and tender ears early in the season to the yellow ripeness at the time of harvest. There was in a majestic valley vegetation to delight the eye with the splendor of many different colors, so vividly rendered perhaps that one almost had the illusion of an intoxicating perfume arising from the flowers, although more likely this was a result of the air coming in through the French doors in the adjacent sunroom that were opened onto the verandah and the lush garden beyond it. The tapestries and the fringed shades of the lamps and the crystal displayed the cosmopolitan character one would expect in the home of an importer. In a far corner, just before the archway leading into the sunroom, was a grand piano of highly polished walnut.

"Alas, the piano has been silent since Marcelina has been gone," Isabella remarked, "but it has been recently tuned, and perhaps, later, she will play it. She is such a fine pianist, I am sorry, almost, that she chose to take up another field of study. As a girl, growing up, she loved the outdoors, and was interested, even then, in antiquity, but she was very devoted to music. She began her first lessons when she was six."

Isabella said she must make arrangements for lunch and then for dinner, since Luis Valera and Sir Wilbur Tennington would be joining them later. Fallon was offered to avail himself of a guest room where his bag had been taken, should he feel the need to freshen up, but, for the moment, he declined. Isabella said Chuco, the *majordomo,* would be serving refreshments presently, and asked Fallon and Marcelina what they would prefer. Marcelina suggested coffee, and Fallon agreed. Isabella nodded, smiling, and retired from the room, leaving them alone.

Fallon had wanted to hear Marcelina play ever since she had mentioned to him her love and need for music. Now Isabella had as much as proposed it.

"It has been a little while, you know," Marcelina explained a bit reticently. "In my little apartment in San Francisco, I have only an upright piano on which to keep in practice . . . but I shall try."

The white gloves and wide-brimmed hat she had been wearing had been left in the foyer upon her entering the house along with her small handbag. Her white traveling dress subtly accentuated her small breasts and callipygean figure. She sat down now at the keyboard, paused for a moment to gather herself, and then began to play. It was the *étude de concert* by Liszt known as *"un sospiro."* Fallon had probably heard it before, although he might not have been able to name it.

There was a bit of acting in the music, but none of posturing, love but not passion, innocence without sweetness, here a moment of nearly celestial drollery, then a flaming moment of the dance, a cascade of delicate colors, a *sursum corda* that shivered now and then, terrifying Fallon with the *cordolium* of irretrievable loss. Marcelina's movements were swift, at times audacious, and then lingering, as a dancer sinking down upon the stage after a most graceful leap. So flawlessly executed was the music in its way that the gentle breeze stealing in from outside and the brightness of this room in a land where for generations human beings had worshipped the Sun as the one true god faded for Fallon, as if Marcelina had taken to extinguishing one by one the candles which lit the world.

Marcelina and Fallon had their coffee in the sunroom. Isabella joined them. After some conversation, Marcelina and Fallon went to their rooms to freshen up, and returned to luncheon on the verandah. The conversation was dominated by Fallon's talk of various field trips he had taken, and Isabella told him of life in Lima. Later Fallon took Marcelina for a drive, enjoying the sights of the city, the Palace, the Botanical Garden, and the Andalusian-Moorish buildings.

When they returned to the O'Day home, Thomas O'Day had come back by taxicab from the hotel where he had left Tennington and Valera. Sir Wilbur had insisted that they would come for dinner that night by taxicab, rather than having O'Day or Fallon drive over to pick them up. Fallon, after conversing briefly with O'Day, went with Marcelina for a walk in the garden, and then they sat for a time on the verandah.

Dinner was a cordial affair, while groups of dancing native Peruvians silently observed the diners from the walls. The table was nicely decorated with flowers from the garden, and upon the tablecloth, as white as Andean snow, among the gold-veined crystal of the goblets, the tall green wine glasses cast gentle shadows in the candlelight, like spirits in a mountain pine forest. The food was very good, and the *pièce de résistance* was ocean codfish prepared from a secret recipe of which the Andalusian *cuisinière* was understandably proud, followed by marzipan and crystallized fruit.

It was after dinner, when Isabella led Fallon and Valera out onto the verandah, the air still warm from the heat of the day while cold, brilliant stars shone overhead in the tropical nocturnal sky, to enjoy an after-dinner drink and to smoke, that Marcelina was asked to join her father and Sir Wilbur in the study across the hall, behind the drawing room. Valera had wanted to be present, but the Englishman had counseled against it, and, of course, Fallon did not know the reason for this conclave but was both curious and concerned.

The study was furnished in dark mahogany with floor-to-ceiling bookcases on two walls — O'Day was a voracious reader of fiction in English, Spanish, and in translation, as was Isabella. It was a lofty, yet cozy, room with two tall windows at the farther end that overlooked the lawn and garden. From the damask-clad wall on either side of the entrance were portraits in oils of Isabella's departed father and mother, gazing into the room out of broad gilt frames, the one with almost military gravity, the other with a youthful grace and striking beauty. These two had been Marcelina's special friends since she was a little girl, and she was surprised, as she glanced at them illumined by the red-shaded lamp on the reading table that her grandfather wore a puzzled look upon his face, and her grandmother seemed openly worried.

There was a deep-seated leather chair, which her father usually occupied as he did now, a less comfortable dark-wood chair customarily turned toward the library table that now faced toward the leather chair, and the cloth chair upholstered in vicuña that Isabella often occupied and in which Marcelina now seated herself. Chuco served Sir Wilbur with a snifter of Courvoisier, O'Day with Jameson over ice, and Marcelina with coffee stirred with honey, as she preferred it.

Sir Wilbur brought out his bulldog pipe and pouch, fingering the crimp cut into the bowl. O'Day rarely smoked, but

Marcelina lit a cigarette.

"Smoking is something my daughter picked up living in the States," O'Day remarked.

"She might as well enjoy it while she can," said Sir Wilbur. "I have reason to know that the States have banned spirits of any kind and, in many places, tobacco as well." He shook his head in bewilderment. "You know, it is said that the English drove the Puritans to the New World, and they certainly have taken an iron hand over what is potentially the greatest nation on earth."

"Most Americans drink in spite of Prohibition, Sir Wilbur," Marcelina said, exhaling smoke and smiling shyly.

"I suppose," said her father, "you wonder what this is all about, Marcelina. Well, I'll tell you. To my amazement I learned today that Don Esteban de Ferrar was a passenger on the *Sea Queen* . . . even though we didn't see him at the dock, nor have we been visited by him. I don't know why. Usually he lets us know when he is coming to Lima."

"I know he was aboard ship, Papa," Marcelina admitted. She put out her cigarette. "I sha'n't tell either of you that I wasn't aware of it. He visited me in San Francisco before I sailed with Sir Wilbur's party. However, his presence there or on the *Sea Queen* was not my doing, and he was not the reason I asked *Tío* Luis to let me accompany him and Sir Wilbur to Haucha. *Tío* Don Esteban knew all about the García parchment and the lost city before even I did. He told me he had been searching for the García parchment for years, and that Sir Wilbur had unfairly managed to get to it before he did."

"Nonsense," commented the Englishman, puffing on his pipe. "His claim I regard as spurious."

"We needn't argue that point, Sir Wilbur," put in O'Day. "What I want to know from you, Marcelina, is whether or not you have betrayed Luis's confidence in going over the particulars of the map he has constructed of the route to the lost city."

There was a silence, and for a moment tears glistened in Marcelina's large blue-gray eyes, although otherwise she was composed.

"Sí y no," she said then, very quietly.

"Marcie," demanded her father, "either you did, or you did not."

"Is it not possible, Papa, for me to have done both?"

"No," he replied, "it isn't."

"Nonetheless," replied Marcelina, "that is what I did. He appealed to my loyalty to my family, to the love Mama has for me, that he has for me. To my love for my family. I felt it was impossible for me simply to tell him, no."

"So you did show him the route, then?" asked Sir Wilbur.

"Not really. I did provide him with a map in detail . . . but, Papa, the details were only right for the beginning . . . as right as anyone would know who was familiar in the least with the Incan road through the Cordillera."

"And then . . . ?" prompted O'Day.

"And then it goes the wrong way. *Tío* Luis knows the topography very well, and I know some from my own experience and more from what he has taught me. *Tío* Don Esteban was born, after all, in Peru, and he does know the country as well as we do, but not the mountain passes, and there he will become lost if he follows the route I laid out for him."

"Did Don Esteban threaten you?" O'Day asked.

"No, he didn't have to, but, Papa, you know I am afraid of Abdullah Simbel."

"With good reason," her father agreed. "Frankly, Sir Wilbur, I do not trust that associate of Don Esteban's any more than Marcelina does, and, although it may be indelicate to mention it before you, Marcie, you've become a woman of the world now, and I have told Isabella and now I will tell you, I feel there is an unnatural bond between those two men. Don Esteban always felt contempt toward most women, with the exception, perhaps, of Isabella, toward whom he has always been affectionate and, from the way he's behaved in the past, toward you, his only niece. Yet, what you have done, Marcie, could have repercussions on you, once he finds out the map you gave him was a forgery. For that reason, I think it is for your own good that I withdraw my consent to allow you to continue on this expedition."

"I felt that was what you would say, Papa . . . if I told you what I had done. I said as much to Chris Fallon."

"My dear girl," said Sir Wilbur, his face seamed now with sympathy, "Chris said nothing to me about it."

"Please, Sir Wilbur," Marcelina clarified herself, "I didn't tell Chris that Papa wouldn't want to let me go, after what I had done . . . or, surely, that you wouldn't . . . only that I myself had been thinking of bowing out . . . even though I did so much want to go along."

The Englishman took his pipe from his mouth and looked thoughtfully at Thomas O'Day. "Might I ask, sir, just what repercussions you think there might be from Ferrar against this young woman?"

O'Day took a sip from his drink before replying. "I'll have to admit, Sir Wilbur, I'm not sure. What I do know of the man is that he is monomaniacal, once he gets a fixed idea in his head as to what he wants, and that he is utterly ruthless. In fact, he left Peru originally under something of a shadow of disrepute . . . nothing for which he might be legally prosecuted, mind you . . . and he is still the absentee landlord of the family estate . . . Don Esteban and Isabella are descended from Francisco Pizarro's lineage through their paternal grandmother . . . but there were some irregularities in Don Esteban's dealings concerning land holdings, and he left a lot of hard feelings behind him when he emigrated. I understand he made a second fortune in the recent war . . . as I told you earlier today."

"Please pardon me, Mister O'Day," interrupted the Englishman, "but just how do you think Ferrar could bring harm to Marcelina if she accompanied us to Haucha?"

"Do you mean," Marcelina asked, an upward springing in her voice, as life ought to be for the young, while the irises of her blue-gray eyes opened widely to the very depths of her soul, "that you would think me a fit person to go along after what I . . . after what I've done to you . . . and to everyone?"

"My dear girl," the Englishman assured her, "what have you really done . . . except inestimably help us?"

"I don't follow that, Sir Wilbur," O'Day put in. "Marcie came damned close to ruining everything."

"On the contrary, what she did . . . if it distracts Ferrar and gets him off our trail . . . accomplishes more than I or anyone else would have been able to do. When I learned he was on the *Sea Queen*, I didn't believe for a moment that he had decided to relinquish his claim to the García parchment, however fraudulent that claim may have been. It was my opinion that he would likely dog us every inch of the way, causing us no end of turmoil by having to elude him at every turn. Even if he pursued us at a safe distance, he might show up at Haucha a few days after we did, or a week later, and make no end of trouble for us. You must realize, sir, that getting there is only part of our logistical problem. What happens after we once are there? Do we really want to deal with a madman waving a gun at us? Quite definitely not. Fallon's family were ranching people in the American Wild West. He is familiar with this kind of rough play, but I, for one, would prefer to avoid a confrontation, if I possibly can."

"Spoken just like an Englishman," O'Day commented without humor.

"Possibly you are correct," Sir Wilbur agreed. "But may I remind you that the British have sought economic and social stability . . . I would add good government . . . in all of the crown colonies. What did Spain want in the New World? I can answer that question in a single word . . . and the answer is *not* rhetorical. The Spaniards were interested in gold. That's it. Nothing more. They plundered Mexico. They plundered Peru. And what now does Spain have to show for the literal tons of gold it laid claim to? Nothing. Spain, today, is one of the poorest nations in all Christendom." He paused to put down his pipe on the oval table beside his chair. "But this takes us too far afield. My original point is . . . whether doing so knowingly or not . . . Marcelina has been of the greatest possible service to our entire undertaking by having effectually removed the one impediment that had arisen before us . . . or, I should say, behind us. If I may cast a vote, it would be that Marcelina be allowed to continue with us. I am sure Chris Fallon, knowing all the facts, would support me in this."

"Perhaps for a different reason," Marcelina said quietly. An impish smile creased her lips.

"Oh?" said her father.

"I would say that Luis Valera would be of an identical opinion," Sir Wilbur resumed, unwilling to have the conversation sidetracked again. "With Ferrar off on a wild goose chase . . . only because of Marcelina's fortuitous intercession . . . I cannot see that she would be in any danger from him or his black minion. Moreover, if revenge were to become Ferrar's motive, because of what has happened, Marcelina would be safer with us than even here at her home in Lima."

"Papa, I honestly do not believe *Tío* Don Esteban would harm me," Marcelina interjected, assuring herself and them, as the young are wont to do.

Thomas O'Day had become uncomfortable in his rôle as

adjudicator at a family assize. "Perhaps we should consult your mother before we decide, Marcie."

"No, Papa. If we do that, it will only upset her. Don Esteban is her brother, and she is fond of him. I should not want to hurt her . . . and telling her of this can only hurt her and worry her."

O'Day pondered that for a moment before conceding. "If you want my girl along, Sir Wilbur, well . . . you have my permission."

Marcelina's gratitude shone in her face. Sir Wilbur winked at her and raised his glass in silent tribute. Thomas O'Day was no less pleased to see how his words had affected Marcelina, for there is no greater joy in all the world for a father than when he has truly made his child happy.

Chapter Nine

Many days later they arrived by motor car at a lonely frontier outpost, a village called Tacho Alto beyond which stretched an arid desert and above which, dimly in the distance, rose mighty mountain peaks. Here they set about finding a local guide and any additional equipment needed for the passage beyond the desert into the mountains and across the great mountain rivers and streams. Chris Fallon had made an excursion into the jungles of the Amazon but was unfamiliar, except theoretically as also was Valera, with the rugged section of the Peruvian wilderness into which they would be heading. Sir Wilbur and Fallon, therefore, left Valera and Marcelina together with the car at a primitive café and made a circuit of the shops until they learned from a mild, honest-looking Italian shopkeeper that there was an old Indian named Quinto who kept an inn down the street, a tough old fellow — but tractable, if you got on his right side — who had guided a number of geological expeditions from the United States into the wilds of the Andes. Quinto was honest, said the Italian. Upon that one could depend for a certainty.

Tennington thanked the Italian, and he and Fallon headed for the hostel indicated. As they neared it, they saw a thin, white-clad figure burst from the front entrance and run down the street toward them, yelling taunts back over his shoulder. So little attention, in fact, did he pay to what was before him that he collided with Tennington, almost knocking him down.

Sir Wilbur caught him by the arms. "I say, watch it, boy."

The youth cast a frantic look backward over his shoulder. "Let go, *señor*."

But the Englishman retained his grasp on the lad, just as an

102

emaciated figure emerged from the hostel, bellowing at the top of his lungs.

"Ramón! Ramón, *tú bribón . . . !*"

The boy kicked and struggled to free himself from Tennington's pinioning arms, but the Englishman held him securely as the lean Indian came up puffing. He was mild-looking, and there were deep lines in his thin face. He looked to be past middle-age, with a ruff of white hair around his temples and the cloudy eyes of a coca-chewer. He wore soiled white cotton clothing with a soiled *poncho* over his neck.

"Ramón, I shall beat you," said the man in Spanish. He beamed at Sir Wilbur. "A thousand thank yous, *señor.*" This he spoke in English. "The leetle rascal ees . . . heh-heh . . . playful. Most playful. Een fact, so playful that he dropped a number of nice beeg flies eento the open mouth of Quinto when he ees taking *siesta.*"

"Is he kin of yours?" Fallon asked.

Quinto looked pious. "He ees the only nephew of poor Quinto. Hees father ees dead. Quinto can only do hees best to raise the leetle fellow. I theenk maybe the *magistrado* could do better."

Tennington released the boy, who dodged under the outstretched arm of Quinto and retreated to a respectful distance, ready to run if necessity should demand.

Quinto sighed wearily and shook his head in resignation. Sir Wilbur said: "Quinto, we'd like to talk to you."

"Come eenside, *señores.*"

The *huésped* led the way inside his little red-tile roofed edifice and motioned the men from the north to a table. It was pleasantly cool in here, but dark, with only a little musty light filtering through the fly-blown windows.

"*¿Aguardiente, señores . . . o pisco o chicha?*"

"No. We're here to ask you to help us with an expedition,

Quinto," Tennington said.

"An expeedition, *señores?* Ah, you would search the mountains and study the rocks, eh?"

"Not rocks," said Fallon.

Quinto's face clouded. "Surely, *señores* . . . you are not more of those madmen who seek Incan treasure?"

"This is different . . . we have a map and rather exact directions," explained the Englishman. "It is just that we still have special use for one familiar with the passes and ravines of the Andes."

"Others have had maps . . . they mean notheeng. Maps are easily drawn and foisted off onto gullible treasure-seekers."

"This one is real," Fallon assured him. "But it is not treasure that we seek, but rather a lost Incan city, cut off centuries ago from all contact with the outside world."

Tennington produced the copy of the augmented map drawn by Valera and spread it out on the rough, warped surface of the board table. Quinto bent over, examining it intently. He picked it up and crackled the paper.

"Thees map ees very new!" he said, frowning.

"This isn't the original," explained Tennington. "The original is an ancient Spanish parchment. This has been augmented by us. However, I can vouch for its authenticity and the route as it is indicated."

Quinto showed definite interest now. "Perhaps, *señores,* there ees sometheeng to thees map . . . I shall study eet."

They remained silent while Quinto perused the map, mumbling occasionally under his breath as he repeated the names on the map and muttered an occasional low ejaculation in Spanish.

Finally, he said slowly: "The landmarks are reel, at least, *señores.* As to the location of the plateau indicated, I theenk that I know the plateau, although I have never been on eet . . . nor have I any desire to be on eet."

"Why not?" asked Tennington.

"There are many theengs, *señores*, of which you white people, weeth all your science, cannot cope. Such are the theengs
lurking in thees region where you are heading. My people have
a respectful fear of eet, and eet ees well that they have, for there
are those theengs weeth wheech no man may interfere."

Tennington sighed. Fallon appeared dubious.

"*Sí*, you may scoff, *señores* . . . eet ees your right . . . *pero* eef
you do not fear the unseen dangers, there are others wheech are
very real."

"Such as . . . ?" Sir Wilbur prompted.

Quinto drew the map before the Englishman and began
pointing out various places with a skinny forefinger. "First,
señor . . . here ees the desert. Eet ees very hot and very wide.
There ees no water . . . there are no plants except on the level
places where there are prickly cactus and long spiny thorns the
length of a man's hand. So sharp and tough are they and so numerous that they will tear your boots to shreds and your feet,
also . . . eef they do not entirely cripple you first. There are
other places . . . rocky and rugged, and een these areas are
small, sharp rocks as treacherous as the thorns een the level areas. There ees great hardship."

Tennington smiled faintly. He was reflecting that perhaps it
had not been such a good idea to bring along Marcelina, or
even Luis Valera for that matter. "Suppose we were to survive
these dangers?" he asked suggestively.

"Then, *señor*, you weel face the great mountain barrier . . .
here . . . a greater barrier than the one you can see before you
from here. Eet ees a remote arm of the Andes, and just beyond
lies a valley of wild jungle that only two men have ever seen, for
only two men have ever crossed that mountain barrier. The reason for thees ees that by the time they have conquered the

desert, they are een no condition and of no mind to go farther. I have guided to the closer mountains white men who are searching for rocks to study, but they go no farther. There have been the treasure-seekers, too, but they are soft men who give out and often die.

"These mountains are as terrible as the desert . . . perhaps worse. They are very steep and rugged, and men may lose their hold and plunge to death far below. At the summits, they are very cold, especially at night, and, ecf you estay steel, you will freeze to death where you are standing. Descending eento the valley on the other side, eet ees easier traveling, far less narrow and less rugged, but here, perhaps, you weel face a terror greater than the cold."

The two men bent forward, fascinated, and Quinto was satisfied, for he loved to tell a story and keep his listeners enthralled. The old raconteur plunged on. "There are giant condors that make their nest high on the slopes here, and I mean giants, for the full span of their weengs ees a dozen feet. They are absolutely fearless, *señores,* for while condors are prone to attack only dying or helpless animals, thees weel attack men who are ascending or descending the mountainside, and, when one ees occupied keeping hees balance, eet ees deefeecult to fight them off."

Sir Wilbur was nodding his head. "Remember, Chris, García in his narrative mentioned a great bird who pecked a man to his death. Giant, powerful creatures . . . condors, what? But go on, Quinto. Suppose that we survive the mountains, too, and the giant condors."

"Next . . . the jungle," Quinto continued implacably. He moved his finger on the map. "Here lies the most terrible dangers of all. Terrible beasts and reptiles roam eet . . . and none are more terrible than the dread Quivaris."

"The Quivaris?" questioned Fallon.

"*Sí.* They are a tribe of wild men who live een the valley een the wall of the great plateau where they make their homes. They are terrible-looking men, *señores.* I theenk, perhaps, they are more animal than man. To get to the plateau you must by-pass their village, for their village ees located een the same cleef wall that you must scale to reach the top of the plateau . . . wheech, by the way, ees a sheer wall."

"That bad?" asked Sir Wilbur.

"Perhaps worse, *señor.* Never do I again hope to see such a terrible people."

"You?" inquired Fallon. "I thought you said only two men ever got over the barrier mountains . . . or were you . . . ?"

"*Sí, señor,*" said Quinto slowly, as though some dark memory stalked him. He sat back slowly, his flimsy chair creaking under his lean bulk, and seemed to be recalling. "I was one of those men, and that was some years ago. The other man was my tween brother, the father of Ramón. We were adventurous young fools and desired to see what, eef anything, lay beyond the thorny desert. We set out alone, across the desert weeth such supplies as we could carry comfortably on our backs.

"From what I have already told you, you may obtain some notion of the pain and hardship that we had to endure to traverse the desert and mountains and the terrors of the jungle. During most of the treep, Pedro, my brother, was creepled, for he stepped on a thorn wheech drove up hees foot, almost to the ankle. When trying to get out the thorn, eet broke off, and a part remained een the foot. Eet festered and swelled.

"Pedro and I came of a common stock, *señores.* We were Quechuans who had felt the hand of hardsheep and want seence our earliest recollections. Eet was a terrible struggle, and perhaps we both were more dead than alive when we finally found ourselves een the valley, but we made eet. Sometimes, even now, I wonder what accursed devil made us go on after

107

the accident to Pedro's foot. Perhaps we thought eet would get well, and, too, we were young and fooleesh enough to remain undaunted by seemingly such a small theeng.

"By the time we reached the jungle, we had much reason to regret our fooleeshness. Pedro's foot was swollen to three times the normal size, and both of us were een very poor condition, pheesically and mentally. How we escaped the dangers of the jungle, I do not know, but we deed not escape the . . . Quivaris."

The very memory seemed bitterly dolorous to the old Indian.

"A hunting party of these wild men sighted us, and weeth Pedro's foot as eet was, we could not escape, and we were almost too weak to care. And then they took us to their village in the cleef, and . . . ah . . . but I weel not attempt to tell you of the horrors we saw and endured een that terrible place.

"Pedro died soon, and they took ees body. What they deed weeth eet I do not know, and for long afterward I was a helplees prisoner, too grief-streecken and miserable to care. When thees state passed, and I began again to take an eenterest in theengs, I began to suspect that they were reserving me for a fate so terrible as to be unbelievable. Weeth thees conviction, I bent all my efforts toward escape. Finally, I left the village of the wild men behind, and, knowing they would pursue me, I thought only of putting distance between myself and that village of the Quivaris.

"I was again restored to health and strength, for the long weeks of imprisonment een the village had geeven me a chance to recover, and, being young and healthy-minded, I deed thees quickly and well. But een the suddenness of my escape, I lost myself een the wilderness, and eet was many weeks before I found the way we had come over the mountains. During thees time, I lived off what I could get, hunted by both beast and man, for the savages scoured the valley een search of me. Never een my life had I endured such a hopeless fight. I lived een eet all the time, and I do not know now why I lived, or what kept me fighting for life.

"When, at last, I again crossed the mountains and found myself on the desert without food or water, I was ready to lie down and die. A thousand times I was ready to geev up. Yes, eet must have been the espirit of life . . . *espíritu de la vida* . . . that, alone, kept me going on.

"When I slipped into complete unconsciousness, too weak to go farther, I woke up long afterward een a peon hut, and two *mestizo* herders who lived there have said they had found me raving with fever. That was many weeks before, they said.

"When I was again able to hobble about, a year had elapsed seence Pedro and I had set out across the thorny desert een search of adventure. Eet might have been thirty years." At this, Quinto shook his head solemnly.

The boy, Ramón, had stepped in at the door and was now eyeing the two strangers curiously. He was a small, bright-eyed boy dressed much like Quinto. Fallon judged his age to be less than fourteen. Puzzled, he turned to Quinto.

"You say this boy, Ramón, is the son of your twin brother Pedro?"

"That ees correct, *señor*."

"But how can that be? You just said you and Pedro were young men when you set out."

"That ees true, *señor*. Neither of us was over twenty."

"But . . . you told us Pedro perished in the valley . . . how could Ramón be his son? Wouldn't that make Ramón close to thirty?"

Quinto smiled wanly. "Ah, you are judging by my appearance, *señor*. How old, then, do you judge me to be?"

"Oh . . . close to sixty . . . maybe more," guessed Fallon.

"*Señores* . . . I have not seen thirty-five summers."

"What?" exclaimed Sir Wilbur. "Come, come, my good fellow."

Quinto replied: "*Señores* . . . I have lived through an experience that aged me many years een a few short months . . . but they were not short to me. They were an eternity of terror. My face had become lined, my form shrunken, my hair growing out white . . . not the gray of age, *señores*, but pure white . . . then I lost most of even that, so that now I have only the little wheech fringes my temples. All that, *señores*, occurred only thirteen years ago."

Quinto's narrative was sobering — if true. The Englishman's face seemed to register mild disbelief, and perhaps he could not be blamed. Chris Fallon was silent.

Quinto, noting their incredulity, smiled and nodded. "Ah, you are theenking, thees Quinto, he ees one beeg liar. But there are those in thees village who have known me all their lives, and they will bear out the truth of what I say."

"Then . . . ," wondered Sir Wilbur soberly, "you would never return to the valley, Quinto?"

"What do you theenk, *señor?*" asked the Indian quietly. "I feel as old and tired as I look . . . and, as for getting anyone else to guide you . . . eet would be eemposseeble, for they all know my story, and they fear the unseen. I myself lead expeditions no farther than the mountains. Eef you weesh, I weel lead you thees far . . . but no farther."

"Perhaps, Quinto, you, too, believe in demons," observed Sir Wilbur. "Yet you seem an intelligent man."

"Eentelligence, *señor*, is no weapon against that wheech cannot be seen. I have been educated by a Spanish *padre* who has a meession near here, but, though he has taught me much, I do not believe all I hear, for, as you say, I am an eentelligent man, and I have learned to theenk for myself. While preesoner of the

110

Quivaris, I saw sights so terrible, and suggestions of rites so hideous, that even you, *señores*, with your cold logic and reasoning would be shocked."

Tennington was not inclined to argue this point; therefore, he only nodded. "Guide us, then, to the mountain barrier, Quinto . . . from there, we shall find the place we seek."

Quinto arose from the table and leaned toward them, speaking in a low and earnest voice. "*Señores*, thees search of yours ees folly. The government weel confeescate any treasure you find should you survive the perils of your journey . . . wheech you weel not."

"You did," commented Fallon, also rising.

"The Peruvian government is thoroughly familiar with our mission, I assure you, Quinto," Sir Wilbur said, getting up himself. "We have with us an archeologist from San Francisco whose claims for certain artifacts would, I have been assured, be respected."

"And Marcelina O'Day," added Fallon. "She was born in Peru, as was the archeologist, Luis Valera."

"You have brought a woman weeth you?" Quinto said in open disbelief.

"A young and healthy young woman," Sir Wilbur assured the Indian.

"But only by marvelous fortune and by the grace of the great God, *señores*, for a hundred times deed I escape death een that wild land beyond the mountains. You are more, true, and you have guns, yet you are worse equipped than even I was, for the lives of the *americanos del norte* have been too soft, and, eef the attempt to enter that region exacted such a cost on me, imagine what eet would be for a young *señorita*? Eet ees folly, *señores*, and devilish to take a young woman there who could not defend herself."

"We, too, have survived dangers, Quinto," Fallon affirmed,

"and I am sure we can protect ourselves and Marcelina from any dangers we encounter."

Quinto sighed. "Eef I cannot dissuade you, so eet must be. I shall handle matters of such equipment as you may need."

They discussed what their needs would be with Quinto, and he assured them the expedition would be ready to leave in the morning. They also arranged with him to rent two rooms in his hostel for the night, one to be shared by the men, and one for Marcelina.

As they left the hostel, Fallon asked Sir Wilbur: "How much of this should we tell Luis and Marcelina?"

"All of it, Chris. I'm no longer so sure I did the right thing in talking O'Day into letting his daughter come along. I thought the journey would be rigorous, but, if Quinto is to be believed, our encounter with Ferrar was child's play compared to what lies in store for all of us. Perhaps Luis, too, should not come. He could drive the car back to Lima with Marcelina, and they could wait for us to return."

"If we lose the car, we'll have a distance to go from here on foot or, at best, on horseback."

"Inconvenient, perhaps, but necessary, I think, under the circumstances," Sir Wilbur concluded.

Chapter Ten

Tennington and Fallon found Luis Valera and Marcelina O'Day walking along what there was of a main street in Tacho Alto which, notwithstanding some human traffic, domestic animals — dogs, cats, chickens, and in one case pigs — roamed freely. They all gathered at the car, and Fallon drove to Quinto's hostel where he parked in an open-air shed alongside the adobe building.

Once inside, again in the hostel's central room at the table where Tennington and Fallon had first spoken with Quinto, Sir Wilbur asked everyone to sit down so he could discuss why there should be a change in their plans. Valera was totally disinclined to return to Lima with Marcelina, and the girl, although only twenty-one and made fully aware of the harrowing terrain, the giant condors, and the fierce Quivaris, seemed undaunted. True, she admitted, she *was* young, but the others were no more experienced in these matters than she was, and she had no husband or child dependent on her to dissuade her from the attempt. She had once thought of withdrawing because of shame and guilt over what she had done concerning the map that, however inaccurate, she had made for her uncle, but this was not a question of something like that. Women of her mother's generation might well have shrunk from such an undertaking, but she was lithe, athletic, sufficiently strong for a girl, and her father had taught her how to shoot a pistol with accuracy. Further, as a group, they were certainly well armed, with two high-powered scope rifles, a shotgun, Sir Wilbur's .55 Webley revolver, Fallon's Colt .45 mounted on a .38 frame, Valera's .45 automatic with seven bullets each in two clips, and

Marcelina's own nickel-plated .32 Smith & Wesson revolver for which she had a leather holster.

Even when Quinto joined them and narrated for a second time what was to be expected, and illustrated the ordeal he himself had been through with the physical ravages he had suffered, neither the professor nor his young protégée was deterred. They had come too far and were too close now to turn back. Marcelina looked to Chris Fallon who in San Francisco and later on the *Sea Queen* had once tried to discourage her, but this time he did, indeed, keep his mouth shut, impressed in spite of himself at Marcelina's plucky willingness of the heart.

Quinto remained adamant that the men were committing the worst kind of folly by persisting in wanting to go where no one had gone before them and lived, but it bordered on heartless cruelty to ask an innocent *señorita* to go thus to certain death. He had never before seen a woman, young or otherwise, wearing pants and talking this way about guns and being unafraid, and he felt for her the terror she was refusing to feel for herself, as if he were following behind her into a cave deep in the bowels of the earth and holding aloft only a fluttering candle.

"Señores y señorita," he said, "I see eet ees not posseeble to estop you from going, even eef you have me as your weetness for what lies ahead." Then, through some strange convolution of his own thinking, he surprised all of them. "My nephew Ramón, who will soon be fourteen, weel accompany you also on the first part of the journey."

The Englishman, who had been feeling more than a little frustrated by his inability to convince Valera and Marcelina to stay behind, now burst forth with a spontaneous show of temper. "My God, man, you have done all in your power to persuade us of the hardships of this journey! You insist, in any event, that Miss O'Day is too young and inexperienced. Now

114

you propose to take Ramón, a boy and, I am sure, far less able to take care of himself than this young lady?"

Quinto sighed and shook his head. "I could not leave him alone een Tacho Alto, for he would get eento trouble. As for hardsheeps, there ees far less hardsheep for the hardy Quechuan stock of Peru than for you, *inglés,* or *americanos del norte.*"

"Hold on," broke in Valera. "I was born and raised in Peru."

"So was I," said Marcelina.

Fallon murmured: "Perhaps you will find all of us of tougher clay than you imagine."

"Perhaps, *señor,* but I do not fear for Ramón, so much as for myself, eef he estays behind een Tacho Alto. That would be my great regret."

"But who will watch your hostel here while you're gone, if Ramón goes with us?" Tennington wondered.

"Eet shall be necessary, *señor,* for you to pay us both enough for our time and trouble so that thees place . . . she can be closed for as long as eet takes us."

Sir Wilbur speculated that perhaps Quinto had been merely entertaining them with the stories of his former ordeal with his brother. One thing now seemed definite. The early part of the journey, on which Quinto would guide them, could not be so terribly difficult for Marcelina O'Day if this native Peruvian was willing to bring along his nephew who was both younger and even less prepared, physically, for the terrain than was the girl.

Early the next morning, the expedition left Tacho Alto and started into the desert.

"Eet ees well," said Quinto, walking by the side of Chris Fallon at the head of the group followed by Sir Wilbur

115

Tennington, three loaded pack mules lead by Ramón, and Luis Valera and Marcelina O'Day who brought up the rear.

Fallon was inspecting the vast, rolling landscape of sandy waste ahead. "Where are these stickers you mentioned?" he inquired.

"Those, *amigo*, weel not be seen for many days yet . . . but you weel know when you come to them!"

The character of the land, as they progressed deeper into the desert, altered gradually, although almost imperceptibly. The flat rolling aspect gave way to gentle irregularities, consisting of swelling sand dunes. Here the vegetation was less, and the surface of the sand underfoot was loose and yielding, rendering travel more difficult.

Three days later, as Quinto had predicted, they ran into the region of stickers — the spiny thorns whose razor tips made nothing of even stout pampas boots.

"Goodness!" groaned Valera who was walking behind the Englishman with Marcelina now behind him and Ramón and the pack mules behind her as they worked their way with infinite caution over the rise of a dune. "I've been pierced a dozen times."

"You have little to complain about yet," said Tennington complacently. "Once in the Gobi desert I ran into a species of thorn similar to this, although the spines were not as long or as sharp. But the tips, when they pierced the flesh, released a small quantity of poison into the body. The sores they made festered and were horribly painful, while the tiny scratches you are receiving are only annoying."

"Look, *señores!*" Quinto called behind, excitedly pointing a finger ahead, just as they attained the summit of a rise. Before them in the hazy, illusive distance loomed a gaunt, towering range of the Andes. Quinto indicated a deep rift between two of the snow-capped peaks. "There, *señores y señorita*, ees where you weel cross."

116

Ramón grunted: "Eet does not look so far away."

Quinto chuckled. "We are yet seex days from eet, *muchacho*."

In the days that followed, it seemed they would never attain it. The alluring peaks that had beckoned so tantalizingly near seemed only to retreat proportionately as the expedition advanced. Their progress was also deterred considerably by the omnipresent thorns that made quick work of their clothing and footgear and even their flesh. The unmerciful sun beating down unremittingly on their lowered heads only added to their discomfort, although Sir Wilbur wore a pith helmet, Fallon a Stetson, Valera, Marcelina, Quinto, and Ramón sombreros. Water they had packed in abundance upon the backs of the mules. Indeed, water consisted of one half of the total weight of their gear and supplies that had been fairly limited to facilitate traversing the mountains.

On the fifth day, they entered the region of which Quinto had told them — a region far more perilous even than the thorns. There was absolutely no vegetation here whatsoever. The ground was black, solidified lava, weathered in places by wind and rain. At one time, apparently, the area had been volcanic, although now even the craters appeared to have been eroded. The terrain itself was treacherous for it was so irregular as to slow passage to a minimum, and there were slender pinnacles of rock here and there protruding upward. One had to be consciously alert at every moment, for to lose one's balance and fall would probably mean death by splatting one's body neatly on the impaling, jagged edge of an upstanding sliver of stone — and it was easy to fall here.

Ramón, sweating copiously from this arduous travel, remarked: "*Caramba,* couldn't we have gone around thees place?"

Quinto called back to him: "*Muchacho,* thees area extends

117

for more than a hundred miles either way . . . eet ees far easier to cross thees area, wheech ees only ten miles wide despite eets great extent een length. Steel, eet weel require all day to cross eet, so have patience, for we have only been on eet for less than two hours now. Quinto can only guide by the best route."

Quinto and Ramón had both discarded their habitual grass *usutas* for heavy boots like those worn by the others. Although even these suffered sadly, they accomplished their purpose in that they protected the feet by deflecting the viciously sharp pieces with their hard-leather soles.

As Quinto had predicted, they left the lava country behind them by nightfall, but the following day they found themselves still in irregular, rocky country, and it grew worse. Days passed. Tempers grew shorter, bodies became haggard and dirty, and clothes became ragged. Marcelina's white jodhpur breeches were mostly brown, but she impressed the others in not complaining, her angular face often set in a determined expression, but her sense of humor was also very close to the surface, and frequently she would cause the others to laugh at some remark of hers.

The day came eventually when they found themselves growing appreciably closer to the coveted range that was their goal, and the hour arrived when they were in the shadow of a towering peak of the Andean sierra. That night they camped at its base.

After the evening meal, Sir Wilbur, hands on hips, stood looking up at the rift that appeared to be the lowest point by which they could ascend. At that, it must be close to twenty thousand feet in height.

"Hot night," Fallon remarked, wiping his forehead. He, Luis, and Marcelina were sitting around the cook fire with Quinto.

"I'd say, take advantage of it while we can," Sir Wilbur said, moving back into the circle around the fire. "Tomorrow, it will be freezing!"

A sudden cry abruptly shattered the still darkness far to the right, and all thought at once of Ramón who had left the bivouac area to gather more firewood.

"Stay here!" Fallon snapped. "Quinto and I will see what's wrong."

Quinto had already disappeared in the direction of the sound.

The others waited tensely, standing now in the light of the flickering flames, staring intently into the surrounding gloom where Chris Fallon and the Quechuan had disappeared, attempting vainly to pierce the darkness beyond the firelight.

Presently, they heard approaching footsteps scraping awkwardly over the rock surfaces as they returned. Quinto and Fallon appeared abruptly, emerging from the darkness carrying the limp form of Ramón between them.

"Bitten by a snake!" said Fallon briefly, as they set the unconscious boy down near the fire. "I saw that by my flashlight . . . don't know whether it was poisonous or not . . . got to be sure. The boy's fainted. That's good."

As he spoke, he was hurrying to a pack which he wrenched open, producing a box of snakebite equipment.

"Incise . . . cauterize," he muttered, swiftly rehearsing the treatment. "There . . . heat this knife till it's red hot." He handed the knife to Sir Wilbur.

It was fortunate, indeed, that Ramón was unconscious, for there was no anesthetic. The anti-snakebite toxin that Fallon had packed with the other first-aid materials was injected. Apparently Ramón had been struck in the leg through a rent in his boot.

When he awoke, he was feverish. All that night and into the next day he raved or slumbered feverishly. They erected a shelter of brush over him to protect him from the blazing sun, and not once did old Quinto leave the boy's side.

The second day the boy was rational and slept most of the day. For a total of three days they were compelled to remain where they were. Time was suspended. The others read while Valera and Tennington frequently played chess with a small set the professor had brought along. Marcelina, wishing for all the world that she might find some place to bathe, went on exploratory walks with Fallon, and some of the time they talked. They were both grateful to have discovered in the other someone to whom they could converse for hours and hours without every becoming bored or irritated with each other's company.

On the third evening, after Fallon had checked Ramón's condition again and found him vastly improved, Quinto said that he and the boy would set their faces toward home the following day.

"I weell take the mules and sell them for you, *señores*," he suggested to Fallon and Tennington. "There will be places now too icy and steep for even the mules to scale. Even you weel have trouble, especially when you reach the snowline. I would also suggest that you cache the greater part of your food here, for the smallest additional weight weel tire you even more queeckly. When the boy's father and I scaled the reeft thirteen years ago, we had scarcely anything, although we were nearly dead from exposure and starvation by the time we had descended eento the valley. The air ees so theen that you will tire queeckly enough up there."

Fallon and Marcelina, having explored into some of the rocky crags nearby, had actually come upon a waterfall of pure clear water only that afternoon. Since their drinking water was almost exhausted, and since the little that remained was distastefully rancid, the discovery had been an elating one, and that night, with Marcelina going first, they all were able to bathe.

Early in the morning, Quinto and Ramón packed their share of the supplies onto the backs of the mules, while the others checked their equipment. Beyond the firearms, each had a small supply of quinine, a hunting knife, compass, canteen, water-proof matchbox, and a quantity of desiccated food in a small pack on their backs. This last had been a special provision of the Englishman's, and he insisted they divide the food equally among themselves, in the event that they should become separated. To this end, each also carried his own water, blankets, and any extra garments that would be necessary on the cold high portion of the route, as well as a long rope to facilitate climbing.

Quinto bade his friends farewell — for he regarded them as such now — and shook hands with each in turn. "You weel require more than good fortune on thees trek, *amigos y amiga*. I weesh you would yet alter your decision."

Sir Wilbur shook his head negatively. "*Hasta luego*, Quinto."

A half hour later, Quinto and Ramón were headed back in the direction of Tacho Alto while the others began their perilous ascent of the rift. They presently found that Quinto had not erred in his judgment of even a small weight proving an encumbering setback to their progress. They perspired freely and felt their legs becoming alternately numb or aching. Valera and Marcelina especially suffered the commencing agonies of novice mountain climbers.

The rift itself they soon found to be a rugged but fairly negotiable route. In places it was precariously steep. Quinto had informed them that the other side was in places a sheer face of rock, with a perpendicular drop to the valley below, and that in some instances they might have to form a human ladder to descend.

By nightfall, they had scaled approximately half the distance to the crest of the rift. It was when they were sitting about their campfire in a nook in the rock and preparing the evening meal that they heard a cry from down the trail.

"*¡Señores!*"

"What?" gasped Sir Wilbur, springing to his feet and pulling his Webley from its holster. Fallon, likewise, rose, albeit more slowly, staring with shining eyes into the oblivion beyond. In a few moments, Ramón appeared in the firelight, breathing heavily, and evidently exhausted.

"Good Lord!" cried Tennington.

"Ramón . . . had to come, *señor*," gasped the boy. "He is now the sworn . . . servant of . . . *Señor* Chris."

"What!" asked the Englishman in some astonishment.

"*Señor* Chris saved the life of Ramón . . . Don Weelbur. Ramón must serve *Señor* Chris until the debt ees repaid."

"But your uncle . . . ," began Fallon, "besides, your leg . . . it should have proper care. . . . I reminded your uncle of that this morning."

"*Señor* Chris has taken proper care of eet. *Tío* Quinto knows Ramón has gone, and why. He say . . . all right."

"I doubt that," replied Fallon dubiously. "Sit down and eat, and I'll look at your leg."

The American said little after his new examination of the Indian boy's injury, and plainly he was irked despite his lack of further comment. Evidently sensing this, Ramón moved carefully about, performing small camp tasks and making himself as inconspicuous as possible, saying nothing and attempting only to please.

The trek to the summit of the sierra rift continued early the next morning. The travelers were cramped by cold as well as by climbing aches now. The rising sun scarcely obviated this condition or relieved the gray depressed state of mind that had fallen upon all of them. They were beginning to feel their ears ringing with a sore, persistent ache induced by the height.

All that day they climbed steadily. Despite the arduousness of their progress, they camped just below the summit of the rift that night. Here, on a ledge that provided shelter from the howling wind that had come up, they were still not able to stop the aching of their ears or of their lungs from the rarefied air. Fallon and Marcelina did not dare smoke. Sir Wilbur did smoke half a pipe, but then gave it up. The last few yards had been the most difficult, for the rocks were slippery with ice, and footholds had to be hacked out. On the very crest, Fallon predicted, the wind and the ice would be worse than ever. Therefore, it was best they remain on this ledge till morning.

When morning came, it was bleak, gray, misted. Once the first sunlight dissipated this miasma, the group left the ledge and ventured upward the final remaining few feet. Fallon stepped out onto a firmly set outthrust of rock, and from this saddle-like formation between the two great peaks gazed out across the land beyond.

The valley existed; that was unquestionable now; but from this tremendous height it was misted and vague and illusive. Human beings were, indeed, finite and dwarfed beside this spectacle. The watchers were assailed by the swift sensation that they were of very little consequence in nature's scheme of things — that, in the face of this, they were but toys — pawns for the elements. Chris Fallon recalled another impressive landscape he had looked upon from the summit of a barrier, but the memory paled to insignificance beside this one.

"We're not so much," said Luis Valera, breaking the silence with a thought that must have rested heavily in the minds of all of them.

Their gaze moved up now to the far side of the valley. There lay the grim wall that must be scaled to the great plateau — and beyond that plateau must lie Haucha — the forgotten city of the Incas. Thus far, García, the old *conquistador,* had done well by them. He had possessed a penchant for accuracy. But there were still the dangers of the valley to be traversed — and the fear of the Quivaris.

The plateau was inter-mountain, while the Andean range towered on either side. Far off to the right and near to the plateau, they could distinguish hazily the black hulk of a peak that seemed to be emitting ominous sounds. Presently, despite the obscuring mists, they determined that the peak was spouting a rather red glow that hovered like a fiery nimbus just over its summit, in addition to the great, spewing clouds that rolled out in massive, smoking billows, black and of such a seemingly deliberate lack of haste as to seem almost ponderous. Those clouds rose, frayed and disentangled, and dispersed to merge with the gray mist.

"Volcano," murmured Sir Wilbur unnecessarily.

"Just so it doesn't erupt in the next week, Tenny," Fallon remarked jauntily.

"Make that the next *month,* Chris."

The sight was sufficiently awe-inspiring for them to withhold further commentary. The next thing they observed was the sheer slope that lay below, and the new sight was not reassuring. The best thing that could be said for this acclivity was its ruggedness. Innumerable crevices and protuberances afforded possible holds for hands and feet where, otherwise, there was no means of descent. Fallon looked down, found the view depressing, and looked up to the bleakness beyond which was scarcely less so. The grayness of the country beyond — relieved only by the orange glow of the volcano that formed the only touch of color — did little to buoy the spirit.

"Do you really think we can do it, Sir Wilbur?" Valera

asked, shadowing his face with a hand.

"Oh, by all means, we shall." He looked about at Marcelina.

"Yes, Sir Wilbur, we shall," she told him with what Valera felt to be surprising confidence.

One by one they slid over the rim and began the descent. With numbed hands and feet, they lowered themselves by degrees. The sun's light was cold and did not touch them with the merest suggestion of warmth. Once the stiffness left their muscles, they continued more easily, though their breathing was still hampered by the thin, cold air. Fallon went first, giving Ramón aid, although his leg was much improved. Sir Wilbur followed, helping Marcelina. Valera came last. They found that the holds supplied by nature more than compensated for the almost perpendicular inclination of the cliff surface. There were jutting ledges not infrequently, and with these they were also provided with occasional resting places.

Progress was slow and methodical. Rests became more infrequent, as the stopping-places became fewer. At times, the valley below seemed to yawn under their very feet, yet always there was a protuberance or ledge whereon to find a foothold. There were places where, as Quinto had observed, it was necessary to form a human ladder in order to make the descent, places where there was a sheer drop for a matter of yards from ledge to successive ledge. Soon, far from feeling frozen stiff, they were bathing in their own perspiration. The bulky packs rendered the process doubly grueling and deadly tiring. They saw why Quinto and his brother, unencumbered though they were, had still had a difficult time.

As they paused to rest on a precarious outthrust of rock, Fallon nodded toward the almost sheer slope below. "How do you like the looks of that?"

Tennington smiled and then encouraged: "This is the roughest place so far, true, but once we're past it, we'll have some of the easiest going yet."

"But how are we going to get past eet?" wondered Ramón.

Marcelina shook her head. "It does look imposing," she said, and smiled grimly.

"We have our ropes," Fallon reminded them. "That's why we sweated so much, bringing them along."

Tennington glanced at his watch. "Almost noon." He looked down to a broad shelf of rock many yards below — separated from them by a sheer drop of the wall. "If we can reach that shelf, we'll have it. Then we can stop and have a bite to eat."

They picked their ropes from the packs.

"Wait," said Fallon. "I think one rope will do it." He dropped one end of his rope over the edge of the ledge, lowering it to its full length. It landed only a foot from the shelf. "Good!" he exclaimed, and knotted the uppermost end about a round rock formation almost a foot in diameter. "It might slip," he observed. "Tenny, keep an eye on it. I'll slide down the rope first and see how safe it is."

Fallon descended in safety to the shelf. Then he steadied the rope for Ramón's careful descent. Marcelina followed, then Valera, and finally Sir Wilbur. But without the Englishman there to steady the round rock to which the rope was secured, Sir Wilbur had only halfway completed his descent when Fallon shouted: "Look out, Tenny! The rope's slipping!"

Chapter Eleven

Tennington did not have to look up to corroborate Fallon's words. He could hear the rock grinding where it was set in the cliff, and he could feel the tiny telltale jerks as the rope slipped little by little with his every movement off the rounded stone.

There was only one thing to do, and the Englishman did it. He loosened his grasp on the rope so that he was sliding down at an alarming rate, almost at a dead drop. Three yards from the shelf, he released the rope and leaped the remaining distance, landing on the shelf with a jar that shook the great slab of rock where it was embedded in the cliffside. His legs ached from the impact, but, even as he came erect, Fallon's body slammed him with a greater impact, knocking him out of harm's way. As Tennington had released the rope, it had worked loose while, crashing and rolling after him, was the great rock that had been pulled completely out of the wall. It plunged downward, crashing on the exact spot where Sir Wilbur had first alighted. Fallon and Tennington picked themselves up slowly, unbelievingly.

"We were lucky that rock remained fast as long as it did," the Englishman said, eyeing his stinging, rope-burned palms.

"Never again!" Fallon said. "When it comes time to scale back up this cliff, we'll have to find another way."

By this time the others had come around to see if Sir Wilbur had sustained injury. He brushed off the incident, saying they were fortunate he had gone last, rather than one of them.

After they had eaten, they viewed their descent. As Tennington had predicted, the worst part was over. The escarpment was still steep enough, but exceedingly rugged, and the very steep places could be bypassed. The vaporous mists around them had further dissipated in the interim, and the valley below and beyond was revealed in a panorama of succulent green grandeur, a luxuriant jungle. And beyond the valley was the gray framing wall — the great plateau beyond which, they believed, was Haucha. The view from this vantage point was also less intimidating, a little less awe-inspiring, now that they were nearer. However, the great looming clouds from the volcano still brooded in the distance, like an ominous mantle of portending doom, a thought perhaps prompted in the minds of them all, though none voiced it.

They were tired, begrimed, and foot-sore when finally they paused much closer to the valley to bivouac for the night. Heretofore, on the heights, they had been obliged to cook their food with heat tablets. Now, they were able again to secure brush for fuel, for there was soil here, of a rocky quality to be sure, and a few tough and tenacious pines had found rest, some of them dying after they had grown too large for their roots to be capable any longer of drawing sufficient nourishment from the rugged ground. The tallest trees would require hundreds of gallons of water to continue to survive. It was from the deadfalls that Ramón was able to gather firewood, a task in which Marcelina assisted him.

After eating, preparations were made to retire soon, weary as they all were. The sun's final golden rays had illumined the valley beyond, briefly but beautifully, then the tropical twilight fled swiftly, and darkness settled over the little promontory where they had located their camp. Chris Fallon, however, wandered to the edge of the promontory and looked up now at the stars above, more of them, and shining more brightly, than he had seen them shine in a long time. Marcelina joined him. She had lit a cigarette and was pleased, at this lower altitude, that she was able to smoke it.

"They are different here . . . aren't they . . . the stars?" she remarked.

"Yes, they are," he answered. "I was just thinking so myself, amid what you might call a *fantaisie macabre*."

"About what, Chris?"

He laughed. "About stars and sand fleas, actually."

"They are the same?"

"Only in one way, I suppose . . . not stars and sand fleas, really . . . but sand fleas and the Eumenides. They are the same in that they both like blood. Looking out into the darkness, against the star shine, I had the illusion, for a moment, that I could see them . . . the Eumenides . . . out there, perched on great branches in the sky, their huge black wings wrapped about them. I wondered, if I listened very hard, in this silence, if I might hear the whistle of their wings in the air."

"Fear of the unknown . . . or of the volcano in the distance?" she asked quietly, dropping her cigarette and extinguishing it with the toe of a boot.

"Not fear so much as hope," he said. "After all, they have been near so often in my life. As when that rope gave out today, and the rock came crashing after Tenny. In a way, I suspect, they might even sometimes protect us."

"Only if you charm them, Chris, the way Orpheus with his music charmed the shades in the Underworld, and even Hades himself, so that he was allowed to take his beloved bride, Euridice, back with him to the world of the living."

"But you know the provision . . . that he dare not look back at her even once, as she followed him."

"Yes," Marcelina said, "provided that he didn't look back."

They were standing close together now. Her face was turned up toward him, faintly visible in the star shine, although her features were vague and her blue-gray eyes were dark pools.

He would feel later that he should not have done it. Perhaps, as Orpheus, he had violated a convenant, and so stood now to lose everything. But he leaned down to kiss Marcelina, and she responded with such passion that he spontaneously thrust up against her. Then she was gone, back toward where the fire still burned, and what sense of hope Fallon had now was fled, and, even if he did not hear the whistle of huge black wings in the silent air, he did feel, nevertheless, an unshakable premonition of foreboding. Had he committed the truly mortal sin? Had he looked back too soon?

The next morning, the world was again gray and misted and the outlook thoroughly bleak. With uncleared and unwarmed spirits, they proceeded, and, happily, the going was more and more easy and the slope less and less steep. When, at last, the mist was gone and they now could view the verdant, sun-lit valley, their spirits rose immeasurably.

They were edging along a ledge below which was a steep drop of five yards when the first inkling came of fresh danger. Fallon, in the lead, was just lowering himself from this ledge onto a spur of rock seven feet below. He was hanging by his fingers from the ledge and was preparing to drop the few inches remaining, when he happened to glance down and saw a snake coiled on the spur but a foot from his left leg. He didn't know whether or not the reptile was poisonous, but he did know that if he moved suddenly, which he must do to drop onto the spur, the snake would probably strike, and his aching fingertips could not grasp the lip rock of the ledge much longer without slipping. Therefore, he used the final moment of his grip to swing his body out and away from the spur, dropping clear by plummeting past it.

He had escaped the serpent's fangs, but, even as he dropped, he was well aware that certain death might await him to either side of the spur, for there were no viable means of support below him. He clawed frantically at protruding rocks as he felt his body sliding down the sheer surface of rock. He grasped at a limb. It tore away in his hand. Then his feet struck a solid irregularity in the cliff wall — an outjutting rock with about a square foot of space where his feet could stand.

He looked about frantically. On every side he could see only the sheerest drop, and there was no ledge near enough toward which he could jump. He was trapped on this meager bit of stone.

"Easy, Chris!" Sir Wilbur shouted from above. "We'll have a rope to you in a minute."

"Watch out for that snake on the spur!" Fallon called back.

He dared not look up; neither did he dare to look down. He could not brace his back against the wall because of the bulky pack. He had to lie flat on his belly against it. Presently Tennington called: "Here comes the rope, Chris."

But, instead, there was an ominous flap of wings, and a great, black, naked-necked bird careened in toward Fallon, the right wing almost brushing his face.

"A condor!" shouted Tennington. "Watch it now, Chris. They are usually too cowardly to attack men, but, if these are as dangerous as we've heard, we may have to do some shooting before we're out of here."

As Tennington finished calling down to him, another condor and another of the massive black carrion-creatures swooped into view, and all gravitated in great circling routes toward Fallon, apparently seeing his helplessness and sweeping in close toward him.

Marcelina, huddled behind Sir Wilbur, recalling her conversation of the previous night with Fallon, wondered if he had had a premonition, or if, perhaps, he had by some freak of the imagination actually mistaken these dreadful birds for the Eumenides.

Fallon's Colt should have been at his side, but, since they had been making this difficult descent, he had transferred it to his pack. His rifle was strapped to his back, but he could not easily reach it, for he could make no movement that might shift him too far outward. He could only strain against the wall. One of the condors now swooped in and brushed severely against his shoulder. It almost upset his precarious balance. He set his teeth and could only pray for something to hold onto for his fingers still could find no place to grip.

Tennington, meanwhile, was struggling desperately to free his rifle from his back, as was Luis Valera, for they had done the same with their weapons as had Fallon. Sir Wilbur commanded Ramón to drop the rope to Fallon and asked Marcelina to throw rocks at the condors.

The trio of feathered killers now were taking turns, circling in to torment Fallon, probably to break what little purchase he had. A wolf pack could not have been more methodically sadistic in this effort to make him lose his balance. Two would come at him from different directions, while the third came from above.

Ramón stared at them, mouth agape, trembling in terror. "They are not birds . . . they are d-demons." He was transfixed by an almost supernatural dread.

Tennington said angrily: "Drop the rope."

Too late. Fallon had been able to draw his knife and now was half turned to meet the sideward lunge of one of the giant birds, but in so doing he had presented his back to another. In an instant great, rending talons tore through his clothes and settled into the flesh of his upper back.

Tennington had his rifle free by this time and a snap shot sent one of the condors plummeting downward, but the one that had settled on Fallon's back was pulling him off the rock by the beating of great wings. In an agony of pain, Fallon fought back savagely and did succeed in driving the bird to loose its hold, but in the process lost his own equilibrium.

It was at this moment that Ramón had finally dropped the rope. Fallon seized at it frantically, even as he fought to regain his balance. In vain. He was too overextended. His outstretched fingers fell just short of the rope, and he toppled backward, groping helplessly at the air.

He pitched backward and down, and, before he even had time to register the fact that he was falling to a very certain death, he landed on his back in a rocky depression only feet below the outjut. He remembered, then, that he had not known exactly what lay beneath him. He sat up, aware for a long moment only of the excruciating pain in his back, not so much from the brief fall as from what the creature's talons had done.

Above him, Sir Wilbur's high-powered rifle cracked out again, and another condor pirouetted earthward. The third, perhaps recognizing the need for discretion, looked ponderously around, and glided majestically away. But Fallon scarcely noticed this. He had even momentarily forgotten his back. He was thunderstruck by what he saw now. There was a shallow crevice in the cliff wall where he had fallen and in this reposed a grotesquely twisted object — a skeleton in what could be nothing other than the metallic remnants of ancient Spanish armor.

He stared at it, unspeaking, scrutinizing it slowly. The moldering skull grinned at him mirthlessly. Little remained of the bones which were practically decomposed. The brass helmet and breastplate and battered buckler were corroded almost away, and only these metal portions of the ancient soldier's garb remained at all. At his side lay a short, straight sword in a rusty scabbard. Under the finger bones of one long-dead hand lay the rusty barrel of a 16th-Century musket, the stock long since decayed and gone. Still, the *conquistador*'s remains lay as they must have fallen more than four centuries before. Only the fact that it was in a crevice, somewhat sheltered from the elements, had permitted any remnants whatsoever to have endured.

"Chris, are you all right?" Marcelina called down, her voice shrill.

"OK," yelled Chris and, drawing a deep breath, repeated: "OK."

"Here, Chris," called Tennington. "If I swing this rope over a little, can you grab onto it?"

The rope swung in Fallon's direction.

"Got it," he called up to the Englishman.

It was only a matter of moments before Fallon had ascended the rope and stood safely now with his companions on the narrow ledge. He looked down at the spur below. The snake had slithered from view.

"What kind was it?" he asked.

"Fer-de-lance," responded Tennington. "Deadliest snake in all South America." He smiled faintly. "For all our mishaps, Chris, I count you a pretty lucky guy . . . to use your vernacular."

Fallon then told them about the skeleton.

Tennington nodded with interest. "One of the ill-fated members of García's expedition. Remember, Luis, García's mention of the giant birds that pecked one man to death? Those condors attacked Chris just as their progenitors of four hundred years ago must have attacked that poor fellow. Ironic, isn't . . . why, great heavens, Chris, that creature tore your back to pieces."

This time Marcelina attended the injured as she dressed Fallon's wounds with medical preparations they had brought along. Valera commented on the potential danger of such wounds in a tropical climate. Fallon wanted to say he had confidence in his recuperative powers, or total faith in the effectiveness of Marcelina's ministrations, but he remained silent. He was commencing to appreciate what old Quinto must have felt. The trip had given *him* white hair, *and he was younger at the time than I am now,* Fallon reflected soberly.

Presently, they continued the descent. Once they saw a herd of llamas below, standing tail to tail as they always gathered when alarmed, yet looking as though ready to flee at any moment. They looked so astonishingly like camels that Fallon and Tennington had seen and even ridden in North Africa, save for the long, shaggy coats of pale red hair that covered their bodies.

The end of the afternoon found them weary, standing at the verge of a rock sector, the last lap of their journey downward, but they could see that they were facing a terrible upheaval of boulders which, as even the optimistic Tennington remarked in a discouraged voice, would be rather rough to negotiate. But Fallon, peering down the jagged surface, thought he could make out a faint rift in the sheer face. Apparently this cleft, zigzagged and irregular as a rope of lightning, was either a crack induced by a shifting of the rock surfaces or eroded by rimlets of rain water. At any rate, it was the only route by which they could hope to continue the descent.

"What do you think?" he asked Tennington.

"I'd say, let's get moving," replied the Englishman. "If we do, I think we stand a good chance of reaching the bottom by nightfall."

Accordingly, they shouldered their gear and recommenced the precarious descent, this time into the rift. It was rugged here, although by no means so much so as if they were descending by any other route, in which case the venture might well prove impossible. With Fallon in the lead, then Tennington, Marcelina, Valera, and Ramón following respectively, they made slow but steady progress. This turned out in reality to be by far the most simple going they had experienced, yet all were sapped by the equatorial sunset that now streamed in golden effulgence across the ancient rocks.

Then, as they attained a turn in the rift, they were suddenly confronted by an obstruction — a broad, flat wall that was a great boulder that had been loosed by some long-ago avalanche to plunge down the mountainside until it had lodged securely in the rift. It now effectively stayed their progress into the valley, for it was too high and sheer to scale and so tightly did it block the passage that it was impossible to find an opening on either side of it.

"It appears we'll have to backtrack," Luis Valera observed, sitting down on a rock and heaving his pack to one side.

"No," said Tennington, "there must be some way."

"I think there is," Fallon said. "If we can move away the rocks embedded at the sides, perhaps we can clear an opening large enough to let us through. At any rate, it's worth a try."

If the others had doubts on this score, they quelled them and set to work on the right side of the obstruction where it met the wall of the rift. As Fallon had supposed, the stones of the wall at this point could be pried loose. As they worked and pried, the rocks and earth began to loosen so that they began to work a narrow tunnel through to the opposite side. Just how far they would have to tunnel, they did not know, of course, having no way to determine the length of the obstruction, but Fallon judged the length of the giant boulder to be no greater than its width. After the first stones, they ran into soft earth. Taking turns in ten-minute shifts, except for Marcelina and Ramón, they dug their way along, the foremost man scraping the dirt loose with a flat, jagged rock and feeding it back, the others behind him thrusting it into the open with their hands in a sort of relay system.

In this manner, they progressed some three yards, and more, paralleling the wall of rock, working with almost frenzied haste to be through before the swiftly departing sunlight vanished entirely and it would become too dark to work.

Sir Wilbur was digging at the front when his scraper suddenly went through the dirt and emerged into the open.

"This is it!" he exclaimed, and set to work feverishly, laboring to enlarge the aperture. Presently an opening sufficiently wide to admit the body of a man was formed, and Tennington tried to wriggle through it. As he did so, there began a fearful grinding, as though the very mountain were grating on its massive base. The great boulder shook, stirred, moved. It shifted then, agonizingly, as though on the very verge of motion.

"Don't move!" Tennington shouted back to the others.

With a sigh of sucking air and a groan of tortured earth, the massive behemoth of rock swayed free. Then, as though hesitant to move after its long imprisonment, it stirred slowly, ponderously, outward. With a violent wrench it moved free of its resting place and, once set in motion, roared and crashed its way along the narrow defile. Finally it plunged wildly downward and abruptly disappeared from view. An instant later there followed a terrific, indefinable crash — then silence, save for a few pellets and loose dirt falling into the depression left behind.

The five stood dazedly in the little embrasure they had hollowed out in the wall.

"That was close," Fallon said. "If that stone had not rolled before any of us had stepped through, we would have been carried along in front of it like chaff."

"That was a danger we hadn't anticipated!" admitted Tennington. He pointed to a shallow depression in the ground. "You see the stone was hanging by no more than an eyelash. When we dug around it, we apparently supplied the final bit of impetus required to send it moving."

Recovered sufficiently from the sudden shock of what had

just happened, they went back to pick up their packs and gear, and once again they resumed their way downward. Before many paces, they came to the brink of a drop-off. In the nearing dark, they could see, by peering below, that the boulder had plunged straight down a short distance and landed between the forked branches of a giant gnarled oak, splitting the trunk from top to base in a massive, crooked V.

"Have we reached the bottom?" wondered Sir Wilbur.

"Not quite," said Fallon, "but the amount of vegetation below indicates the terrain is beginning to level out."

They descended down the drop and found a cleared space among the rocks and bushes to camp. Here they prepared a meager supper from the remainder of their fast-waning supplies.

"We'll hunt tomorrow," said Tennington. "There'll be game down there and game birds."

The next morning, Tennington and Ramón hunted up more dead brush with which to replenish the fire. After a meal eaten in relative silence, they shouldered their packs. Except for Ramón, their hand guns were again at their sides, and the three men had rifles slung loosely from shoulders. In this fashion they proceeded down the slope. The most arduous portion of the journey seemed now to be ended, but not the most dangerous. Below lay the jungle with its unknown animal terrors — and the Quivaris.

Presently the terrain, sloping off more at every successive step, rolled onto a space of weed-covered rocks, and beyond this the vegetation increased, and there were trees and foliage. Here Chris Fallon called a halt and produced the map that Luis Valera had drawn. He pointed toward the wall of the great gray plateau, looming across the valley.

"We'll strike out for the north end of the wall. From there

138

we'll work along to the south and search for a way to scale the wall. There was an osier bridge connecting that plateau with the natural entrance to Haucha, but, as García relates, it was severed centuries ago. However, there may be another way across that García never knew about, or descendants of the Incas may have created a new means of access since then."

As they continued on, it was not too long before they found themselves having entered the jungle that filled the valley between the mountain saddle they had just descended and the plateau toward which they were heading. The trees were gigantic and gnarled, with great looped lianas draped from limb to limb, and myriad musky tropical blooming flowers mingled their fragrances with that of rotting vegetation. Occasionally there was the raucous shriek as a startled, gaily-plumaged parrot flitted away in alarm, and once a chattering monkey tribe beat a hasty and noisy retreat.

Marcelina was considerably unnerved by these outbursts, and she walked now with a hand on the snap of her holster in which she carried her small pistol. Once an anaconda slithered up a tree trunk close by, and a number of pacas darted across their path into the underbrush.

In single file, they continued in silence. To Fallon's consternation they presently came upon a poorly defined trail beaten through the brush. Since the trail apparently led in the direction they were going, he guided the way into it. Then, as they passed beneath some low-hanging branches, he heard a terrified cry to the rear. He stopped at once and with Sir Wilbur hurried back past Marcelina and Luis Valera to see Ramón, who had been walking behind the others, being hauled up into the branches of a huge tree, his body encircled by the folds of a massive snake.

Chapter Twelve

"Boa constrictor!" said Fallon. "Fast, now . . . or Ramón dies!"

His crisp cold voice snapped Valera out of a stigma of lethargic horror, and the three of them brought up ready rifles. Fallon fired first, into the boa's gaping mouth, then Tennington scored, and Valera, each with a body hit. But it was Fallon's shot that had found the brain of the serpent.

"Quit shooting!" he told the others. "We might hit Ramón. The snake's been shot through the head. That's the best we can hope for with a rifle, anyway."

Fallon was right. For a long moment, the boa constrictor's muscles went lax all over its great length, and its tail, which was entwined about a bough in the tree above, loosened its grasp and fell to the ground beneath. But Ramón was still ensnared in the folds of the snake's body, and, though it had not had time to commence the constricting of its coils so as to crush its prey into pulp that would slide easily between the serpent's distended jaws and down its commodious food tract, it would in a second begin the wild lashing of its death throes that would be quite capable of dispatching a grown man.

Therefore, Fallon moved swiftly. He slid his pack to the ground in a second and from its indispensable contents produced a heavy machete. He sprang forward to the coils of the snake and struck at it viciously, hacking at a fold until he was blood-spattered. And then the serpent's death lashing began. Its massive tail came up and caught Fallon between the shoulders, knocking him off his feet. He bounded upright immediately and resumed hacking at the coil. With a terrific twist, it wrenched away from him, carrying the helpless boy with it.

Fallon now caught it with a hand and slashed again and again, concentrating his efforts on a single portion of it, and suddenly his machete went clear through the reptile's body, severing its vertebrae cleanly and decreasing the dying serpent's mobility. He dropped the machete. With seemingly superhuman strength, he tore with his fingers at the writhing portion that held Ramón, and he pulled it off the boy, and hauled him safely away.

The boy was half fainting, and both he and Fallon were splattered with the snake's gore from head to foot. Sir Wilbur, without wasted motion, located the first aid articles in Fallon's pack. Marcelina came forward to assist and within moments the job was done with the boy.

As the Englishman was returning the first-aid articles to Fallon's pack, Chris moved to his elbow. "Be easy on the kid, Tenny. He . . ."

Tennington wheeled on him furiously. "I wish I could say he did something right . . . just once! What the devil is it with that boy and snakes!"

He closed Fallon's pack and handed it over to him. Fallon adjusted it to his back with quick movements. Then, without a word, he proceeded down the trail, followed by his now equally silent companions, Ramón limping alongside Marcelina, with Luis Valera this time bringing up the rear.

Presently Fallon remarked over his shoulder: "Watch the trees as we go. Any liana twisted in the branches might turn out to be another snake."

Apparently no one thought the comment deserved a reply, for no one said a word, but Tennington angrily construed the ensuing and unbroken quietness into a hostile silence. He squared his shoulders. *Let them,* he thought in his frustration. *This is no place for that boy.*

Fallon, as a matter of fact, did feel a bit of unbidden irritation as he considered the Englishman's mood. But, then, there was perhaps some justification for it. Sir Wilbur had not thought it a good idea for Quinto to bring Ramón along in the first place, and the boy had held them up once already. Now he was with them, again without being invited, and Fallon had been on enough excursions to know how, should similar accidents keep occurring, the boy might come to be regarded as a jinx.

The jungle grew thicker and denser as they penetrated still farther. The oppressiveness of this wilderness began to beset them. The trail, vague enough when they had encountered it, was growing tangled and almost impassable. Fallon, at the fore, now had to resort to his machete to slash a way for them.

For nearly three hours, they proceeded in this fashion. It was hard going, and, though perhaps not the most difficult portion of their journey thus far, it was thoroughly as uncomfortable. Where they had frozen on the mountain heights, they now sweltered in tropical heat. Sweat streamed freely within clothing that was wringing wet as they forged their way onward.

Then, ahead, Fallon sighted the encroaching, sullen gleam of sluggishly moving water. With an abruptness that nearly precipitated him into the murky depths, Fallon suddenly broke from the bush onto the bank of a river. It was the river mentioned by García and on the map, and it had also been told of by old Quinto, but, notwithstanding, he hadn't expected it to appear so abruptly.

Fallon stepped back, machete in one lean hand, wiping his forehead with the back of the other. Tennington slowed up behind him with the others.

"We're stopped," the Englishman said. "Looks like we'll have to swim."

"Swim, nothing," retorted Fallon.

"Why not?" Tennington asked.

"Believe me, there're reasons," Fallon said dryly. "Come on. This is the time for us to find food." He jerked his head upriver.

They proceeded up the slow-moving river, paralleling it and keeping to the bank. It was difficult going, since the jungle crowded up to the very edge, and they frequently had to force their way. Presently, however, their uncomplaining diligence was rewarded, as Fallon shouldered his rifle and brought down a plump curassow. Then they found an open spot near the water, a glade-like clearing beneath massive trees, where they prepared and cooked their meal.

It was good to eat well again, a process ever calculated to place one at a renewed state of well being with the world. With considerably heightened spirits, they all relaxed, and Tennington, restored to a good humor, was pleased to take an hour's rest afterward before they moved on upstream.

When the time came to resume the march, they were all glad because of the abundance of insects in the vicinity that had been attracted by their presence. They seemed especially enticed by Marcelina's flavor since she had to slap continually at them, even after they were moving again. Soon her hands and face were spotted with blood.

Sir Wilbur was curious about Fallon's reasons for denying them a cool swim across the river, but he was too proud to ask any questions. Then he recalled their heavy packs and rifles. Of course, that would be sufficient reason. You couldn't swim with equipment. He imagined that a raft might do it, though. Maybe Fallon was looking for some kind of raftwood.

As they proceeded upstream, the water appeared to flow a little more swiftly. From the satisfaction reflected faintly on the stoical Englishman's face, it was this sort of place one might contemplate for a crossing. But then, all of Tennington's puzzlement returned. Fast-moving water was no place to swim across a river. Then he recalled the possibility of crocodiles. That would be reason enough, he thought with a shudder, recalling his own harrowing experience with one of those river reptiles in Africa. He had no desire to risk a personal encounter with a South American species.

Presently, though, to confirm this possibility, he put the question to Fallon. "Crocodiles?"

"No. Not here, anyway." He smiled enigmatically.

"Equipment?"

"No, although that's part of it. These waters are dangerous. A worse danger lurks here than perhaps anywhere else in the world."

Tennington was on the point of inquiring what that danger might be, when the party rounded a curve in the shoreline, where the trees had concealed the other side of the land from their view, so that they had come suddenly upon the sight that stopped all five in their tracks.

The river now had a sandy beach, extending several feet from the shore to the water. There on the sand crouched a huge jaguar, holding between his front teeth a round black object, which on second glance proved to be a big turtle. Evidently the cat had been on the point of prying open the shells with his claws to get at the succulent flesh between them.

The jaguar was lengthwise to them, and he must have been seven feet in length, enormous for his type. He was markedly similar to African leopards, dappled on the head, although his coat was marked by rosettes instead of spots. He was more massive and ponderous of build, however, than a leopard, and his head was broader. The tawny tan of his hide was water-soaked, since he must have advanced into the water to claim his dinner. He stared with unblinking eyes at the newcomers, and made no move to retreat. It was the first jaguar any of them had seen here, and they were all transfixed by the sight of the sleek, beautiful, and terrible creature, which may have been more wariness than good sense, although a sudden movement on the part of any of them might have been the one that would have galvanized the creature to sudden and furious action.

But now the jaguar, flipping his dinner back with a paw, turned slowly to face them, and with a low snarl bared his fangs.

"He has no fear of men!" whispered Fallon. "He's tasted the flesh of man in the past and has found it to his liking."

As he spoke, he was slowly, and without once removing his gaze from the cat, bringing up his rifle. He got no further. The creature was now crouching even lower; muscles as sleekly co-ordinated as the fine springs of a jeweled watch tensed; then the cat sprang. Even as he sprang, Fallon was throwing himself off to one side. But Sir Wilbur, being directly behind Fallon and being paralyzed a second too long, was less fortunate. The beast sprang and bore him backward under its weight, and then Fallon fired.

The jaguar leaped backwards into the air — a leap of pain. He came down in the river with an ignominious splash and blood frayed in a sinuous trickle into the water, staining it red, and then the big cat was paddling away from them toward the opposite shore.

Fallon sighted his rifle to shoot again — then stopped, lowering it. "Too beautiful to kill," he murmured, and then the water was suddenly torn by a wild splashing as the jaguar's smooth glide was destroyed, and he twisted, giving out a terrible scream of agony.

"¡Madre de Dios!" Luis Valera exclaimed, as the jaguar disappeared beneath the surface, and the water now was thrashing in a wild, bloody frenzy. Then, within seconds, and as suddenly as it had commenced, it ceased.

"What . . . ?" began Sir Wilbur, as he arose unsteadily but not hurt.

"I forgot," Fallon remarked soberly, lowering his rifle slowly and staring at the river which had returned to its placid flow, "they would have gotten him anyway."

"What?" asked Marcelina.

"The piranhas," Fallon said, "cannibal fish. Perhaps you saw a few small white bodies clinging to the jaguar before he went down?"

"I've heard of them, but have never seen them," she replied.

Fallon nodded grimly. "Teeth like razors. They can strip the flesh from a man's bones within seconds. I encountered them before in the Amazon. That's the reason I didn't want to cross."

"They were on that jaguar in a second!" Sir Wilbur exclaimed.

"His blood attracted them," Fallon said. "And just to demonstrate how fast they work . . . well . . . the water's cleared, and it's like crystal to the bottom at this point. On the sand down there . . . no, there . . . take a good, long look . . . and don't forget it."

After a moment, peering into the flowing water, they could distinguish the thing on the dark bottom that Fallon was indicating — the skeleton of the jaguar picked clean.

After a moment, Sir Wilbur inquired: "Well, where do we cross? *How* do we cross?"

"Come on," Fallon answered. "We'll work upstream farther, then I should be able to show you."

They trudged in silence for at least another half hour until Fallon finally paused at a place in the river where the distance was not so great from bank to bank, and on the opposite side was a great dead tree, the top having been broken off and washed downstream long before. It had grown on the slope of the bank and was now so tilted that it leaned far over the water. The river flowed very rapidly here, so rapidly that it frothed up

146

in places with flecks of agitated foam. This condition extended for hundreds of feet in both directions.

Fallon turned now and indicated some stout, straight saplings growing nearby. "We can use these to construct a raft. Even if any of us were good enough to swim it, we couldn't do it with our equipment. Also, the river appears to be too deep to be fordable at any spot I've seen."

The Englishman agreed with Fallon on this score, but, as they unpacked their hand axes and threw their equipment and rifles aside to commence felling the saplings, he wondered if the same swiftly rushing flow, sight of which might well discourage the strongest swimmer, might not also sweep a raft and its cargo helplessly downstream?

"How'll we get the raft across?" he asked Fallon.

"Poles might propel it across. Just a minute."

Fallon was occupied in trimming a slim, cut sapling about fifteen feet in length of its leaves and branches. Evidently he had already anticipated this problem. Having shorn the long trunk of its foliage, he strode to the bank of the river and sprawled on his stomach near the water's edge, then thrust the pole straight down into the swirling depths, bracing it with both hands so that it would not be swept from his grasp by the insistently tugging current. Then he whirled. When he had thrust the pole as far as it would go to the bottom, scarcely two feet of it extended above the racing surface.

"And it's probably even deeper in the middle," he remarked. "If the poles weren't yanked right out of our hands, they'd be useless anyway."

"Then how . . . ?" Valera began.

"I think I have it!" Tennington exclaimed. "We can toss a noose across the water and rope that big trunk on the other side. It's old, but it looks sturdy enough, and it should hold the weight of the raft and our gear."

Fallon nodded approvingly. "We're thinking along similar lines, Tenny."

"If we tie the other end of the rope to a tree on this side and get on the raft and edge it across, with us holding onto the rope and pulling the raft . . . and ourselves along. . . . Why . . . what's wrong with that?"

Fallon was shaking his head before Sir Wilbur had finished.

"We might pull ourselves across that way . . . but what would be holding the raft to our feet? Nothing. It'd be swept right from under us. It would be too hard to pull even if we tied ourselves to it."

Wondering how he could have overlooked such a minor, yet important, detail, the Englishman said no more.

But now Valera put in: "Why worry about a raft? We can just go over the rope hand over hand . . . even Ramón."

"I doubt if any of us would make it with all our equipment," Fallon commented with a shake of his head. "I think I know a way. I'll explain it after we finish the raft."

They felled and trimmed the saplings and cut them into the proper length, then lashed the ends together with rope. Then, by main force, they shoved the raft down into the stream, and Fallon secured it tightly to a tree on the bank. It had required three hours.

Fallon said: "First, we'll lasso that dead stump across the river . . . and then tie the other end to the raft itself. Then we get on with our gear . . . one person per trip . . . and push it into the stream. The current will swing the raft right down to the opposite shore."

"But how'll we get the raft back to the other bank?" Tennington wondered.

"We'll tie another rope onto the raft . . . then one of us left on this side can pull the raft back again."

"I told you he was a cowboy," Sir Wilbur remarked to

148

Marcelina, and winked.

Fallon noosed a rope and, after several experimental casts, succeeded in approximating the distance correctly and cast a loop over the dead trunk. He secured the tree end tightly to the edge of the raft and then tied another rope to the opposite end. He pulled tightly on the first rope to ascertain its grip on the trunk and proceeded to heft his gear onto his back and sling on his rifle.

"I'll go across first," Fallon said, "and make sure it's safe." He stepped onto the raft. "Shove it out."

The four on the bank combined their strength into a vigorous shove that thrust the raft away from shore and into the stream. For a long moment it glided gradually outward. And then the current caught it, and it was swept abruptly downstream and into the middle of the current. For a long moment, the midstream current held it thus, and it seemed that the raft would either be suspended helplessly in the churning force of the water and refuse to swing on, or else the tug of the water would snap the rope. But then a swirl of water caught the raft, and it gravitated onward toward the opposite shore, propelled by the current and by the centrifugal action of the taut rope, and, in a moment more, it had glided safely into the calmer water near the bank. Here Fallon reached out, grasped a low-hanging branch, and pulled himself and his craft in very close to shore.

Tennington had retained a tight grasp on the free end of the other rope which now spanned to the raft, and, as Fallon stepped off onto the opposite bank and waved an arm, he, Valera, and Marcelina threw their weight into it and tugged the raft back across the intervening yards of frothing water.

"You next, Ramón," Sir Wilbur directed, "and be careful to stand in the middle of the raft."

Ramón likewise completed the crossing without mishap,

and again Tennington, Valera, and Marcelina pulled back the raft. Marcelina made the next trip, and then Valera, and Sir Wilbur had to pull the raft back by himself, and with considerable effort without anyone else to aid him against the restraining current. Finally, he himself clambered onto the raft and shoved off. But this time there was a mishap. The ancient trunk that held the taut rope could take pressure, for it was thick and still sturdy, but its long-dead roots were settled with only the main taproot still seaming it to *terra firma*, and now that root snapped. The trunk was torn from the soil and yanked into the river with a furrowing splash, and the raft, having at that moment reached midstream, shot away downstream, trailing rope and trunk behind it. Sir Wilbur, as it broke away, flung himself off as far as he could toward shore and struggled to turn away from the current, but the current would not be thwarted, and he was swept downstream, his companions on shore staring after him until he disappeared suddenly around a bend.

As one, they snapped about and tore along the bank downstream, and, though their progress was pitifully slow, impeded as they were by the heavy underbrush, they stumbled and thrashed frantically onward. Fallon in front gasped: "If he can only . . . get . . . to shore . . . fast . . . when he hits those shallows . . . before the piranhas. . . ."

Marcelina, close behind Fallon, groaned: "My God, Chris, those fish!"

"He's a good swimmer, Marcie. Once he's free of these rapids, he should be able to get to shore before they could ever. . . ."

"The jaguar didn't!" panted Marcelina.

Chapter Thirteen

For long moments, as he fought on through the dense brush with the branches and boughs lashing at his face and tearing at his clothes till his face was smirched with raw welts and his skin scratched till blood was drawn, Fallon's mind was a dull, vacuous nadir of despair that refused to focus itself on the grim and unavoidable truth. Sir Wilbur had been swept beyond reach or sight so swiftly that he must have long since been washed into the calm water. The rapids provided a hideous, senseless dirge in his ears. He stumbled and fell and came upright and plunged on without knowing that he had fallen, and his thoughts reeled with strangely conflicting memories: the long years of companionship between himself and the Englishman — thoughts of their expedition to Egypt and Ethiopia, a hunting trip they had taken together in British East Africa — and always through these mental images moved Tennington and himself. And he thought, too, of the sleek, powerful jaguar trying to propel itself to safety on the opposite shore of the river — and of the violent thrashing, and a moment later nothing but a litter of bones picked clean lying on the clear sandy bottom. And he saw again the blood fraying into the water from the big cat's wound — and he saw again the spots of blood on Sir Wilbur's hands, from insect bites, from hewing wood for the raft, from tugging on the rope.

Every terrible thought climaxed suddenly as Fallon burst from the bush and rounded the bend of the river, stopped, and saw ahead, far ahead, nothing — nothing except frothing rapids circling down to the calmer water.

Nothing.

And then — before he could momentarily feel even a fleeting reaction — he heard a single, strangled call from scarcely three yards to his right — and there, as he glanced across the river, was Tennington, his head bobbing alternately under and above the water. It was when he had been above water that he had given the call, only to have it choked off as he was again submerged beneath the rolling surface of the tugging current.

Then Fallon saw that the Englishman was hanging onto a dripping vine, one end of which trailed in the water while the other was looped about a thick tree branch hanging low over the river. He had not seen him immediately because the thick, gnarled trunk of the tree with its low foliage and network of parasitic vines tended at this point to screen his view of the river.

Marcelina O'Day, Luis Valera, and Ramón had come up now behind Fallon and were also watching the man's struggle in the river. It was plain Sir Wilbur was having a time hanging onto the vine, which required both his hands, and still keeping his head above the current. He was trying to pull himself up the vine, but with the terrific backward drag of the current and his back pack it was all he could do to retain his grasp on the trailer. He must already be half drowned.

Fallon realized the predicament. The vine grew too far out on the branch for him to reach from where he stood, and the tree bent so far out over the water that the branch was at too great a distance to get a good grasp on a tree limb. The trunk itself was far too thick to scale. There now was only one possibility, and it was fraught with danger. If he missed . . . but he didn't pause to think, for Sir Wilbur couldn't hold on much longer.

Fallon leaped, and his leap carried him out over the water. He could hear Tennington's yell in front of him, but he didn't miss. His fingers closed unerringly over the bough, and he drew

152

himself swiftly onto it and grasped the slender retaining vine that clung between Sir Wilbur and death. Fallon squatted there on the branch and threw all his weight back on the taut vine. Below him foamed the river. If the vine suddenly snapped, he would be pitched off balance into it — or if Sir Wilbur lost his hold and there was suddenly a counterbalancing weight. . . .

But there was no time for reflection. Fallon just strained at the vine and, for a long moment, couldn't get enough leverage. Then the strength of desperation and his straining weight told, and Tennington was being pulled up inch by inch. Fallon set his teeth, but, try as he would, he could gain no more than those few inches, and his aching arms and fingers felt torn from their sockets. But now Sir Wilbur was up far enough so that he could work his legs free of the current's force and thus pull himself hand over hand slowly up the vine, somehow forcing his own cramped and aching muscles to lift his weight. Fallon, throwing himself flat on his stomach on the branch, braced himself and extended his hand down toward his friend. Tennington grasped Fallon's wrist, and Fallon did likewise, and bit by bit he hauled Tennington upward till they both lay sprawled and gasping on the broad, rough-backed surface of the bough.

They rested for only a few seconds. Then, marshaling their faculties, they looked painfully down at Marcelina, Valera, and Ramón on the bank but a few feet away. There still remained the problem of getting safely onto the bank again.

"Jump as far as you can toward the bank," Valera called up to them. "Try to grab my hand."

He sprawled flat on the bank and extended his hand as far as he could to the trunk, then hesitating, crouching at the base of the limb, as he stared at the rushing water below. "Don't think . . . jump!" he insisted.

Fallon sprang immediately, catching a glimpse of frothing

water as he descended, then the swirling depths closed over his head with the roar of his own splash still echoing in his ears. He fought instantly to the surface, throwing one hand upward. But the current caught at him immediately, and his hand missed Valera's by inches as he was yanked away. Hurling himself frantically forward, he threw his remaining vestige of strength into two powerful strokes toward shore, and, this time, his grasping fingers closed over Valera's extended hand. He was pulled, dripping, from the water and clambered onto the bank where he fell face down, utterly drained of his final reserve of energy. Marcelina fell to her knees beside him.

It was now Sir Wilbur's turn. He made a jackknife leap from the branch, and, when he came up, he was much nearer to the bank than Chris Fallon had been. Without difficulty, Valera drew him onto the slope. He lay there beside Fallon, panting from exhaustion. Ramón came to his side.

Presently Marcelina was able to draw Chris Fallon to a sitting position, who shook back his dripping black hair from his forehead. "Thought you were really gone that time, Tenny," he grumbled.

Sir Wilbur pulled himself up while Ramón was beside him, although not touching him. "Thought I was, too. Grabbed at the first thing I saw . . . that vine."

"Thank God you're both all right," Marcelina said.

A pair of great-billed toucans, bustling in the foliage overhead, appeared to agree.

Since the day was waning, they decided to camp at this spot. They were by now a truly sorry-looking group, covered as they were with mud, damp from water, with scratches and welts on exposed skin, and besieged constantly by annoying insects. Marcelina's reddish-brown hair was bedraggled, and she was amused by the folly that had made her believe white jodhpurs might ever have been appropriate for this journey. She was able

154

to wash her face and hands, however, and, after that, felt better. And not for one moment did she regret having come.

A fire helped somewhat to drive away flying insects, and they were able to make a meal from birds that had never before heard the roar of a hunter's rifle. It occurred to Chris Fallon that the sounds of rifle fire might also be heard by the Quivaris, but he dismissed the concern from his mind because of the pressing need for game.

It did not occur to any of them, not even Ramón, that Quinto might hear the sound of those shots, but he did from the very promontory where Chris Fallon and Marcelina O'Day had exchanged their first kiss. He wasn't there voluntarily, but rather as a captive, and his captors heard the shots as well. Certainly nothing was further from Marcelina's mind that night as she sat on the ground before the fire near Chris Fallon, her legs drawn up beneath her. By this time they both knew they were in love, and so they dared not wander away together from the firelight. It was as if their only hope for comfort and security in each other was here, around the fire, and in the quiet between them.

Sir Wilbur Tennington, obviously recovered from his ordeal, rolled them all out early the following morning, ignoring a reluctant remark from Valera about the jolly-fellow British. After a hurried repast and, having assembled their packs and consulted the map, they set out again toward the towering plateau wall on the opposite side of the valley. All that morning and well on into the afternoon, they made their way through an almost impassable wilderness, Fallon hacking out the way with his machete. There was an amazing profusion and variety of animal, as well as vegetable, life.

It was late in the afternoon that the jungle began to thin as the terrain sloped gently upward. The trees became less dense, and they were of a hardier upland variety, some even conifer-ous. It was also then that it began — that odd, spine-creeping sensation sometimes attributed to a sixth sense, an uncanny and inexplicable feeling that gives the constant impression that some intelligent being is watching your every movement, and, though they all felt it, not one of them mentioned it to the other.

Coming to a sylvan glade set in a rocky sector, they made camp. It was only late afternoon, but the oppressive sense of alien eyes watching induced in them all a desire to halt and re-connoiter. Ramón prepared a fire while the others prowled about, gazing suspiciously at the rocks strewn about the edge of their campsite, though, again, none gave any evidence of their fear by word. Marcelina, who had awoken that morning want-ing very much to bathe, a patent impossibility then as now, felt the prying eyes, but there was no effrontery at which to be an-gered, since the observers, if there were any, could not be seen.

By the time the meal was prepared, the time of the brief twi-light was approaching. It was after they had eaten that Chris Fallon openly suggested that tonight, for the first time, they should post a guard, each of the men taking a three-hour watch as sentry. All agreed.

"You may be excused from guard duty, Ramón," Tennington interjected, in a more kindly manner than he had used with the boy in a while. He could see no sense in need-lessly subjecting Ramón to the hardship of enforced wakeful-ness after his recent siege of fever and the hardship of all that had followed since. In this Fallon concurred. Ramón probably needed sleep more than anything, and, too, Ramón, more tired than perhaps any of the others, was more than likely to fall asleep while on duty.

The watches were divided between Valera, who would take the first, Tennington who would take the second, and Fallon who would take the last. Valera picked up his rifle and sat down by the fire, while the others shook out their blankets before going to sleep.

"Don't forget, now, Luis," Fallon admonished gently, "if you find yourself getting too tired, wake me up."

"Believe me, Chris," returned the archeologist, "many times in my life I have been able to watch for an hour" — he smiled assuringly at Marcelina — "and more than an hour."

"All right, Luis," mumbled Tennington, perhaps a little testily, his voice muffled as he rolled into his blankets, "just don't go to sleep."

Valera settled himself somewhat grumpily by the fire, wondering what kind of infant they imagined him to be. He stared into the fire. The embers, red and gleaming, were commencing to crumble, and a lethargy began to steal over him. He blinked, then, and snapped erect, realizing that he may have underestimated his weariness — especially after a hard day of hiking.

He swiveled his glance around toward the rocks, instead, and stared at them idly. Beyond the flickering circumference of firelight there was only dimness from which could be heard the voices of myriad nocturnal creatures. Eerie sensations playing up and down his spine were becoming increasingly pronounced.

There! That was a movement — of some nature — he had caught in the darkness, just beyond the rocks. Slowly he raised his rifle, swallowed hard, and began to take aim. Then a small rodent danced across a rock, scampered across the clearing, passing within scarcely a yard of where Valera sat, before vanishing again in the shadows.

The professor's ensuing spasm of relief was almost stifling. As it was, he managed a feeble chuckle and settled back again, with the uncomfortable knowledge that the thin-frayed tempers of his companions would scarcely have been improved had they been awakened by him from sound slumber with a false alarm. He contrived to stare intently into the darkness from whence the rodent had issued, and, as he felt the grip of excitement relax, began to think. That rodent certainly didn't explain the ghastly sensations that had been besetting him for most of the day.

He began to grow drowsy again. Three times he almost drifted off, but caught himself just in time. To obviate the possibility, he then got up and walked about the clearing a little. This, though, soon proved to be impractical, since his limbs were sore and aching from the day's vicissitudes, so he returned to the fire and reseated himself by the fire, sitting, however, bolt upright to preserve wakefulness. When his back presently began to ache from this unnatural posture, he slumped down again, only to be immediately claimed by drowsiness. From then on it cost him an even greater effort to maintain watchfulness. Time and again he would drift off, only to snap erect again as exhaustion claimed him. He took to glancing at his pocket watch. Time seemed to drag. His thoughts wandered to Francisca. Perhaps she was in bed, missing him. How many years had it been now that they had drifted off to sleep, secure in each other's proximity? Why hadn't he encouraged her to come when he had agreed to let Marcelina accompany them? Of course, the girl should have stayed behind in Lima. Ramón should not have rejoined them. This was no place for a boy and a girl not much older than he was. Luis Valera was actually so far gone with these distant ruminations that Tennington's voice came to him as suddenly as a slap.

"Time for my watch, old man."

The Englishman was emerging from his blankets, yawning, and apparently had not noticed Valera's momentary somnolence, for which he was thankful. He was also glad the Englishman had not depended on him to arouse him for the next watch. In fact, Tennington must actually have thought he was being noble about it, for he remarked, as Valera rolled heavily into his blankets, his voice very quiet but kindly: "You took five minutes longer than your watch, Luis. Next time, don't be so self-sacrificing. You need sleep as much as any of us."

Sir Wilbur had little difficulty. He had taken long watches before, and it was a matter of his experience that he remained awake and alert in just as unconscious a state of mind as the conscious state with which Luis Valera had sought to stave off sleepiness. Part of the time, he smoked his bulldog pipe, and the hours of his watch passed easily for him. After he had aroused Chris Fallon for his watch, Tennington went back to sleep just as easily as he had stayed awake.

Fallon had been fortified by six hours' sleep and had no difficulty in keeping awake. He relaxed in a sitting position by the now nearly dead fire which he replenished without any danger of going to sleep on the job, but the return to wakefulness did tend to make him restless, that and his thoughts, as his eyes would venture just short of where Marcelina was sleeping. She was here with him, and his fear of losing her, as they had almost lost Tenny yesterday, troubled him, but less when a gray light began to tint the sky with a gentle neutrality, and he got up to stalk quietly around the clearing.

Not once during that long night had one of them caught a glimpse of any mysterious being spying on them, and now, with dawn drawing near, Fallon's keyed nerves began to relax. He decided that the strain of the past weeks must have wrought heavily on his mind to induce such an unreasoning jumpiness. He returned to the fire, which again was burning very low, and sat down beside the mostly charred embers. As the first rays of actual dawn slanted down across the clearing from above the surrounding mountains, he even dozed for about a half hour, then snapped out of it abruptly.

It was dawn now, and he noted with relief that all of his companions were still slumbering soundly and had failed to note his defection. He felt his time was probably up now. Smiling to himself, he rose, picked up two skillets lying near the fire, and banged them together. His companions came out of their blankets fast. Tennington actually rose to his feet, his rifle ready, then grinned ironically when he saw the cause of the sudden disturbance.

Fallon chuckled and strolled off among the rocks to stretch his legs and relieve himself. Presently, he tilted his head, catching the murmur of running water. He investigated and soon located a stream bubbling its way down the sloping land. The water was clear and very shallow, about two feet or so in width. He followed it upslope a short distance, failing to notice that he was now out of sight of camp, and entered a rocky glen where a number of trees grew in a close circle. In the center of the glen he found where the stream had its origin, in a deep, bubbling pool that widened out around the glen, the trees casting cool dark shadows on the surface. The water was very cold as he squatted down beside it to wash and drink. He must tell the others of this, especially Marcelina. The pool was fed from underground. He couldn't see to the bottom.

While he was bending down to drink and speculating simultaneously on the good fortune of finding this pastoral pool, he was aware suddenly of a violent rustle of foliage in a tree looming over his head. Immediately he twisted about to look, but, before his head could swivel halfway up, he felt a terrific weight crash into the center of his back and drive him forward, smashing the wind from his body, and both he and his antagonist were thrown off the edge of the pool and down into the water. Fallon tried immediately in a gasp to regain his shattered breath, but he breathed only water that strangled agonizingly.

He was plummeting downward then into the dark water,

and his opponent's legs were locked around his waist and fingers gripped in a throttling grasp around his throat, so that Fallon was helpless, his wind shut off and water in his nose. He was being carried downward into the icy depths, his consciousness ebbing by the instant. And against the iron strength of the creature who bore him downward, his feeble struggles seemed useless.

Chapter Fourteen

"There won't be much to eat this morning," Tennington remarked, as he was preparing their morning meal. "Wonder where Marcelina went? Chris is gone, too."

"They're probably out walking," Valera replied. "They didn't leave together, but they both went in the same direction, off toward the northeast."

"Well . . . ," Tennington said tentatively as he turned to look in the direction Valera had indicated, but his eyes stopped abruptly, his gaze fixing on the ground a few yards away. There was the shadow of a man — and, glancing off to the right, he saw another man who had must arisen from behind the concealment of a low thicket.

The Englishman started to reach for the rifle leaning against his pack a foot or so away, when, immediately, the two men lifted their own weapons, and from all around the camp — from rocks, grass clumps, and bushes — rose men, until there were nine warriors. Then, suddenly, three more of them dropped from low-hanging branches of trees drooping near the camp. These last must have been there all the time — before the explorers had struck camp last night. Tennington realized every member of their party had been in danger during the night. It appeared now that other warriors had crept up to surround the camp and had only been waiting for this unguarded moment to take them prisoner.

Given a chance to regard their captors at close hand, Tennington saw an exceedingly primitive tribe of jungle Indians. Judging them by their general features and native dress, he had not seen such wild-appearing men, either in Africa or in

Outer Mongolia. For the most part, they were powerfully muscled men, but of a rather squat build, if not exactly short in stature. Their fierce appearance only managed to convey the impression of enormous power in leash. Their hair was black and straight and unkempt, and it fell in tousled tresses to their backs, and in some cases even over their faces. Their eyes, however, glistened opaquely — like the eyes of animals, shining from the recesses of dark caverns. Some of them went naked, while others were almost so with the exception of an animal-skin breechclout about their loins. There was no evidence that they made any effort at ornamentation. All of them were scarred, but these were irregular marks, plainly from brambles or wild animals or knife or spear wounds. The scars did not seem to be self-inflicted decorations from either tests of manhood or tribal markings. Their weapons were crude knives of quartz that were, nevertheless, sharply honed and sturdy, and some carried quartz-tipped spears. One or two had clubs of knotted wood.

The first man Tennington had seen — a very big Indian and, apparently, the leader — raised his arm and gave a command. Immediately Ramón recognized the spoken words as a dialect of his own Quechuan language.

"Do you understand them?" Tennington asked the boy.

"*Sí*, Don Weelbur . . . he commands that we do not move."

There was little opportunity at the moment to speculate on the matter, since the warriors were now closing in about them with ready weapons, regarding them warily, as potential enemies. Two collected their rifles, roaming at various intervals about the camp. Three others approached them closely and relieved Tennington and Valera of their hand guns and knives and systematically frisked them. All of these they had undoubtedly recognized as weapons.

"Ramón," instructed Sir Wilbur, "please tell them that we

come in peace and are only passing through this valley."

Ramón was plainly terrified, but he repeated what the Englishman had said in Quechuan. He had already surmised that these warriors were part of the tribe of the Quivaris about which Quinto had spoken.

The leader replied.

"He says we are to gather our packs."

Tennington and Valera, seeing no way to avoid the command, set about packing their gear. Marcelina's pack, Tennington noticed now for the first time, was gone. Ramón was ordered to gather up Fallon's pack.

When Tennington had slung his pack over his shoulder, he glanced questioningly at the leader.

The leader spoke to Ramón, who was just finishing with Fallon's pack.

"He say we are to carry the packs and go weeth them."

The leader now nodded and motioned toward a group of his men who were already filing from the camp to the southeast. This was the same direction they had been traveling, even if, now, there wasn't much any of them could do about it. The warriors who had appropriated their guns had been admiring them and showing them about when the leader snapped out an order to them, and they fell promptly behind the prisoners following the leader who, in turn, was preceded by several warriors. Ramón, carrying Fallon's pack, was more terrified for those who were missing than for himself. He felt he must protect Marcelina O'Day and Chris Fallon even at the cost of his own life.

The trail they took led up a rocky incline and then across a section of scrub trees and upheaved boulders. As they marched, Tennington had time for speculation. Despite his far-flung travels, only a group of Afghan mountain bandits had impressed him with as much potential savagery as these

Quivaris. Yet, despite their obvious isolation from the outer world, they did seem fairly intelligent and self-controlled people. Their curiosity about the firearms had not been child-like, merely a natural healthy inquisitiveness, and perhaps from some contact in the past they were familiar with how firearms worked. Then he thought abruptly of Chris Fallon and Marcelina O'Day. They had gone off separately — walking among the rocks, Valera had said — and had not been seen since. Perhaps they, too, had been captured by some of these warriors — or murdered. Tennington's stomach seemed to recoil at that thought. Then he considered that Fallon might well have escaped, and Marcelina with him. After all, he had seen no indication among their captors that they knew of Fallon and Marcelina — the way things were distributed, Ramón, who had no pack of his own, was carrying Fallon's, and Marcelina's had vanished. On the other hand, they *must* have known of them, for they had evidently been spying on the expedition for hours, perhaps longer.

Tennington was at the point of putting a question through Ramón to the leader concerning the two missing members of the party, when it occurred to him that Fallon and O'Day might just possibly have escaped those sent to capture them. If so, the leader was probably ignorant of this, and there was no point in calling his attention to it now. After all, Fallon, and to a much lesser extent Marcelina O'Day, if they were still alive and free, might perhaps be their only hope of rescue.

Luis Valera's mind was teeming with similarly fearful speculations. He had believed what Quinto had said about the Quivaris, and he knew from his years of having lived in Peru that in the hinterland mountain fastnesses and jungle valleys there were still primitive tribes that had been ignored while Peruvian civilization grew up in other parts of the country. As it was, he could see no immediate hope for their escape, and he

165

was mortally afraid for Marcelina and cursed himself for ever having let her come this far with them. These savages had jumped them too efficiently. It indicated to him that they had scouts flung beyond the borders of their tribal village, if they lived in a village, and not still in caves as Quinto had indicated. In any case, they must have known of their entrance into this country from the very first moment they had set foot in the valley. Even if the three of them could successfully make a break from this war party, they would be hunted down within a very short time. These primitive warriors undoubtedly knew the jungle in this valley as well as he had come to know the environs of Lima or San Francisco. Any attempt to elude them here would be laughable — and disastrous. He knew Quechuan well himself, but he thought it prudent, under the circumstances, to rely on Ramón as the interpreter. It had been his long-standing belief that a clandestine knowledge of a language gave a person a kind of power over those speaking it.

They had toiled up a slope for a good hundred yards by now. It was not a steep slope, but a gradual undulating upgrade, and presently they surmounted it. Before them stood the great cliff wall of the plateau, an ominous-looming mass backed by the sunlight in the eastern sky. It could not be more than two miles distant now, and from here it seemed more than ever like a high, sheer, perpendicular wall. Tennington, notwithstanding his inherent optimism, was beginning to feel less and less confidence in any successful outcome to this venture. Even if they escaped from these people, how could they hope to ascend such a sheer wall — and, if what had been written was further borne out, bridge a chasm between that plateau and another still out of sight?

However, the temper of their captors was yet to be tried. Tennington could only bolster his state of mind with two hopes. The first was that these people might not yet have had sufficient contact with civilized man to hold a grudge against them in general, as most primitive peoples had, because of civilized man's ruthless tyranny in exploiting the resources of land seized in most cases from the natives. The second was that the whole attitude of these Indians had thus far been one of quiet, but not brutal, force.

The march continued now across rolling, horizontal country, spreading out level at the foot of the plateau wall — level, that is, in general topography, not in detailed contour. There were massive rocks and rugged spurs upjutting and littering this section, so that traversing it was far from simple, and what might have been, otherwise, less than an hour's journey might consume better than two hours. The only vegetation in sight at this point was decidedly semi-tropical, of a scrubby nature, twisted and stunted and grotesque, having found meager and tenuous roothold, groping between gigantic rocks to the soil beneath.

Having drawn so near, Tennington thought that now he could see the base of the plateau pierced with a number of equally spaced portals. Then he realized that this was, indeed, not conjecture. The framing cliff wall marked the entrances to dozens of man-made dwellings, and he could now see people — men, women, and children — going about their various business. So, as Quinto had said, the Quivaris were cave-dwellers — presumably the most primitive form of human social evolution. Quinto had said the Quivaris were a dreadful tribe of men, more animal than human. Now, *they* were in the hands of the Quivaris. Recalling the terrors of Quinto's imprisonment, which Quinto had only hinted at, and the terrors which Pedro, Quinto's brother and Ramón's father, had failed to survive, Tennington's heart began to sink as though crushed by a lead weight.

They moved on until, in plain view of the village, they were seen by others who immediately ceased their various tasks, and clustered about captors and captives, halting their progress as they reached the verge of the cleared square before the entrances to the caves. They gestured and talked excitedly in their Quechuan dialect that Ramón mostly understood but did not translate. At any rate, these other tribal people did not offer to molest the prisoners by prodding or railing at them, as Tennington had halfway anticipated from his acquaintance with other primitive peoples in former times.

The entire tribe had now assembled and appeared to be several hundreds in number — all scantily clad, if clad at all, and with the same primal and wild-looking appearance. A glance assured Tennington that their means of preparing food was no less primitive.

The leader of their captors, apparently a stoical man impatient with all this hub-bub, raised his spear and proceeded to prod a way through the encircling crowd. When this did not prove successful, he belayed some of them across their heads and shoulders with the haft, and now swiftly a path was cleared that enabled the warriors to proceed with their captives to the mouth of a cave in which they were pushed.

The ceiling of the cave was so low that, with the exception of Ramón, they had to bend their heads and sometimes their backs. As far as the Englishman could tell, the tunnel into which they were now being prodded insistently from behind had been hewn out long ago by the hands of men and was not a result of erosion. It was difficult to tell how far they were precipitated forward through a winding passageway where they could hardly distinguish the faint outline of the tunnel walls which were illumined only by flecked light.

Tennington was in front, and he had to grope his way unsteadily along the uneven floor that he could not really see beneath his feet. Ahead of him all was blackness. He wondered suddenly if this was the Quivaris' means of disposing of them — perhaps to thrust them along through darkness until they plunged into an unseen pitfall where they would be left to perish of starvation and thirst — in utter darkness. He continued onward, feeling every step out ahead of him with the utmost caution. From in front, there came no sound — while, from behind, above the sound of shuffling footsteps, was the echo of the villagers' voices becoming more remote.

Presently, he could no longer feel the walls with his hands, or see them, and beyond all was pitch black. Tennington stopped here, and behind him Valera and Ramón also came to a stop. Ramón cried out as one of the warriors poked him with a spear blade to move him along. Tennington resumed, then, again feeling tentatively ahead.

"Come on," he whispered to his companions.

They crowded after him, and then they all heard bare feet shuffle on past them. Tennington wondered if this might be an opportunity for escape, that it might be possible to lose their captors in the darkness of the tunnel, but this momentary thought was squashed quickly as a torch-bearing warrior came forward, leading them into a large room hewn from the rock that was obviously at the end of the tunnel.

The leader for the first time then changed his expression to a wicked grin, seeming all the more malevolent in the flickering gleam of the torch. He looked directly at Tennington.

The man with the torch stepped now into the middle of the room, and so the three captives could see the interior more plainly. It was a great rounded bowl with a vaulted roof about fifteen feet above the rocky floor, but the immediate impact came from a series of poles lining the walls on the far side on which were strung a number of small, roughly oval objects about the size of apples. Before Tennington could conjure up a thought as to the identity of these objects, the leader spoke di-

169

rectly to him for the first time.

Ramón translated hesitantly. "We are to remain here, Don Weelbur. Warriors guard the entrance to thees cave. If we try to leave, we'll be killed."

It took Tennington several seconds to respond, then he said haltingly: "Why have we been brought here? We do not seek trouble."

"We have found it," Ramón translated the leader's reply.

The leader then spoke to his men, and they all began to file from the room.

"Can you leave us a light?" Tennington asked.

The leader hesitated a moment after Ramón translated, then he took the torch from the torch bearer and set it in a niche hollowed in one wall. Then they did leave, and the three captives remained in the vaulted room with the wavering torch-light casting elongated shadows from the grotesque little objects on the poles.

Once the Quivaris had gone, Tennington took down the torch and stepped over to the far wall to examine the objects more closely. Valera and Ramón followed him. Tennington held up the torch to the apple-size objects and then stepped back in involuntary astonishment. Every one of those things was the head of a man, shrunken to one sixth its normal size. He thought he saw now why the leader had left them the torch. It was simply to give them a view of the heads that would serve as a goad to shock and horrify them. And soon the torch would go out and leave them in utter blackness — both the blackness of the cave and the blackness of despair. He could take it. He wondered how the other two would.

He reinserted the flambeau in its wall bracket and then proposed to his companions that they sit down beneath its light.

"Sir Wilbur," Valera asked, "what do you think has happened to Chris Fallon and Marcelina?"

170

"Perhaps they had the good fortune of my uncle and have escaped," offered Ramón.

"We can hope," replied the Englishman.

For a time they remained sitting that way, without speaking. Tennington wondered if there would be a chance they could jump the guard later on. Perhaps when night fell — he glanced at his watch. At least the day had progressed, but it would be many long, weary hours till nightfall, and long before that the torch would burn out. Still, his watch did fortunately have a luminous dial. He would be able thus to gauge the coming of dark. Darkness, at any rate, would be the time they had best gamble everything on an attempted escape.

While the torch still burned, curiosity finally prompted him to arise again and, once more taking it with him, he walked over to examine the heads more minutely at close range. This time Valera and Ramón watched him but did not rise themselves. Tennington went down the lines of poles, examining, in turn, each face. The features, though reduced and shrunken, retained to an astonishing degree individual differences that had characterized these persons in life — especially those heads that were more recently treated — in perhaps the last ten years, or less. Some of the heads were obviously very old — as much as several decades — a few perhaps several generations. Yet, in the yellow torchlight the grotesque little specimens were in a way hideously exaggerated, so that all appeared to resemble horrible little demons — thrusting their heads forward from the wall like minions of darkness.

Tennington was glad to step back, after a minute or so of this, and pace about the room to observe its other features, but there was actually nothing else to observe on those barren rock walls.

"See anyone you recognize?" Valera asked, half humorously.

Tennington grunted negatively, but returned presently to the heads, and again examined them intently in the light of the torch that had by now burned halfway down its pitch-soaked length.

Suddenly he paused.

"You know, Luis, one of these heads does look familiar," he said hoarsely, "but I can't say why."

Valera now got up and walked over to join him, followed by Ramón.

"Isn't that old Quinto?" Sir Wilbur asked the boy.

"No, *señor*," the boy said quietly, his voice trembling. "I think eet ees *Tío* Quinto's tween brother . . . my father."

Chapter Fifteen

As Fallon was borne downward into the Stygian depths of the pool by the weight of the mysterious assailant clinging to his back, one idea came to his disordered mind. His knife hung at his side, and now he drew it, straining his arm desperately around till he could slash viciously backward toward one of the bare brawny legs of his antagonist clamped tightly about him. Instantly there was a savage twisting, and the incredible grasp on him loosened. A quick writhing on his own part broke the man's hold entirely. Then Fallon felt his feet touch the bottom of the murky depths, and, crouching, he jackknifed both legs hard, so that the force of it sent him shooting upward toward the surface. His nose was closed with water, and he was choking and retching on it, so that for a moment he blacked out, and it was only his upward impetus that kept him moving. His head broke the surface abruptly, and, coughing and wheezing, he fought to stay there.

His head and his eyes cleared. He turned at the sound of a splash near at hand to see his attacker, a great-shouldered man with a brown, fury-contorted face about which wild strands of glistening black hair clung. He had likewise emerged, fighting to keep on the surface. It was apparent to Fallon that the man was no swimmer and that he was wounded, for the water about him was pink-tinged.

Seeing Fallon, the man lunged after him, and Chris now caught the glitter of a golden-bladed knife in his hand. The knife flashed downward. A backward contortion by Fallon caused the blade to slash only water, which frothed up thinly on either side. Fallon wheeled back to the attack and caught the man about the neck. The fellow twisted violently, and both of them went under. Fallon could feel the man's twisting as he began to wield his own knife with vicious desperation. When Fallon felt the man's body relax, he kicked away from him, coming again to the surface. This time he propelled himself to the edge of the pool, and pulled himself up to safety on the bank. There he leaned on a rock, dripping, gasping, attempting to regain his shattered wind. The water, convulsed and crimson, subsided slowly. There was no sign of his antagonist.

Fallon recalled the *golden* knife, and wondered about that. It was, then, that he heard Marcelina's voice and saw her rushing toward him.

"Chris . . . what happened? Are you all right?"

She was hastily beside him, crouching down, reaching out to touch him.

"Got jumped by someone behind me, I guess, or jumping down from that tree," he replied. "Had a knife . . . a golden knife. We fought. He's probably at the bottom of this pool." He looked at her, and his eyes fell to her jodhpurs. "Is that blood? Did someone attack you?"

"No," she said, pulling back but not standing up. "My cycle began last night while I was sleeping . . . it's early. At any rate, I have pads with me in my pack and left camp as soon as I discovered what had happened . . . to attend to myself. I knew you had left camp before me. When I finished, I heard what sounded like water and followed after you. I saw this pool just as you were coming up."

"I'm soaked, but otherwise all in one piece," Fallon said, gathering himself and rising.

Marcelina also stood up. "Do you think there are others?"

"Probably. I didn't see anyone when I was on watch, but I've sensed for some time we were being observed. That man, whoever he was, tried to kill me. If there are others, then every-

174

one is in danger. We'd best get back to camp."

Moving cautiously through the rocks and foliage, they made their way back to the clearing only to find it deserted. A few smoldering embers marked the campfire. For a long moment they stood stunned in the middle of the camp. Fallon saw at a glance that his own equipment was gone. At least Marcelina had her back pack.

"What do you think happened, Chris? If there was an attack, wouldn't we have heard something?"

"They may not have been attacked. More probably they were taken by surprise."

"Not killed? Oh, my God, Chris . . . !"

"There's no blood, no bodies, no signs of a struggle." Fallon was moving about now, trying to read from signs on the hard earth what had happened. "If they've been taken captive," he said, "they can't have gone very far."

There were several minor articles left on the ground that did indicate the others had left or had been compelled to leave in such haste that they might well have escaped anyone's notice. It would have required a large party of men to take on an armed group by force, and Fallon knew the others must have been taken by force; otherwise, they would have signaled. But by whom? There had been no sign of anyone or any indication that the terrain was inhabited until the incident at the pool. A single person, or a few persons, might have escaped observation, but a large group of men? Then Fallon recalled how the man at the pool had jumped him — in complete silence and with no indication of his presence until the moment of contact.

Such woodcraft suggested not only on uncanny ability to move in complete silence, but also a knowledge of the territory that was intimate and flawless. Fallon now had no doubt the man who had attacked him was of the same party who had captured the others, and with this realization several factors became obvious — factors that sent a chill up his spine and stopped him from bolting immediately after the others. If these natives had kept such a close surveillance of their territory, a dozen of them might well be watching the two of them right now from the concealment of nearby rocks and bushes. Furthermore, any sudden blundering pursuit of the others and their captors might well precipitate violence. Finally, as meagerly armed as he was with only his knife and his Colt which had been in the water as had been the shells looped in his belt, any attempted rescue effort must be carefully planned.

A moment's continued speculation relieved him of the first concern. If the natives had known where he and Marcelina had been, they would have sent back men to capture them before now. There was no doubt they knew of Marcelina and himself, since they must have had the entire party under surveillance for some time, but perhaps they had deliberately sent out the man who had attacked him at the pond and depended on him to kill Fallon and possibly capture Marcelina. The confidence that must have been placed in that particular warrior was proven by the fact that he had been expected to kill Fallon without help, and Chris could not blame them for thinking that way since it had been mainly luck which had seen him safely through the encounter.

"Chris," said Marcelina quietly but with urgency. "What is it? What do you see? Is there some kind of trail?" As she spoke, she came very close to him. "Almost everything's gone, but I still have my revolver."

"Good. Mine has been in the water, but the ammunition I have is supposed to be waterproof. I'm not about to try and shoot it, however. The important thing is we're both armed."

"We should try and follow . . . shouldn't we?"

"Cautiously . . . *querida*."

Her blue-gray eyes flashed at him. "Do you know what that word means, Chris?"

He reached out and drew her to him.

"It means the danger is very great, and I don't want you hurt in any way. I cannot leave you here, Marcelina, because it is not safe . . . and, if I take you with me, you must know we run the risk of being captured just as Tenny and the others have been. Even if both of our guns work, there are probably too many for us to overpower them."

Marcelina put her hands on his chest and drew back. "I can fight, Chris, when I have to . . . and I shall do my part . . . *querido*."

She was smiling. So was Fallon, now.

Before striking out on the trail, however, he swiftly cleaned his revolver, borrowing a dry handkerchief from Marcelina. In addition to the cartridges in his belt, which he also dried, he had a compass, a watch, and matches in a water-proof box. Marcelina also had extra cartridges and a small bag with a shoulder strap in her pack in which she carried soap, wash cloth, hygienic napkins, and even a package of cigarettes and matches in a water-proof box.

"One must be prepared," she quipped as they reviewed their inventory.

Fallon did not reply. Instead, they now set out, following the trail as well as he could make it out that the group had followed away from the camp. It led southeast from the clearing, but soon afterward he lost it in the jumbled rocks. Their only hope was to continue southeast, which he did by the sun, checking with his compass from time to time. They did exercise caution as they went, since Fallon suspected, if he were to judge by what they had already seen, the natives might have scouts stationed at strategic intervals throughout the area. Their best advantage lay in the fact that this was relatively open country. The possibility of ambush from concealment was, therefore, minimized, although behind any one of a dozen huge boulders they passed a man might have located himself without much risk of discovery.

For perhaps two hours they tramped and sweated with the tropical sun blazing down on them from an open sky. Fallon's head was unprotected — he had left his hat in the pool — but Marcelina, at least, still had her broad-brimmed sombrero. They did pause once to rest, but not for long. Marcelina had her canteen attached to her pack, but it was nearly empty, and, not having thought about it, she had not filled it earlier at the pool.

It was when they abruptly topped a rise of rock that Fallon swiftly drew back and motioned to Marcelina to remain still. Slowly, then, Fallon crept behind a swell of lava and looked below. Marcelina came softly to his side. Before them lay a village — or what appeared to be a village from the number of people walking about in front of the rock wall that was the side of the great plateau. A second glance revealed the gaping holes in the base of the cliffside that were the entrances to caves, and with this knowledge an abrupt realization overspread them — these must surely be the Quivaris of whom old Quinto had warned.

As they watched from concealment, they could make out a group of Quivaris moving toward one of the caves and with them were their companions, apparently unharmed. They watched as the villagers thronged about the captives and how a warrior forced a way through the bystanders to the entrance of one cave into which their companions were escorted. Presently the villagers seemed to disperse and return to various activities, and, a short time later, the warriors emerged from the cave without the captives. Some of these went about other business while a few remained to stand guard about the cave's entrance.

Fallon realized he could not attempt a rescue now. It would be better to wait until night. Even though he considered momentarily the possibility of bluffing the savages with his Colt and Marcelina's revolver, he decided against it at once. One man and one woman, even if armed, could not fight off a whole army of armed natives. Then the heated sunlight bearing down upon his back and head became sufficiently noticeable to deserve his attention.

He pulled back, as did Marcelina, and he whispered to her: "Let's circle around the village toward the base of the plateau and find some shade."

They left the volcanic rock outcropping and worked around to the side, crawling part of the time on hands and knees in the more open spots while trying to exercise caution of movement as well as a constant vigilance for possible sentries. They were their companions' only hope for freedom now.

After a time Fallon came to wonder suddenly why they had seen no sign of sentries. Then he decided that the Quivaris must have posted an impregnable line of scouts only at the outermost frontiers of their country, depending on that line to stop any intruders. Now, however, that they were safely through that line, they could approach almost as close to the village as they might wish without fear of discovery. Marcelina was quite as deliberately cautious as Fallon, as if she had become as accustomed to life in the wilderness almost as much as in the home of her parents in Lima or in a classroom in San Francisco. She kept pace with Fallon, proceeding just as he proceeded, and the only times he would look back at her were when they would pause briefly.

They reached the plateau wall nearly two miles south of the Quivari village. There they found some pleasant green shade trees beneath which they rested and cooled off and found that, while they had received more scratches and bruises crossing the rocks, they were not serious.

Refreshed after a time, they arose to explore the surrounding terrain. It was more verdant here, less rocky, and had almost a park-like appearance. Only the gnawing hunger in their stomachs was unsatisfied, and they were aware of a growing thirst. Fallon could find no sign of game, big or small, though he would not have dared to fire a shot anyway so near to the village. But they did find a brook trickling over a pebbly bed, and here they were able to assuage their thirst, and Marcelina filled her canteen. Then out of curiosity they decided to follow the brook downstream.

Presently Fallon spotted a gaping gulf in the ground ahead. He could see that the stream ran over the edge of the gulf, and they could hear the splash of water on rocks below. Reaching the brink of the gulf, they peered down. The gulf was a great, irregularly round orifice, many yards in diameter. It was walled with massive rocks that must have been placed there by humans. The stream flowed over the edge and dropped down in a miniature twinkling cataract to splash solidly on an upjutting rock. The great hole was filled with a dark pond, all of fifteen feet below the ground where they stood.

In the center of that pond, partly on and partly off a great rock which was too small to accommodate its tremendous length, sprawled a gigantic crocodile, more than twice the length and girth of any Fallon had ever seen. It was a dull gray, and lay with closed eyes, as completely still as death. Fallon wondered how a creature of this size had gotten into such a comparatively small pool, and how it lived — if, indeed, it was alive, so still was it sprawled. An image suddenly came to him out of a book he had once read by François Châteaubriand, about how the heart of the most serene human being resembles a natural pool in a wilderness savannah where the surface is perfectly calm and pure, but where you can see in the depths at the bottom of the pool an enormous crocodile that somehow is able to find nourishment in those waters.

Some movement off to the left attracted Fallon's attention, and he motioned to Marcelina for them to move behind the concealment of a tall, dense thicket, from where they could still see plainly. Two of the Quivari women now came into view, bearing bulky objects wrapped in bark cloth slung across their backs. They stopped at the brink of the pool, loosened the cloths, and held them over the edge of the hole, dropping out the bulky contents which were now revealed to be large chunks of raw meat. These fell into the pool with loud splashes, and immediately the women turned and left. Neither Fallon nor Marcelina was watching them closely any more, however, so focused was their attention upon the gigantic reptile. As they watched, the crocodile's whole length was galvanized into a sudden movement, and he crawled forward to slither off the rock in a gliding splash as he plunged after the meat.

Now they both knew how the saurian was fed — that he was being kept here by the Quivaris for an unknown purpose. Fallon did not wish to stay to see the crocodile finish his lunch, but, instead, signaled to Marcelina that they must follow the two women back to their village. This way they could probably get nearer to it than from any other approach. They trailed silently behind them at a safe distance, Fallon in the lead, Marcelina farther behind him. In this way, should one of them be attacked, the other might be free to come to that one's aid.

Great hardwood trees spread a dappled shade over the ground underfoot, and it was an altogether pleasant scene. Fallon paused at the verge of the village, behind a towering boulder beneath a shade tree, from which he could plainly view all the activities of the Quivaris. Marcelina had soon caught up to him, and here they settled down, speaking only for a moment in hushed whispers, to wait for nightfall.

But time and the silence did seem to drag. They did not dare to smoke. Once or twice, they saw a hunting party, or what appeared to be a hunting party, a group of warriors setting off toward the jungle with their spears. The thought of food whetted their already acute appetites, and the hunger pains were great for both of them. Still, although the hours dragged, there came a pleasantness in the pastoral afternoon, with only a few insects to disturb them and a cool breeze coming up to refresh them. Fallon even fell into a doze.

He awoke suddenly, and found they were in the gray of dusk with the final vestige of sunlight filtering crimson and golden across the western forest. Marcelina was sitting beside him, alert now, if she had been musing. Fallon peered out from their shelter toward the village. Cooking fires had been started, bright orange in the colorless cloak of descending twilight. The entire population of the Quivaris seemed in a mild furor of excitement. He glanced at his watch. The entire afternoon had passed.

The supper period was agonizing for both of them, although Fallon did reach over to squeeze Marcelina's hand and to smile encouragement at her in silence. The savor of cooking odors was wafting downwind from the village. But following the evening meal, the people began vanishing slowly into their caves until the village appeared almost deserted. Fallon was puzzled. Marcelina, still visible in the dim light, seemed to ask: *Could they be retiring already?* No — there was a group emerging from their cave — and another. But what a transformation.

They now wore golden and gem-studded garments and ornaments, the origin of which Fallon could only conjecture, but Marcelina whispered softly: "Incan."

Just that one word. A score of warriors now were hurrying up with firewood they were piling in a massive heap at the center of the broad and spacious clearing surrounding the entrances to the caves. In an astonishingly short time, they had assembled a massive amount of dry timber there to which they presently set the torch. The great shoots of flame curled upward, entwining sinuously about the stark timbers rearing high, and casting a ruddy glow over the entire scene.

The glow did not quite penetrate back to the shadows of the rock where Fallon and Marcelina were crouched, but even here the landscape was illumined for the moon had became visible above the rim of the plateau — a big, generous, full equatorial moon that articulated even details in a silver radiance.

Then they saw their companions brought out, being hauled with a terrific clamor from the cliff wall. An ornately bedecked native stepped forward then and addressed a lengthy and — to Fallon and Marcelina — senseless monologue to Sir Wilbur Tennington. By this time most, if not all, the tribe had assembled.

Fallon, every nerve keyed high, pressing Marcelina to remain behind, began now to edge out from their concealment toward the clearing. He moved very carefully. He suspected that this whole elaborate fandango presaged some heathen religious rite the highlight of which would be the burning deaths of their comrades. At any rate, now was the time to make his play. Forward he moved, keeping to the deeper shadows as best he could.

Nearer and nearer he crept, from rock to rock. Then he paused almost at the edge of the firelight and started to pull his Colt. But, before he could complete that maneuver, a heavy figure launched onto his back and drove him bruisingly to the ground. In a moment he felt a powerful arm fasten about his neck and hold him helpless in a crushing grip.

Chapter Sixteen

Sir Wilbur Tennington bent down, holding the torch still nearer the head to regard the shrunken features. There was no doubt — this was Quinto's face in miniature, or rather, as Ramón had said, the face of Quinto's brother, Pedro, Ramón's father, whose fate had been unknown. That had remained for them to discover here — but the really astonishing fact was that the similarity should be preserved in this shrunken specimen after all these years, and still more astonishing that the specimen should resemble so exactly Quinto as he looked now. This, too, was answered for Tennington when he reflected that the premature aging of Quinto's features through his terrible experiences corresponded by coincidence to the shrinking and drying and aging process involved in the curing and preservation of the head of Pedro.

Luis Valera, also studying the head, tough-nerved though he was, was not unaware of a series of chilling shudders convulsing his backbone. He tried to concentrate on the minute artistry, the intricate skill involved in the preparation of these skullless, heat-cured specimens. In a people as utterly primitive as the Quivaris, it was doubly remarkable. Among the Jivoro, a noted head-hunting tribe of the Andean foothills, it had become a developed form of art, such as it was, but less so than this.

Ramón, after identifying the head, became silent, but tears formed in his eyes and coursed down his cheeks. He was torn by sudden grief but also awed by the horror of it.

Tennington sighed finally and shook his head. "I say, Luis, these heads do give us some indication of what has happened to others who have fallen into the hands of the Quivaris."

"I fear you're right, Sir Wilbur." He looked in consternation at the Englishman standing in the flickering torchlight. "What about Chris . . . and Marcelina?"

"Chris Fallon weel rescue us!" Ramón said earnestly. "They haven't taken heem prisoner."

To this, Tennington did not reply. He couldn't. There was nothing to comment to this steadfast faith Ramón had expressed in Fallon. On the other hand, the Englishman could far more readily believe that Fallon was lying out in the rocks somewhere with a spear thrust through his heart, and Marcelina as well. He didn't want to think it, but he couldn't help himself. He had no doubt that the Quivaris had every square yard of this region under surveillance by one means or another, which meant that Fallon and O'Day must surely have been either killed or captured, and since, had they been captured, they would surely have been imprisoned here with them by this time, Tennington could come to only the one conclusion.

Ramón was beside him now. "You do really theenk *Señor* Chris weel save us, don't you, Don Weelbur?"

"I am sure of only one thing, Ramón, and that is Chris Fallon has not been taken captive as we have. I am sure, if it is possible for him, he will do what he can to help us, but we sha'n't wait beyond nightfall. Before that time, Luis and I will do our damnedest to overpower the guards so we can try and get to our firearms. Once we have them back, at least we'll have a fighting chance."

"Don Wilbur es correcto, muchacho," Valera said in Spanish to Ramón. "We must not give up hope. Perhaps we should have resisted when they came upon us at our camp, but, assuredly, we shall resist them now that we know our lives are forfeit if we do not."

There was nothing to do but wait. Tennington replaced the

torch in the hollow niche in the wall and glanced at his watch. It was approaching noon, but in this pitch-black subterranean room, all hours would seem alike. Then he sat down against the wall beside the others.

The torch burned itself out eventually, and they were left in complete darkness. This was the hardest of all to endure. The explorer glanced repeatedly at his luminous watch, but time moved ponderously.

Several hours passed. The enforced idleness only emphasized their lack of water or nourishment, but these pangs were mingled for all of them with excitement and fear. Finally Sir Wilbur glanced again at his watch and got to his feet in the darkness.

"I'll take a look now," he said quietly.

The other two arose to accompany him. With Sir Wilbur in the lead the three of them groped their way inchingly along the wall till they had located the passageway. After many yards of walking forward, they could distinguish the faint gleam of firelight washing the rocky passage well ahead. They could also distinguish voices that seemed to become louder with every step they took. Apparently this was not the best time for an attempt to escape.

Suddenly a group of warriors burst into the tunnel and started toward them.

"Get ready to *fight*," snapped Tennington.

As the first man tried to seize him, the Englishman caught him, twisted him ungently about, and hurled him back at his companions, knocking one of them staggering into the rock wall where he hit his head and slumped down. Valera wrestled with another for a spear, got it, and beat the man over the head with it, driving him to the ground. Then he swung the spear around in a glittering arc before him, so that the warriors, retreating from that lethal swing, left a magically cleared space around the two men and Ramón.

But their triumph was brief. In a few moments there came a swarm of warriors from the entrance to the passage, and the three captives were forced with their backs against the wall, where they were pinioned and Valera was disarmed. Then they were brought outside, held between warriors, and led along the cliff wall.

A few yards away a great fire sent broad yellow-orange banners of flame and spark showers streaming high into the dark blue canopy above. The whole village appeared to have gathered near it, but there had been a great change. The men had assumed gaudy headdresses and ornaments of what appeared to be solid virgin gold. Even their weapons were now gold-shod, and there were valuable stones set in many of the trinkets they wore. The women, who before had worn little, now wore golden breastplates, girdles of plated gold very ornately wrought, and jewel-encrusted headdresses that confined their formerly tousled hair and lent them an aspect of quiet dignity.

While it was apparent to Tennington that some sort of ceremonial was in progress — undoubtedly a ceremony of human sacrifice — what startled him most was the new apparel of the Quivaris. It came to him all at once, as it already had to Luis Valera, that this finery was Incan in origin. It corresponded to samples of Inca relics he had seen, and it suggested another possibility. Could it be that the Quivaris were but a degenerate off-shoot of those ancient and proud People of the Sun? Perhaps, but this could only be conjecture — while the fact was there could be no doubt now the Quivaris had had access to the lost Incan city of Haucha. That meant they really were close to it, that it must actually be atop and across the plateau, that Haucha did exist. It also meant, Tennington speculated, that there must be some means of ascending the perpendicular wall to the plateau and bridging the chasm that had once isolated the city. He looked at the firelight playing with subdued glitter on the dull surfaces of virgin gold — the ornamentation of a vanished people now adorning these savages. The same firelight weirdly and cruelly distorted the faces of the Quivaris, so that they resembled nothing so much as an unholy aggregation of demoniacal beings. Then he wondered, ironically, what good all this new knowledge would do any of them?

An abrupt silence spreading over the assemblage drew his attention to a slight man drawing through the crowd toward them. On viewing him, Tennington did not have to guess that he was the chief of the tribe. That fact could scarcely have been more evident. As he approached the three captives, the gathered Quivaris parted so that there was always a clear space in which for him to pass.

When he stood before them, Tennington saw that this man was a chief in more than just appearance, ornate enough in itself. He wore a golden loin plate, wristlets, anklets, and a necklace, all of gold, and weirdly inscribed. An odd medallion of gold rested in the distended lobe of one ear. He affected a feather mantle over his shoulders and a feathered headdress that defied description. His face, moreover, was not the face of a savage. The deeply recessed eyes, set beneath lowering brows and further accentuated by high cheekbones that were artificially shadowed beneath to give his naturally narrow visage an almost gaunt appearance, glowed with fiery intelligence. Immediately the Englishman sensed the potentialities of the man. For the rest, he was slight of build and not tall, yet well-muscled and proportioned, though no more so than his stalwart warriors. Upon the next few seconds or so, Tennington thought, might hinge their fate. It rested in the hands of this man.

The man spoke: "I am Cadika."

Ramón was brought forward to stand before Cadika. Terrified, again near tears, he told Sir Wilbur what the chief had said.

Tennington responded: "Tell him I am Wilbur." He did not employ his last name, suspecting that the Quivaris could not pronounce it easily. "And that this is Luis."

Cadika regarded the Englishman with whatever curiosity he felt reflected only slightly on his face. "You have come far?"

"Yes," Tennington replied slowly, "to be roughly greeted."

Cadika smiled — not a reassuring smile. "You have found death. Our young men, before they can become warriors, must spend a period of time alone in the jungle guarding the frontiers of our country. When strangers approach, word is relayed back to our village, and a party is sent out to take the newcomers captive."

Ramón translated as best he could after the chief paused.

Tennington stiffened. "Do you greet all strangers thus?"

"Only enemies."

"We are not enemies."

Cadika shrugged and, with an enigmatic expression, remarked idly: "We shall not press the question. It would be of no moment if we did. By the law of our people, you are not of our tribe and, therefore, you are enemies."

"We did not come to fight with you."

Cadika shrugged again, still smiling. "Why you came is of no moment. The fact remains that you did come, and you must die."

Ramón translated as quickly as he could, first one way, and then the other, and, although Cadika's words carried great finality, he found himself hoping the Englishman might be able to talk all of them into being freed.

Tennington squirmed. "We only seek the lost city of Haucha which, it has been said, lies beyond this giant wall that towers above us."

189

Cadika's smile evaporated. "What do you know of Haucha?"

"Enough," Tennington assured him. It was a subtle baiting of the chief, and a deliberate move on Tennington's part, but unfortunately it was also a fatal move.

Cadika grinned with even greater cheeriness now. "Then doubly you must die! The city of Haucha is sacred to the Quivaris. Such was the trust placed in us long ago by our masters, the Incas. The city of Haucha was one of their homes with a shrine to Haucha in the Temple of the Sun. It is for that purpose we are here . . . to guard the city of Haucha from others."

Some of these words were strange to Ramón, so, instead of translating them, he translated only those he understood. Tennington somehow managed to perceive the gist of it. Valera, on the other hand, although he did not speak, understood all that was said.

"Why do you guard Haucha?" Tennington asked.

Cadika ignored the question and asked: "Why does this other man not speak?"

Ramón explained that Luis Valera was a man who knew much about the Incas.

Cadika cocked his head to one side and nodded at Ramón. "I shall speak slowly so all will understand. Long ago our masters, the Incas, ruled all the world from westward to the Great Water, about which we are told by legend, and to the Great Mountain far to the east." He pointed in that direction. "Once atop this plateau and across a great chasm they lived in Haucha. They did not need to fear enemies or the savage creatures of the jungle. There was only one pass to the top of the great wall, a pass easily guarded. Up there were fields and pastures, and they had their herds, their llamas, vicuñas, and alpacas. There was much to eat, much to drink, but also, because they needed to fight neither beasts nor men, there was much

190

idle time on their hands, and because they were an ambitious people with restless, questing minds, they delved into the secrets of nature.

"The Sun smiled then, and he blessed their work, and they discovered things which my poor people and, aye, even you strangers will never understand. Finally, armed with that knowledge . . . and the knowledge of how to organize their people . . . they left their mountain retreat and went out to conquer all the land. We, the Quivaris, were people who lived as the beasts in the great forest. Under the Incas, we prospered and became more and greater. Everywhere, the Incas spread learning and prosperity, and all the tribes of the land shared this plenty.

"But at one time when the empire was split by internal strife and was in a weakened state, the cruel white men from over the Great Water found it. They came in great canoes with wings and rode over the land of the Incas on four-legged beasts, the like of which no man had ever seen, and no lance or arrow could penetrate their metal clothing, no lance or spear could prevail against their sticks that spat thunder and death.

"All the people believed these white men gods. Even our masters, the wise Incas, thought so for a while. Then the diseases and fevers of our land began striking these white gods down, and we saw them for men . . . very cruel and wicked men. The empire of the Incas was crushed . . . crushed for the yellow metal the white men wanted. They tortured, murdered, destroyed, and pillaged for it. The great Inca cities, sacked and stripped of their wealth, fell into decay.

"But one group . . . to retain their pride and their lives . . . fled from the oppression of the invaders into the wilderness, back to the place from which they had come . . . to Haucha. The white men pursued them with a party, but terrible were their losses, for the men of other tribes along the way, warriors who had let the Incas through, fell upon the white men when they tried to pass. They fought them bitterly, so that only their thundersticks saved them from death. The fevers and wild beasts also claimed many white men.

"Yet, they did reach the great wall beyond which lies Haucha, and here we, the Quivaris, could have stopped them, but the Incas gave us orders to let them into the passage leading up to the plateau. We did not understand, but we did so, and the wicked white ones entered the passage and approached the great bridge when the Incas, waiting atop the cliffs, loosed an avalanche upon their heads. None was left alive, and the pass was sealed. Then it was that the Incas told us they had planned this in advance of the coming of the white men. Knowing that Inca rule was ended, they arranged to destroy the great bridge whereby they would seal off the way to the home of the Incas forever. In Haucha were stored the greatest treasures of all the Incas. Greedy men from afar would kill and loot and stop at nothing to get them. The descendants of those wicked men are today all around us, but the Quivaris have survived. We have done so because we kill anyone . . . *anyone* from the outside . . . who comes here."

Both Tennington and Valera had listened intently to this narrative as crudely, and perhaps inaccurately, as Ramón had rendered it. Valera could not constrain himself as Ramón stumbled over these last words as he translated them.

"Ask him, if there is still a way to gain the top of the plateau and cross over to Haucha?" he prompted.

Sir Wilbur nodded at Ramón who now put Valera's question to the chief.

Cadika nodded sagely: "The silent one speaks! Yes, there is a way, very dangerous, which only the Quivaris know. After the slaying of those white men, we continued to go back and forth onto the plateau, for our duties were to till the fields and to

192

shepherd the herds of our masters atop the great plateau. In the morning, we would take the secret trail to the top and work through the day. In the evening, we would return here to our village.

"But one morning those in Haucha were no longer able to use the ropes to transport food across the great chasm. We were able after some time to cross over to Haucha only to find some of our masters ill . . . many already dead. They said a great sickness had come with them. They told us to leave and return no more to Haucha, lest we, too, perish of the disease, and we were glad to do as they said.

"For many days, we ventured no more to the city of Haucha, now a place of death. But one morning, the chief of the Quivaris, my ancestor and a very brave warrior, went up alone to the city, for none was willing to accompany him. He found all the Incas dead. Everywhere were corpses and the scavengers who fed on them, and the great buildings were only echoing tombs of silence and death. He went to the Temple of the Sun to find nothing but silence and dust. As he prepared to leave, a groan attracted him to a room at the rear of the temple. There he found the high priest dying, but before the great one died, the last of his people, he placed a trust in the hands of my ancestor . . . a vow that he and the Quivaris would always guard the way to Haucha so that one of the temples of the Incas might sleep forever in splendor.

"So we have done, honoring them ever since. We shun the dead city as a place of phantoms, and woe be to anyone who would attempt to find it."

"We did not come for treasure," responded the Englishman wearily when Ramón had concluded this narration.

"Then why did you come?" asked Cadika, and continued before an answer could be made. "Your quest was foolish. Even should you get past us, you will never escape the Ones

193

with Teeth Like Knives who live atop the towering plateau and who once were the guardians of the Temple of the Sun."

Tennington wondered who the Ones with Teeth Like Knives might be, as Ramón translated, but the chief was wondering something else. He abruptly pulled something from beneath his feather mantle and flourished it before the invaders' eyes. The firelight gleamed on the steel barrel of Tennington's rifle. Cadika lifted it carefully in one hand.

"This is like the thundersticks the men from over the Great Water used to conquer long ago. You will show me how it is used?"

Tennington only laughed.

"You will show me . . . or die slowly."

"You will kill us, anyway . . . it is all one to me now how I die."

Cadika considered these words and decided they were the words of a sullen and angry man. Having no wish to risk maiming his captive so that the secret of the wonderful thunderstick would be forever lost to him, he decided rather to bargain. He eyed Tennington shrewdly. "Show me how to use this thunderstick, and I will set you free."

"How do I know you will keep your promise?"

Ramón's eyes gleamed as he translated. Perhaps Don Wilbur would save them.

Cadika's brow clouded. "The chief of the Quivaris does not lie!"

"How do I know that?"

Cadika said angrily: "I have given my word before my warriors. If I break it, they would kill me . . . along with you."

Tennington believed in that primitive sense of honor. "It is well . . . but also you must free my friends."

However, Cadika's mounting anger burst all bounds with this. He hurled the rifle to the ground. "You ask too much!

Now you shall all die and swiftly . . . !" He broke off, not wishing to reveal more before his people. "My warriors tell me," he added, "that there were two more of you."

"What happened to them?" demanded Tennington.

"That," admitted Cadika, "is no less than what I would like to know myself. But the warriors who were with the party that captured you all assure me. They say they saw a man and a woman wander off from your camp, but there is no chance that they could have escaped. There were scouts located in hiding all around you, and one of them would surely have seen them."

Tennington's heart lifted. If there had been no word of Chris Fallon and Marcelina O'Day, it was possible they had escaped, after all. Valera and Ramón were visibly cheered at this thought.

Cadika went on: "It is possible that the man or men who attempted to capture them killed them in the attempt and disposed of their bodies, saying nothing to the other warriors. It is a law of our people that the lives of all strangers who enter our land are not ours to take . . . they belong to Pahatahala and are to be reserved for sacrifice to him. If this law is violated, it will mean death to the warrior who kills a stranger."

Tennington's restless mind speculated on the identity of Pahatahala. Could this be another name for the Sun? Since the Sun had been the god of the ancient Incas, it was not unlikely that the Quivaris also worshipped it. But if so, why were they holding this ceremonial at night?

Cadika continued: "Why did you come?"

Tennington shrugged. There was no point in withholding that information. Besides, he could get a certain satisfaction from informing the Quivaris that their ancient masters, the Incas, had not been as thorough about covering their tracks as they had thought.

"There was one man, Cadika, who escaped the avalanche in

the pass. He returned safely to Cuzco and recorded the way to Haucha before he died."

"And fools, following that record, have come to seek treasure and have found death," declared Cadika.

"And how do you propose to kill us?" Tennington asked.

"You will be slain in sacrificial rites to Pahatahala."

"And who is Pahatahala?"

Before Cadika could reply, there was a deep and subterranean rumble through the ground beneath their feet, a noise and slight quaking that extended throughout the terrain.

"Pahatahala himself has answered your question," smiled Cadika. "Pahatahala is the fire mountain."

The volcano, Tennington thought, and lifted his gaze to the massive crater with its red glow vivid against the dark skyline, above which sparked great billows of smoke. It lay off to the north, almost adjoining the plateau.

"Long ago," Cadika said slowly, "when our masters, the Incas, died, we knew that the Sun no longer smiled upon his children, for, if so, he would not have allowed his chosen people to perish. For a while, we were desolate and without a god. Trouble beset us . . . fever, poor hunting, poor fishing. Then one day the Taholu, another forest people, came from the south to attack us in great numbers.

"They were far superior to us because the fever had depleted our people severely. For two days and two nights, we fought the Taholu, and finally the remainder of our people was backed into a pocket in the cliff near the fire mountain. Our food was gone. We were tired and at the mercy of our enemies.

"Then the fire mountain roared and spat boiling wrath down upon the heads of the Taholu and burned them all beneath liquid rock, slaying nearly all, and the rest fled. Thus we were saved, and through the mercy of Pahatahala, the fire mountain. We knew that the Sun could have had nothing to do with it, for it was night, and his face was hidden. The fire mountain favored us, and, since then, we have known that his favor is ours, and we are the chosen ones. It is to *him* that you will be sacrificed."

"You will hurl us into the crater, perhaps?" Tennington asked sharply.

"No," smiled Cadika. "When one of our people dies, we hurl his body into the crater to lie forever in the embrace of his god. But such as you shall not be so honored. Bring them to the fire!"

A half dozen brawny warriors hauled the captives forward and hustled them through the mob of jostling, sweaty Quivaris. Up to the fire they were dragged, so close that the heat was already almost unbearable. Cadika stood close by now, the ruddy firelight bathing his ornamented form. Tennington, with a shock of horror, realized the means of sacrifice now. They would be hurled into the heart of this roaring furnace of a blaze, there to die twisting in helpless agony. The terrible truth of the situation was also sliding over Valera and Ramón.

"Throw him in first!" commanded Cadika, indicating the Englishman.

Chapter Seventeen

Fallon was sprawled on his stomach. The warrior at his back fought in complete silence. For the moment the warrior devoted his effort to holding Fallon securely. After the initial surprise, Fallon realized this was a showdown, and he struggled savagely to break the warrior's grip. Thrusting himself upward and backward, Fallon knocked off the warrior's headpiece as they rolled out of the aura of firelight and into the shadow of a low-slung rock nearby. Breathing gustily, they continued to toss about, Fallon seeking to break the warrior's hold, the warrior attempting to retain his implacable grip. Fallon's hand fell to his Colt, grasping the butt tightly, but the warrior's hold on him prevented him from drawing it.

A shadow moved up behind them, and a small, nickel-plated revolver smashed down rather smartly onto the warrior's skull. He went limp. Fallon was still beneath him.

Marcelina now stood crouching silently as Fallon shoved the limp warrior aside and drew himself up. He realized that they might be in plain view of the villagers, so he glanced that way. The chief was speaking to Tennington and Valera. Ramón appeared to be translating. The struggle had attracted no one's attention.

Fallon crouched down and signaled mutely for Marcelina to remain crouched where she was. She kept her revolver at the ready. Glancing down at the unconscious man, Fallon noted that he, like the other natives, was ornamented and bejeweled. He had been wearing a particularly gaudy headpiece with a devil's mask wrought of thin sheet gold covering his face and with feathers at the back — undoubtedly ceremonial dress dating back to the ancient Incas. Once on one's head, it would completely cover the face except for openings for the mouth, the nose, and the eyes, and the decorative feathers concealed most of his head.

Fallon retrieved the headpiece and then dragged the warrior farther back into shadow. Hurriedly stripping the warrior of his regalia, he signed to Marcelina to withdraw even farther back, which she did. Putting his lips next to her right ear, Fallon whispered to her briefly.

Moments later a tall, lean, muscular figure in the ornamentation and apparel of an Incan ceremonial costume, his face concealed by a golden devil's mask and in all appearance like the other Quivari warriors assembled in the wide clearing before the caves stepped cautiously from behind the rock and advanced softly into the very midst of the assemblage. Part of the exposed skin was very pale in striking contrast to the deep brown of his hands and neck and to the copper-colored bodies of the Quivaris. Fallon could not really be certain of the efficacy of this disguise. The best he might hope for was that the burnished coloration cast by the flickering firelight would perform the necessary deception at least long enough for him to get sufficiently near to his comrades to give them a fighting chance, if not effecting their successful escape. His clothes he had cached back in the shadows where he had left Marcelina, retaining only his knife and cartridge belt and Colt buckled around his waist and half concealed by a decorative belt. Marcelina was to keep an eye on the warrior. Perhaps it would have been more prudent to have knifed the unconscious man, but Fallon had been reluctant to do it.

As it was, none of the throng paid him much heed as he gravitated among them, not hurrying in a way that would draw attention, but circuitously moving always closer toward the three captives. It was his plan to get as near as possible, then slash their ropes. Perhaps a shot from his revolver would demoralize the Quivaris sufficiently to attempt an escape. But this intention was thwarted by Cadika's abrupt command that caused a half dozen warriors to seize the captives and drag them forward to the fire.

Fallon realized their intent just as Cadika gave the order to cast Tennington into the heart of the fire, and it was then that he charged forward to knock down one of the men holding the Englishman, simultaneously pulling his knife and slashing the bonds securing Sir Wilbur's wrists. As he had hoped, the Quivaris were momentarily shocked into rigidity at the sight of one of their own number saving a prisoner, and then an angry bellow swept the throng of warriors, and they moved forward to converge upon Fallon. When the nearest was but two yards away, and raising his spear, Fallon drew his revolver and fired once into the air. He had only waited until the attention of all were upon him before loosing the shot, and its effect was instantaneous and worth the delaying strategy.

The Quivaris broke in every direction and fled, and Chris immediately wheeled and cut Valera and Ramón free.

"Get out of here . . . fast!" he told the three of them, and then swiveled his attention back to the Quivaris.

The warriors and women had broken wildly for the shelter of their caves, and a few had even sought escape into the rocks beyond, but now, seeing that no one had come after them following the sudden noise, many paused in flight and turned to stare in hesitation at the strange creature who had released their prisoners. Perhaps many of them supposed that this was some supernatural manifestation, that the Inca spirits were displeased by the attempted sacrifice of these men and had sent this messenger to save them. But Cadika recalled that two of these invaders had not been captured, and he recognized that the object in the apparition's hand was like those taken from the prisoners.

Cadika was not as brave as some of his warriors, but he was perhaps the most intelligent of the Quivaris. He knew of the thundersticks from legends told among his people, but perhaps this small thunderstick only made a great noise, yet inflicted no harm. He seized a spear from a ready warrior and advanced toward Fallon, raising his weapon. His warriors watched in awe. They were courageous men, but simple ones, too, and none dared face forces beyond their comprehension.

Fallon turned in time to see Cadika nearing him, spear half poised over his shoulder, and then, as the Quivari chieftain's arm tensed as though for a cast, Chris tilted his gun up from his hip just the slightest and fired. Again there was the noise that had terrified the onlookers, but this time there was an accompanying bellow of pain from Cadika, and he dropped his spear and brought his hand down to stare at it. It seemed to have been pierced by a sudden and invisible shaft, and blood streamed thinly down his palm.

Cadika was very angry now, and, though he prudently retreated back to a line of his warriors gathered at the edge of the clearing, he roared furious orders, none of which was obeyed.

"Hurry up!" Fallon snapped to the others. "You're unarmed . . . I'll have to cover your retreat. Marcelina is armed, out that way." He gestured with the hand that still held his knife.

Tennington hurried, but not away, rather over to snatch up his rifle that Cadika had previously dropped on the ground, checked the loads, and took his place at Fallon's side. "That's right," he insisted to Valera and Ramón. "You two start running. We'll be right behind. Join Marcelina and go south . . . parallel the cliff wall and keep close to it. That way we won't lose you."

There was nothing else for Valera and Ramón to do, unarmed as they were, so they turned and started to run from the fire, out into the moon-flooded darkness beyond.

Fallon and Tennington began backing away in the direction their companions had taken, their firearms at the ready. Cadika was still striving to incite his warriors to charge them but without much success. When Fallon and Tennington reached the shadowed part of the clearing where the warrior had earlier fallen, they turned their backs and hurried off in the direction the others had been told to take.

Cadika had again taken up his spear and was almost frothing with rage. He was beginning to stir the warriors. Then, of a sudden, there was a roar and rumble, and a great shudder reverberated through the earth. It nearly rocked some of the villagers off their feet.

Cadika's swift mind instantly seized the psychological advantage provided by this providential act of nature. "Listen, fools! The fire mountain speaks in the voice of thunder. Do you hear his anger that you have permitted the invaders to escape?"

One warrior was foolish enough to suggest that the fire mountain's terrible trembling might be a sign he was pleased and received for his pains a crack across the jaw from Cadika's spear butt that dropped him.

Cadika sprang forward now, roaring for his warriors to follow him, and this time, carried away by his words or his enthusiasm, they followed, yelling excitedly.

Meanwhile, Fallon and Tennington raced on down the trail, believing themselves in pursuit of their comrades.

"They might have . . . ducked into . . . one of these crevices," Fallon declared, indicating the innumerable shadowed fissures that scarred the cliff wall. "We may have . . . passed them."

"I . . . don't . . . think . . . so," gasped Tennington. "You say . . . Marcelina was . . . with you?"

202

"She's . . . probably with . . . them . . . now," answered Fallon, hoping he was right.

They hurried on. The trail they were blazing wound in a perfect parallel to the base of the cliff, and it was illumined in part by the bright moonlight. Though they could see ahead somewhat, they still could make out no sign of Marcelina, Valera, and Ramón. Everywhere was an upheaval of rocks, so that the overall landscape here was suggestive to Fallon of photographs he had seen of dead and barren places.

Presently they slowed to a walk and proceeded at a more leisurely pace, realizing now the necessity for quiet, though each was eager to hear the other's story. Then the shouts of the pursuing Quivaris could be heard behind them.

Tennington turned and looked back. "So they're coming after us. And they know this territory better than we do."

"Do we try to bluff them?" Fallon asked.

"We'd better not. I fear that first fright engendered by your gun has worn off and that we couldn't very well handle them all even with guns. No, we'd best hide."

"Where? Every place is too open, and in this moonlight . . . ?"

"True, but the shadows are pitch-black. A man could duck into a shadow and hide a yard from a searcher without being seen."

Tennington paused as they reached a place where the trail dropped off sharply to one side and where there was nothing but a dark gully below in which they could not distinguish the bottom. They could just see that there was an inclined slope. Tennington beckoned to Fallon, and both slid over the edge of the incline, and here they rested on their stomachs less than a foot from the trail, yet out of view of anybody from above, situated as they were in shadow and indiscernible to any but the closest scrutiny.

They waited tensely there, and soon the Quivaris went tramping by along the trail, every able warrior of the village, it seemed, grotesque, flitting figures in the silvered moonlight, and moving now in relative silence.

Fallon waited until they had gone past and on ahead. Then he edged closer to Tennington. "Where now?"

Tennington glanced at him disapprovingly. "For heaven's sake, take that heathenish thing off."

Fallon realized that he was still wearing the golden devil's mask, and he removed it, letting it roll down the rocky incline. It clattered its way to the bottom. "Never thought I'd be throwing gold away." He repeated: "What now?"

Tennington nodded to the trail, and they clambered up and set off at a slow trot, following after the Quivaris.

"I'm worried about Marcelina and the others," Fallon said softly.

"I'm sure they've had sense enough to hide, just as we did," the Englishman assured him. "The trouble is, this might put the Quivaris between us and the others . . . and if one of them should see the Quivaris coming, he might think it's us instead and be captured. On the other hand, they may get disoriented and run off into the rocks only to get lost."

Fallon growled: "We should have kept on going, rather than stopping. We had a good lead on them."

Tennington shook his head with a wry smile. "They know the country. We don't. The Quivaris' only transportation is their own feet, and they can travel exceedingly well on them. They'd have overtaken us eventually. Furthermore, this is an upland climate, and they're native to it. Look how winded we were becoming!"

Fallon caught the explorer's arm suddenly, bringing them to a stop on the trail. He pointed off to their right, away from the cliff side. There a dark figure was approaching, picking its way gingerly through an avenue of towering rocks.

"It's not one of the others," whispered Fallon.

"Then it's a Quivari," whispered Tennington. He cocked his rifle. "He doesn't seem to have seen us yet. You move on down the trail. I'll wait here."

Fallon moved away reluctantly and paced on, turning a sharp curve in the trail. Here he paused, not wanting to get too far ahead of Tennington. He waited with drawn Colt, listening intently. He doubted that Tennington would need help, but he was prepared.

Then his attention was distracted by a faint noise downtrail in the opposite direction. He turned swiftly, facing that way. Could the Quivaris be returning? No, he could hear nothing new and could see only the cold radiance on the moon-bathed rocks. He turned, and decided to go back to Tennington. Moments had passed, and he had heard nothing from that direction.

But, before he took a half dozen steps, he heard something else — a faint shuffling behind him. He whirled about, Colt ready. The foremost of the Quivaris was less than a yard from him. They had turned back and stolen upon him when his back had been turned.

He had time to fire once before one of the warriors was upon him, grasping his gun arm and twisting it back savagely. His bullet caught another warrior in the stomach, and he doubled up and pitched backward as though struck by an invisible fist.

With no more need for secrecy, the warriors bolted on past Fallon, and the man he was grappling with and headed on toward Tennington with wild, pealing yells.

Fallon and his opponent fell together onto the ground, and the savage twisting of both as they struck sent them rolling over and over. When they stopped, the warrior was on top.

Fallon still retained his Colt, but his wrist was pinned uselessly by the warrior's free hand. The warrior's other hand held a knife which he was trying to drive down into Fallon's heart. Already it was poised inches away and was pressing inexorably, prevented from the fatal thrust only by the fact that Fallon was holding back that arm, but his grip was steadily weakening, and now the knife hovered a scant inch from his chest.

They had rolled into shadows, and Fallon could only catch a faint golden gleam on the knife blade, and the shape of his adversary was a looming, straining hulk over him. Frantically he threw his remaining strength into a sudden sideways twist, and their movement finished it — for they had been sprawled on the very brink of a dark and unseen gully to the edge of which they had rolled, and it had required but that one slight movement on Fallon's part to precipitate them over and into the black gulf below. Down they caromed, Fallon on top sometimes, then his antagonist, down the almost sheer incline, jarring and bruising them as they rolled over and over, still clinging to one another.

They struck bottom suddenly, and the Quivari was beneath Fallon, Chris's full weight landing on top of him. Even though the Quivari's body broke Fallon's fall, Chris was hurled forward now so that his head struck something hard, casting him into blackness.

Chapter Eighteen

As the noonday sun struck its zenith over the heat-slumbering jungle, Quinto rested beneath the humid shade of a poinsettia tree, its great, crimson-flaming fronds seeming to droop in the heat, as though in sympathy with the exhausted Quechuan.

Nearby, Don Esteban de Ferrar sat with his back to a gnarled mahogany. Abdullah Simbel stood calmly by with folded arms. The gigantic Negro, alone of the three, seemed inexhaustible. Not heat, hardship, nor privation could bow or lean his massive frame.

There was little other indication now of the immaculate duo that had set out across the desert weeks before with a well-supplied party of three Indian guides and pack mules. Ferrar's impeccable white flannels were rags. He was thin and dirty, and his face haggard and hollow-eyed. His beard had grown out raggedly. Quinto, whom they had encountered on the desert and who had been forced to join their expedition because of his knowledge of the map Sir Wilbur Tennington was using to locate Haucha, was thinner, and his parched skin, scratched arms, and exhausted posture showed plainly the rigors of the ordeal he had be compelled to undergo. Abdullah's once spotless white garments showed similar wear to Ferrar's, but he still wore his fez cocked at the correct angle, scorning a sun helmet like that worn by Ferrar.

The present journey itself was something Quinto did not care to remember. The return trip — if he survived this time in order to make it back, which he doubted — he put from his mind. The heat — the mountain cold — the snakes — the hunger — the fear — the brushes with death caused by these bar-

barians — they all formed a nightmarish pattern of horror and unreality that his mind could now only dully accept. He had opposed Ramón's decision that he must return to accompany Chris Fallon and his party, including the beautiful *señorita*. He had even been inclined to whip the boy to make him return to Tacho Alto, but he hadn't, so great had been Ramón's sense of duty. He might well be dead now, along with all the others.

The heat of the jungle was terrible, but here, at least, it was shaded and quiet, and he could rest for a time. Ferrar, relentless and driving though he was, was letting up just a trifle now that they had come, as he said, only a day's journey from the plateau that would lead them to the treasure he sought. Despite his insistent fear of Tennington's party beating him to the treasure, he could afford to be a little magnanimous — especially in the face of the utter exhaustion that faced him. He was weakened in a far more serious way than Abdullah Simbel. No matter how terribly he was goaded by his own mad lust, he had found that he could not drive himself beyond a certain point.

Had his niece not deceived him utterly with a map that led in the wrong direction, he might by now even have been ahead of Tennington. Family or not, once he caught up with Marcelina, she would pay a dear price for her betrayal.

"We should eat a little," Ferrar muttered, expecting Abdullah to prepare a meal from the meager remainder of their provisions. Much of what they had brought they had had to leave when they crossed the mountain. Only Abdullah's tremendous strength and endurance had enabled them to get anything at all across.

Quinto came hesitantly to his feet. "Don Esteban . . . may . . . may I scout around just a little?" he asked in Spanish.

Ferrar scowled. "Why don't you stay here and rest?"

"There may be danger. I have told you of the Quivaris. I cannot escape . . . where would I go? But perhaps I shall learn something . . . perhaps even find some fruit or berries we can eat."

Abdullah glared at the Quechuan. He didn't need to say anything. Quinto was in awe of the tremendous strength of the black man, and he recalled how, before they had begun their trek across the mountain, the three Indian guides with them had wanted to turn back. It was then that Abdullah, wielding a machete, had at Ferrar's orders beheaded one of the guides with a single blow. After that, there had been no more talk of turning back.

Recollections of how Ferrar had goaded them on brought to mind how the two remaining Indian guides of this party had expired. On the descent of the mountain, one had toppled to his doom, knocked from the wall by a gargantuan condor. And only yesterday, as they had forded the river at a shallow point, the third guide had been dragged down by frenzied fish with gigantic teeth, although the fact that they had attacked him had doubtless been responsible for the salvation of the rest of them in the perilous crossing.

"I said . . . stay here, Quinto," Ferrar ordered.

The Quechuan submitted, resuming the place he had occupied under the poinsettia tree.

Following a small repast, they resumed once again the weary march through the brush — Abdullah first, hacking a way through the jungle growth, then Quinto, and, with his rifle at the ready, Ferrar.

Quinto watched the big Negro's powerful arm wielding the machete in great, tireless strokes. His fear of the giant was a personal thing from the time he had beheaded the reluctant Indian guide. He knew Abdullah would kill him on an instant's notice.

It was mostly low brush at this point, and by late afternoon they came to a clearing among the rocks only a short distance from the plateau. It was the same clearing where Tennington and his companions had been surprised that very morning by the Quivaris. Because of the relentless way Ferrar had driven them, they had actually gained on Tennington.

Abdullah had unslung his pack and was gathering firewood from dead brush when Quinto, glancing toward the far right, saw three dark figures gliding toward them among the rocks. He gave out a small cry of alarm, and Ferrar, following the direction of Quinto's gaze, raised his rifle and fired. The three figures stopped dead in their tracks at the sound of the shot and the more impressive whine of the bullet on a rock only inches in front of them. Then they turned as one and fled, disappearing among the great boulders.

"Savages who never heard a gunshot," Ferrar scoffed. "They won't be back."

Quinto had had experience with the Quivaris, and he definitely did not share Ferrar's confidence. He feared them more even than he did Abdullah Simbel. He decided that, even if it should cost him his life, he must escape. He was convinced that the Quivaris would return and in greater numbers.

The evening dusk closed down on the encampment, and Ferrar, realizing that they had reached the last of their food, told Quinto he would not be fed. Ferrar demanded he sit back slightly from the fire while he and Abdullah ate what was left. Afterward, drawing an oval cigarette from his gold case and lighting it, Ferrar looked menacingly at the Quechuan.

"What you have told us, Quinto, has been borne out," he said in a low voice, expelling a ribbon of smoke. "From this point on your presence can only hinder us."

Ferrar looked at Abdullah who was sitting alongside him at the fire. Even before the Negro could rise, Quinto had sprung to his feet. Ferrar had forced the moment to its crisis. Abdullah, his grimacing teeth gleaming terribly in the firelight, stepped around the fire and started toward the Quechuan. Quinto, saying nothing, turned and ran down an avenue of looming boulders. Old before his time, as he surely was, the giant lumbering man was quickly overtaking him with bounding steps.

Two rocks loomed ahead in the dusky light, close together with a few scant inches separating them. Actuated into remarkable celerity, Quinto wriggled sideways between the two rocks like a snake and then sped on desperately. Abdullah grunted and wheezed and strained tremendously as he sought likewise to wriggle his own giant frame through the narrow embrasure, and thus wasted precious seconds. Giving it up, he bounded around the obstructions, but, when he once stood on the other side, he had to stop in consternation — the Quechuan seemed to have disappeared in the darkness ahead.

He made his way slowly back to the clearing, there to receive a berating from Ferrar, but it was not as severe as Abdullah had expected. As far as the don was concerned, they were rid now of the meddlesome Quechuan and need not concern themselves with what happened to him.

How long Quinto ran and stumbled around through the jumbled avenue of rocks, he never knew. At last, he fell face down on a great flat slab and lay there, gasping and sobbing for breath. What could he do now? He was alone, at least, and now had only the Quivaris to avoid, as he had once before fled from them years ago.

There was a low rumbling snarl near at hand. He raised his head. The moon had now topped the rim of the plateau, and the whole landscape was almost as bright as it was during the day. There, illuminated plainly, stood a great jaguar, scarcely three yards away. It voiced another muffled snarl as it regarded the man, its eyes gleaming lambently in the moonlight.

The jaguar regarded the man with annoyance. But, apparently, it wasn't looking for trouble, but just wanted to be left alone. With an angry growl, it turned and slunk off among the shadows. While Quinto sat watching, it disappeared.

Once again he came slowly, and even tremblingly, to his feet, but he went no more than a few paces before he sank down again beside a rock, giddy with weariness and nauseous from lack of food. He thought to himself that, perhaps, it was useless even to attempt to go farther tonight, especially with the potential danger all around him — and, besides, where could he go? It would be folly to reënter the jungle in the dark, and yet it was only by means of traversing the jungle that he could once more leave this accursed valley. Then the thought washed over him. Fallon and his party! They could not be more than a few hours' trek ahead. If he continued due east toward the plateau, he would surely locate their camp. Like them, Fallon and his party had been traveling due east toward the plateau. If he struck out in that direction — and he couldn't lose it in this moonlight — he should be able to encounter their campfire.

With renewed hope and vigor, he set off toward the plateau, its great bulk looming black and flat far above. It was closer now, he realized — he could not be more than a mile from it. He had no fear that Fallon would turn him out, and Ramón would be with him. As difficult as it was for him to trust any man, he *did* trust Fallon after the way he had cared for Ramón and the kindness he and the others had shown toward them both.

Quinto paused suddenly. Had he heard a gunshot somewhere off to the left? He had, and now he advanced more cautiously over the rocks, becoming aware also of yells and shouts not far away. He came to a full stop, trying to puzzle this out, his heart pounding wildly. Then, at a hurried pace, he proceeded forward. He was almost under the looming wall of the plateau now. He hesitated. Had that been a party of men running silently by the cliff wall but a moment ago? What had been those shouts and cries he had heard, and which had now ceased?

He proceeded more slowly. There! Was that the shadow of a man ducking behind that huge boulder? In his present danger, there was not much he could lose by investigating. He had no gun, but there was a long-slanted hunting knife at his belt, and this he drew and edged forward toward the great boulder.

As he worked around it, a hand shot out and grasped his wrist. He fought wildly, but in an instant the dark form of a tall man confronted him and twisted the knife from his grasp. Then he was thrown back against a boulder — and a voice said: "You! What the devil are you doing here?"

The moonglow fell on the man's face, and Quinto straightened, staring at him. "Don Weelbur," he whispered.

"How the devil did you get here, man? You left us on the other side of the mountain."

"Ees not Ramón steel weeth you, *señor?*"

"Don't tell me you have been following after Ramón!" Then he looked wildly about. At any moment, the Quivaris might reappear.

"No, *señor,* Don Esteban de Ferrar forced me to come."

"Is Ferrar with you?"

"No, I escaped from heem only thees night. But he ees here een the valley."

Tennington looked downtrail. Fallon would be there. It was best they join him at once. He could get the rest of Quinto's story later. "Come on!" he snapped.

At that moment a gunshot crashed out down the trail, and Tennington spun around. "Chris!" he gasped. Wild yells followed. In an instant, a mob of yelling savages pounded around a bend in the trail and surged toward them.

It was too late to run. Tennington swept Quinto against the

side of the massive boulder and, placing his back against it, grasped his rifle by the barrel like a club. Then the Quivaris swarmed in about them, and he brought the weapon down viciously. It cracked across a warrior's head, and the man went down. Evidently, the warriors now had orders to take the escaped captives alive, for, though they tried to close in, they made no attempt to wield a weapon.

Another man circled in too close, and Tennington brought the heavy rifle down like an axe. Mingled with the resultant crack of wood on bone was the sound of splintering as the stock split in half under the blow. Then there was a gasp from Quinto as a warrior lunged and seized him.

Tennington wheeled viciously, blindly, smashing the warriors from his path with his clubbed rifle as he sought to beat them off. Then a spear-butt descended on his skull, and he fell among the sprawled forms of his downed enemies.

What followed was for Quinto like the embodiment of the worst nightmare from his past. He was knocked unconscious and remained so for a long time. When he awoke, it was to find himself bound, a prisoner in a dank cave. It was the cave of the skulls, but he did not know that, since there was no light. His thirst was great, and his hunger only further weakened him. Sir Wilbur Tennington was also a bound prisoner. In their isolated imprisonment, the two men talked, and Quinto told the Englishman of all that had happened since with Ramón he had left their party. Tennington narrated to Quinto all that had befallen them since Ramón had rejoined them. Quinto was heartened to learn that, apparently, Ramón had been able to escape the Quivaris, as had Marcelina O'Day, Luis Valera, and, quite possibly, Chris Fallon, since, had any of them been recaptured, they would likely have been brought to this cave.

Eventually, some Quivari warriors came in, one of them carrying a torch. The feet of the prisoners were untied. Then, their hands still bound in front, they were guided bodily forward out of the cave and away from the village. The sun was shining. During their transit Tennington found the Quivaris no longer were wearing their Incan ceremonial raiment. The procession was led by Cadika whom Tennington recognized and, of course, Quinto did not. Somehow it had not seemed to concern the Quivaris greatly where Quinto had come from, since no effort had been made to question him at any point in his captivity.

Once the procession halted, the hands of the prisoners were untied, although each was quickly held fast by a warrior on either side of them. Cadika stood alongside, regarding them both. Quinto looked about dazedly. More Quivaris, men and women, were gathered behind them in a large group. Off to the left loomed the plateau wall, about which were trees and bushes. This was a beautiful park-like scene, and yet somehow unreal.

Quinto felt himself pulled forward now by the two warriors who were holding him. They brought him to the brink of a great gulf in the ground, and there below he saw a pool of water in a rock-sided hole and in the center of the pool was a great, flat rock on which sprawled a gigantic crocodile of such proportions that he thought he must be dreaming. Then he was hurled over the brink of the gulf. As he plummeted downward, he thought, somewhat idiotically, that this was the same sacrifice that had been intended for him once before, that it had only been delayed.

Chapter Nineteen

The sunlight slanted down thinly into Chris Fallon's eyes as he opened them. He tried to lift his head, for it was lying on a rock, but the ensuing pain the movement edged into his head where it had made stunning contact with the rock was excruciating. He felt that part of his skull gingerly. Oddly, there was no blood, but there may have been concussion. He must have been unconscious for hours, since the sun had long since risen. He also appeared to be none the worse for the experience, insofar as he could tell, except for the painful headache.

He slowly drew himself upright. Near and slightly under him lay the cold body of the Quivari warrior who had fallen with him. The warrior's neck had been broken. Fallon shuddered, stepped away from the body, and looked up and around him. Apparently, as seen now in daylight, they had plummeted into a pit about twenty feet or more deep and about a yard and a half in diameter at the bottom, widening out toward the top.

He saw immediately that the way this pit must be shrouded in darkness by night had been what had saved him from detection, as none of the Quivaris had seen him and their own warrior topple into it. He also saw that the sides of the pit were absolutely unscalable. If the sheer, smooth regularity of the walls had saved him from broken bones in falling, they also now prevented him from leaving the pit. Speculating about what might have happened to his companions during the time that had elapsed while he had been lying here unconscious brought another awareness, of the need for action, no matter his physical condition.

He began to examine the pit. His immediate concern must

be to get out of it, and at the moment that seemed quite impossible. He stopped suddenly, his fingers running over the lower wall — the side facing the plateau towering above. The side of the pit here seemed to be conglomerate — as though a number of sizable rocks had been wedged into an opening and hammered in tightly, then mortared shut. Excitement gripped him. It appeared now that there had been an opening in the wall of the pit at one time — an opening sealed up by human hands. How or why this had been done did not concern Fallon at the moment — he only knew that it might present a means of escape.

He set to work prying with his fingers at one of the tightly set rocks. The mortar had rotted over the years and fell away easily. But then the futility of this procedure struck him as he realized that, perhaps, no one person could pull these rocks out by hand. Still, if it were possible to loosen even one, the others should come easily. He picked up a good-size stone and began battering at the wedged rocks. Presently, one loosened, and he was able to pull it out with his hands. He found the other rocks about it were thus loosened, and he began to work feverishly, tearing out the rocks until he had bared an aperture about a yard in diameter.

Then he searched about till he found his Colt where it had fallen. Holstering it, he returned to the opening he had excavated and thrust his head into it — but it was pitch blackness inside. Apparently this was a tunnel, sealed up by men in some long-gone age for some mysterious purpose of their own. He found his match box hanging from his belt. He struck a match and held it high to illumine the interior of the tunnel or cave. All he could see to either side and above were stone walls and ceiling, and ahead only darkness.

He crawled in and stood up — the tunnel was broad and high — and took a few tentative steps ahead. Then his match flame guttered and went out. He stopped, hesitating, not wishing to waste another match. He took another step — then stopped again, for far ahead, and on a level high above him, he could see a patch of daylight. He paused for a long time, and presently, as he had hoped, his eyes began to adjust to the darkness, and he could see that he was at the foot of a long, straight, crude flight of steps leading up to the daylight far above. The tunnel simply slanted sharply upward at this point, and it appeared to Chris that the rough, ascending steps had been hewn from the living rock.

He started as swiftly as he dared up the steps and long afterward, it seemed to him, he stepped out on barren, rocky ground. For a few moments he was puzzled as to his surroundings, then the startling answer washed over him. He was on top of the plateau. That rough stairs had been hacked laboriously up at a slant as a means of reaching the plateau perhaps six or seven hundred years before, and heaven only knew how many hours of labor had gone into its creation. The Incas must have sealed it up at both openings after the Spanish invasion to insure that no surprise attack could be launched through it. The top sealing, however, had long since caved in and lay in a litter of rocks and broken mortar on the steps beneath. But this was, at least, the top of the plateau, and he had probably found the only means of gaining access to it.

He moved slowly away from the opening and began to walk across the plateau about a hundred yards to the edge of the wall. There he paused at the brink, looking down. Heights had never troubled Fallon. He looked at the mountain they had crossed so laboriously, the jungle below, and far off to the right was even visible the clearing before the Quivaris' caves. And in all the country below he could see no sign of moving life. He stepped back from the brink and was moving away when he stopped in his tracks at a thunderous roar directly ahead.

He moved about, but at a cautious pace now. The sound seemed to have come from behind a bulge of lava not far away. Then he halted in his tracks — the author of the noise had stepped up into view on the ledge of lava — and it was such a creature as Chris had never before seen. It must be an unknown breed of jaguar now extinct elsewhere. It was larger than an ordinary jaguar, but that it was allied to the jaguar there could be no doubt, for he could distinguish, even from here, the dark, ocellated markings like a water-color pattern on the sleek and gleaming coat, similar to that of the black jaguar common to the jungles. But this was a hardier upland creature and somewhat more massive of build and proportion above the forehocks, through the chest, and about the shoulders, and it appeared to have no neck whatsoever, the head being almost sunk between its great shoulders. Behind the shoulders, it tapered down to a lean, hard abdomen and lithe, powerful legs. Its tail was rather short and atrophied. Its skull, flat and wide, was ugly and primal, and its wicked, slitted green eyes suggested a minacious ferocity. But the most outstanding feature by far, even in comparison to the tremendous size around the anterior, was the two curving fangs projecting downward from its boned upper jaw. These fangs, inches long, were more like tusks, gleaming, white, and sharp.

Fallon, staring at the massive creature, was too astonished to be afraid as he speculated on the genesis of the feline. It was, perhaps, only a form of jaguar bred to the upland, and hence its odd proportions, but there was another explanation that seemed more likely to Fallon. The build and musculature of this weird cat conformed somewhat to conceptions of the saber-toothed tiger, that long-gone and fearless carnivore that had once roamed the entire world in a bygone age and that must have been the terror of the mammal world. It occurred to Fallon that the saber-toothed tiger had, indeed, once roamed this part of South America and that it might have cross-bred with the ordinary forest jaguar, originating the evolution of the hybrid species which now faced him. Or it might even have been that the original saber-toothed tiger had, in actuality, been allied to the jaguar, and it had not altered quite so much in this odd example of prehistoric survival. Whatever the case, Fallon was certain he was facing a creature from the dimly shrouded primordial past — a creature that somehow still flourished in this lost plateau country.

So engrossed had he become in this random contemplation that the beast's sudden movement and wicked snarl almost made him jump. His hand went automatically to his Colt, but, as he was slowly drawing the gun, the strange cat turned and bounded off the lava ridge, disappearing behind it. Chris held his Colt, oddly cognizant of the futility of such a weapon against such a monster.

He began cautiously to circle the ridge and came out beyond it just in time to see the great cat's graceful hindquarters loping out of sight behind a ragged buttress. Fallon promptly set off sharply to the south, quite away from the direction the cat had taken.

Fallon was not thinking of how he might descend again from the plateau now that he had attained it. He was not even thinking of his companions' possible predicament. For the moment, he was most interested in exploring this plateau that had for so long been inaccessible. He continued south and found the top of the plateau — in this direction — as barren and rocky as the country immediately below it. He had to ascend rocks, circle them, jump them. Abruptly he halted on the brink of a chasm and looked downward. It was very narrow and almost filled up with rubble, apparently from that great avalanche of long ago, or a series of minor avalanches over a period of many years.

It came to Fallon that this might well be the gorge spanning the edge of this plateau and the fortified cliff city that had been blocked when the Incas had loosed a landslide and destroyed the connecting bridge to seal off Haucha from the pursuing Spanish *conquistadores* of which Fernando García had been the only survivor. At any rate, the gorge was in this direction and, if the ruins of Haucha were, indeed, located atop the spiring adjacent plateau, he should be able to see some indication of it if he climbed high enough on this side.

His physical condition was not good, and his head still throbbed. However, he turned northward where there was a rise which, with some difficulty, he was able to climb. When he arrived at the top, he halted. About a half mile across on the adjacent elevated plateau he could plainly see a wide, level series of gray, ancient buildings. Sight of these dwellings here reminded him of the ancient deserted cliff dwellings on Navajo mesas he had seen in New Mexico and those, in turn, reminded him that Spanish *conquistadores* of old had crossed the southwestern United States under the command of Hernando de Soto and had stormed one of those cliff fortresses, and that the Navajos living there had loosed an avalanche of rocks upon them from above when they attempted to ascend the cliff wall, killing and maiming many, so that the Spaniards had been compelled to retreat. This Peruvian tableau had not been all that different.

He started immediately in the direction of Haucha, descending into the gorge. It took him nearly an hour to make the descent down rugged terrain and across the gorge before he stood at the base of the cliff on the other side. Looking up at this rugged wall, he saw that there would not be an insurmountable problem in ascending it. It was steep, but irregular.

It was then that he thought of his companions, and especially of Marcelina, whom he had not seen since she had saved

221

his life outside the village of the Quivaris. With a guilty shock, he recalled the danger his companions had been in, and now he realized the time that he had spent so far had been wasted when he should have been locating the others. He turned quickly to retrace his steps, but, before he could take very many paces, he came stock-still.

Now two of the saber-toothed jaguars were about five yards distant, and from the look of them they had been stalking him across the gorge and up to the cliff. There might have been an animal strategy to this, for he was now cornered against the face of the far cliff. His mouth went dry. His Colt was ready, but he knew it wouldn't do much good. Against creatures of this size a pistol shot would produce only an infuriating pain. Fallon looked frantically about. Retreating right or left would be futile.

Then he looked up. The cliff didn't appear very scaleable at this point, but, providing that the cats didn't charge immediately, he might be able to reach a point of safety to which they could not so easily ascend. Holstering his Colt, he grasped a spur of rock with his free hand, located a foothold, and pulled himself up about a yard. With a low snarl, perhaps thinking the prey would escape, one jaguar charged. Fallon half turned, drew and leveled his Colt, and fired. He missed, but, fortunately, the noise of the discharge, echoing deafeningly among the rocks, brought the cat to a stop.

Fallon continued his ascent while the two cats watched, snarling angrily, but apparently hesitant to charge up after him. Then the second beast bounded forward, in two long graceful leaps reaching the base of the cliff, and a third leap carried it upward. Desperately, Fallon grasped at a stony projection over his head and hauled himself up, so that the cat's bared upreaching claws missed his feet by inches, but in the sudden effort he had to drop his gun in order to use both hands, and it clattered downward over the rocks and fell out of his reach.

The saber-tooth jaguar, its leap spent, fell back, but it and its mate now stalked restlessly about below, snarling horribly as they stared up at their prey.

Fallon, heaving his weight upward on the projection, found a broad ledge of rock within easy reach of his fingers, and he pulled himself up to this and stood, he thought, beyond their reach. It was a foolhardy notion. One of them sprang suddenly upward, falling only inches short of the ledge. Fallon would not have believed such a huge cat could have sprung so far, and he now realized fully its power. He knew that another such leap might prove his finish, and he quickly looked up for a means of farther ascent, only to see that there were no more handholds or footholds in reach. He was trapped on this ledge. Below, one of the cats seemed to be preparing to spring again.

A hasty and frantic glance about discovered several sizable loose rocks lying on the ledge where they must have fallen from above. He hastily scooped up one about the size of a football and, lifting it above his head, pitched it at the feline just in the act of springing. The cat, struck hard on a great shoulder, was spun off balance by the hurtling weight and bounded off to one side. Unhurt, but now enraged to a degree precluding any hesitation, the maddened beast sprang again, and this time the curved talons closed over the lip of the ledge where Fallon stood. For a moment the beast clung there, then began pulling itself up, its hind claws scratching and raking against rock.

But Fallon was not idle. No sooner had he released the one rock than he was wheeling about in search of another. Lifting one twice the size of its predecessor, he staggered over to the brink of the ledge with it, just as the jaguar was in the act of drawing itself up over the edge of the lip rock. The great black-velvet paws with their horny claws strained into the rock to support its great weight, then the flat, snarling head reared up, and the cat shifted for the final thrust of energy that would carry its tremendous forequarters safely onto the ledge. It was at that moment Fallon, standing on the very brink with the rock poised high above his head where he had exerted all his power to elevate it, hurled the weighty missile with his strength behind it down onto the saber-toothed jaguar's skull.

There was a sickening sound of crushing bone and brain, and then the blood-spattered rock bounced away, and Fallon saw the hideous pulp that had been the cat's head. For just a moment longer the jaguar clung by reflex action to the ledge; then it pitched backward and toppled downward to land with a solid thud on the floor of the gorge yards below.

The other saber-tooth leaped away just in time to miss being struck by its falling mate. Then it bent over, sniffed the corpse, made a plaintive sound deeply in its throat, and now looked up at Fallon, its baleful eyes almost disappearing in the crinkling flesh of its muzzle as its gleaming, tusked jaws parted to voice a deep and vindictive roar. Fallon glanced hurriedly about, only to realize with a shock of terror that there were no more rocks nearby large enough to inflict any more such damage. His knife, too, would be useless, but he drew it. Then there was no more time to consider the matter because the saber-tooth's body was bracing for a leap that would carry it to its mate's killer.

Chapter Twenty

Perhaps by now Abdullah Simbel realized that Ferrar's mind had begun to totter as a consequence of the ordeal of this excursion and the man's frantic outrage over Marcelina's deception. He had executed one Indian guide at Ferrar's command, and would have finished Quinto the previous night, had he been able to overtake him. But, if he had acted in these instances from the inflexible loyalty he had to Don Esteban, he did not feel that the demand for such wanton butchery was anything that could really have any rational justification.

On the other hand, for Abdullah the outrage over Marcelina's betrayal could be salved only by the girl's death. Once they overtook her, there was little, he thought, that would give him greater satisfaction than to break her neck. But he suspected that here Ferrar, however angry he might be, would ultimately be inclined to show mercy because Marcelina, after all, was his only niece, and he had always loved her, even if only from afar. It was, in fact, the love Ferrar harbored for Marcelina that, despite even what she had done to him aboard the *Sea Queen*, continued to inflame Abdullah's jealousy of the only living person, other than himself, who mattered to Don Esteban. Abdullah realized that Don Esteban had stripped naked the girl's soul — he had said as much — but, somehow, in spite of this, in spite of her betrayal, the don still loved her. It would have been better, indeed, had Don Esteban stripped her body and ravished her and found her wanting, than what had happened, because the kind of love Don Esteban bore for Marcelina was for her soul — which Ferrar had dared to seduce — and in this, in Abdullah's mind, rested the greatest threat to the exclusiveness of his own relationship with the don.

The morning after Quinto's escape from their camp, Abdullah and Don Esteban forged on toward the plateau in the same direction the Quechuan had fled. After a couple of hours, as they topped a rise of land, Abdullah signed with his head to signify a halt. He gestured toward the base of the plateau, now plainly visible, and Ferrar saw the cave dwellings of the Quivaris.

"Aborigines," Ferrar observed. "Tribal natives. Perhaps we can . . . ah . . . persuade them to help us."

They pushed on toward the village, Abdullah in the lead and Ferrar behind, the latter now muttering to himself. As they neared the caves, Ferrar raised his hand, and he and Abdullah flattened themselves behind a spur of rock. From this vantage point Ferrar was able to scrutinize the cave village through his binoculars. Because the Quivaris had removed their ornamental Incan regalia of the night before, they appeared to Ferrar as a mere group of savages whom he surveyed without vital interest.

Yet, Ferrar did see some activity around one of the caves, and he realized that two prisoners were being brought out, each being dragged between two natives. The Spaniard surmised that the captives were probably two from Tennington's expedition, and his curiosity was aroused over the possible fate the Quivaris intended for them, since they were being led somewhere. He beckoned to Abdullah, and the two of them now struck out cautiously across the rocky terrain, at an angle away from the village but in the same direction that the party of Quivaris was taking which seemed to be toward a weedy area to the south, paralleling the plateau wall.

It was not long before these two, keeping at somewhat of a distance and obliquely taking every advantage of concealment offered by rocks, saw the natives and their prisoners vanish into a wooded grove. Toward this they made their way, both now with ready rifles and advancing with caution. As they neared the grove, the terrain was far less broken and rugged. Once they had attained the first trees, Ferrar paused to listen. He could hear the natives muttering somewhere among the thickets and trees ahead. Crouching low, they continued forward, using as a screen a series of low brambly thickets that grew thickly where the shade of the trees had not shut off the sunlight.

Abdullah, towering over Ferrar, was able to gaze over the top of a thicket, and then bent back down quickly. He glanced at Ferrar and pointed ahead. Following the direction of Abdullah's finger, the Spaniard parted the bushes and peered beyond.

There, scarcely ten yards away, a great round pit yawned in the ground, and gathered at one side of it were the natives and their prisoners. Ferrar's feverish eyes widened.

"Tennington," he rasped, "and that damned Indian guide who got away from us."

This statement did not leave Ferrar loudly enough to reach the ears of the Quivaris, and it was at this moment that two of the warriors pitched Quinto off the brink into the pool. Ferrar scarcely noticed him, or the hollow splash as he struck the pool. His eyes were fixed on Tennington. He then looked at Abdullah, slowly and somewhat vacantly.

"Why, they can't kill Tennington," he said softly. "He's mine!"

As he said this, he lifted his rifle, swinging it to a level and firing somewhat hastily at the Englishman.

Tennington was staring dully at the pool as Quinto disappeared below the surface of the water. He had finally given up hope, believing that Chris Fallon must have been killed when the Quivaris had charged last night. Fallon had certainly not been taken and that could only mean he was dead, and, of

227

course, Marcelina, Valera, and Ramón had been left to wander, lost in this Peruvian wilderness, until sudden or lingering death claimed them. And now he would follow Quinto, being hurled into the pool, food for the great crocodile.

He was possessed by this resigned state of mind when the shot rang out close by, and one of the Quivari warriors holding him pitched forward with a slug through his head. Ferrar, in his haste, had obviously missed his target. The other Quivaris behind and around Tennington hesitated only for an instant, then began to scatter. Tennington was swift to react. He swung about, driving a fist into the stomach of his one remaining guard, who was perplexed as to how he should react. The blow decided him. The warrior went down, doubled in agony, releasing his distracted grip on the prisoner.

One other had not fled at the gunshot. This was Cadika. He had been standing by the edge of the pit watching the sacrifice, and now he whirled about, drawing his knife and swinging it viciously at Tennington. The knife cut a gleaming arc through empty air as the Englishman nimbly dodged, and then he came up, his fist swinging hard to connect terrifically with Cadika's jaw. The chief was hurled back off the brink, his scream splitting the silence as he plunged downward, only to be choked off in the waters of the pool as he struck with a terrific splash.

Tennington watched what happened below from the edge, rather than seeking cover for himself from whoever had fired that shot, believing that it was most probably one of his own companions. Quinto had apparently plunged to the depths when he hit the water, which was very dark and deep. Then he had shot up again to the surface, glancing about to get his bearings. The crocodile had slithered off the rock when Quinto had hit the pool, but when, seconds later, Cadika plunged in beyond the Quechuan, it was after *him* that the gargantuan reptile went. Cadika had hung onto his knife and with this he engaged the creature as it reached him. The great maw yawned and closed, and in the water there was suddenly a twisting, bloody froth, whipped around by the crocodile's mighty tail and the struggling chieftain.

Ferrar and Abdullah had by this time emerged at the edge of the pit on the north side, and Tennington felt a shock of surprise at seeing them. "Throw Quinto a line!" he shouted across at them.

Ferrar's eyes narrowed musingly. "Why? I wanted him killed last night in our camp!"

"You damned fool!" Tennington shouted back. "He's the only one who can get us to the top of this plateau. He knows the secret way. Haucha is on the other side!"

Ferrar seemed amazed by this lie, and it spurred him to action. "Abdullah," he commanded, "drop a rope to that savage."

The big Negro put down his rifle, unslung his pack, and produced a length of rope which had been earlier employed in climbing up and down the mountain. He presently dropped one end down into the pit, holding the opposite end and bracing his great form to take the weight of the Indian.

"Quinto!" Tennington called to the Quechuan in the pool. "They're dropping a rope. Over there! Swim for it!"

The battle between the crocodile and the Quivari chieftain had ended by now. Quinto, keeping afloat in the pool, looked up as he heard the Englishman, and then around to the north side of the pit where Abdullah had lowered the rope. Only last night this giant man had intended to kill him. Now he was holding a rope. Death, if he remained in the pool, was certain. He had escaped from Abdullah once before. Perhaps he could again. It was a chance, at least, a better chance than he had if he stayed in the pool. He started swimming in the direction of the rope.

At first, although he was able to grasp the end of the rope, his arms were too weary for the task of pulling himself up hand over hand. Once Abdullah saw this, he began pulling up the rope himself, using his great arm and shoulder muscles, while Quinto could, at least, cling effectively to his end as the rope was drawn up.

Tennington, taking his dazed former guard in tow, was able to work his way around the pit's edge to where Ferrar and Abdullah were located while Quinto was being lifted up the wall of the pool. Keeping a hammerlock grip on the warrior, the Englishman was close by when the Quechuan was dragged over the lip to lie, sprawled and exhausted, breathing very hard, at Abdullah's feet.

Ferrar faced Tennington and the Quivari warrior with his rifle leveled at them.

"Wait," Tennington said. "Wouldn't you spare me, too, if I found the treasure for you?"

Ferrar's eyes coalesced with unstable thought. Tennington was confidently poised despite knowing that his life now depended solely on Ferrar's whim.

"You said this Indian knows the way," Ferrar said, still holding the rifle, referring to Quinto. "That's why Abdullah fetched him up here. I was all for killing him last night and wouldn't have minded in the least leaving him down there with that crocodile. Now, you say *you* know the way. Which is the truth, *inglés?*"

"Quinto understands the dialect of the Quivaris. This man, who is now my prisoner, cannot be understood by either the two of you or by me, but Quinto can speak to him and tell us what he says. I know that the Quivaris, probably centuries ago, sealed off the passage leading to the top of the great plateau. Beyond that plateau is the gorge between it and the mountain city of Haucha."

Ferrar was listening intently, his eyes traveling to the

Quivari warrior being held, without resistance now because of fear of Ferrar's thunderstick, and then over to Quinto who was pulling himself to his feet.

To the surprise of the Quechuan, Abdullah reached forward and helped steady him on his feet.

"Granted you speak truly," said Ferrar, "you have still given me no reason why you should remain alive. We now have this damned Indian guide back, and the Quivari is covered by my rifle."

"And your niece . . . Marcelina?" Tennington asked.

"What about her!" Ferrar demanded abruptly, rage coming suddenly into his eyes.

"You may feel you have a reason for hating her," the Englishman argued quietly, "but you have no idea how it broke her heart to have to deceive you, nor do you know how she has suffered for it."

"Has she been killed?" Ferrar asked, his voice and manner, quixotically, arched by abrupt concern.

Abdullah remained silent, but his eyes gleamed fiercely at mention of the girl's name.

"No, Don Esteban," Tennington said, "she is still alive, but in great danger from the Quivaris."

"Do they hold her a prisoner?"

"No. She eluded them last night when Quinto and I were taken."

Ferrar's glance turned to the Quivari warrior, then to Quinto, who was still trembling slightly but had recovered his breath. "You, old man," Ferrar commanded, "ask this savage what has happened to Marcelina?"

"He doesn't know, I'm sure," Tennington interrupted. "Ask him, instead, about the passage to the top of the plateau."

Quinto did so, but Ferrar's voice overrode his as he demanded of the Englishman: "Is Marcelina on the plateau?"

"I do not know," the Quivari answered Quinto.

"She may be," the Englishman told Ferrar.

"This man says he does not know," Quinto said.

"Abdullah," Ferrar rasped.

The giant reacted at once, grabbing the warrior out of Tennington's grasp and lifting him physically from his feet with his hands at his throat.

"He must tell us," Ferrar snapped at Quinto.

The Quechuan repeated the question to the gasping warrior.

"Don't kill him . . . !" Ferrar ordered. "Not yet."

Abdullah lowered the warrior, but kept his mighty hands locked around the man's throat. Ferrar pushed his rifle forward, aiming it toward the Quivari's right thigh, and fired. The man issued a scream of agony, twisting, trying to break Abdullah's hold, but he was held fast. The bullet had only grazed the man's leg.

"Repeat the question," Ferrar ordered Quinto as he aimed his rifle again, this time toward the man's genital.

Quinto's voice quavered when he asked again the way to the top of the plateau.

Tennington was sickened by this desperate violence but knew he must say nothing.

"No! I cannot . . . !" the warrior screamed. "The fire god will destroy any desecrater of the sacred heights!"

"What did he say?" Ferrar demanded.

Quinto repeated what the man had said.

Ferrar looked now over the edge, down into the pool at the bottom of the pit. He turned back to Quinto. "Either he tells us now, or Abdullah will feed him to that crocodile."

Quinto repeated what Ferrar had said. Somehow the Quechuan appeared to have drawn courage from what was happening.

"I will lead you," said the Quivari hastily.

Abdullah released the warrior, who fell to one knee, his hands going to the blood oozing from the bullet crease along his right thigh. Ferrar turned his rifle first on the Englishman and then on Quinto.

"Abdullah leads with this savage. You two follow. I shall be behind all of you. I will kill anyone who tries to escape!"

An implacable determination hovered above those words. Tennington assumed that Marcelina O'Day had for the moment slipped from the Spaniard's mind. He expected Ferrar to bring her up again, but he didn't.

Abdullah coiled the rope, stowed it in his pack, shouldered the pack, and took up his own rifle. Then they struck south along the cliff wall, traversing a well-worn trail which led beneath towering shade trees. The Quivaris might well be watching them from concealment, but, in view of what had happened to their chieftain and, more recently, to the warrior who was now a prisoner, it was a silent surveillance. Tennington presumed they would know better than to interfere.

Chapter Twenty-One

Although the actual time that had elapsed was much less, it seemed to Quinto, who was half starved and physically exhausted, that weary hours and miles had passed since they had left the crocodile pool. Tennington, too, was nearly spent as a result of the ordeal over the last two days. The Quivari's bullet-grazed thigh was bleeding slowly, and, although he was leading the way, followed by Abdullah and Quinto, he had taken to stumbling. Ferrar, who was behind Tennington, cared nothing for the physical condition of the captive and had refused Tennington's suggestion that they should pause at least long enough to attend to the warrior's injury.

At last the Quivari halted and pointed toward the rock wall. There, a tremendous cleft split it from top to bottom, a splitting induced by some long-subsided convulsion of the terrain.

"There trail," he said.

Quinto translated.

Ferrar nodded and motioned with his rifle. "Tell him to go ahead."

"No," the warrior said in a wailing, fearful tone. "You find the way without. . . ."

Quinto got as far as the first word in his translating when Ferrar interrupted. "Tell him to keeping moving, Quinto, or this rifle will speak and send him more swiftly to his gods than they could seize him."

Quinto repeated what Ferrar had said. The warrior by this time was apparently so weak that he lurched and almost fell. Abdullah with one hand caught him by the right shoulder and forcefully propped him up. Then he shoved the man forward.

Limping unsteadily the Quivari led them between the towering walls down a narrow and rugged pathway where those following all stumbled repeatedly over the rough-edged stones littering the fissure's floor.

They hadn't gone very far when a cry from behind apprised them of a new danger. A party of Quivaris that had evidently been following them clandestinely had seen where the party was going and apparently the threatened desecration of a sacred place had given them a courage to attack that had been lacking since the encounter at the crocodile pool.

"Hurry!" snarled Ferrar from the rear.

The warrior at the front almost plunged to his doom for, as he sprawled over a boulder, he landed on the brink of a great rift in the ground. The rift was not deep, but it appeared to be filled with mire. Presently they all had bunched up at the edge of the rift. There was enough light in the fissure to see that the rift extended to the looming walls on either side, and that it was all of a half dozen yards across to the opposite side.

"Was bridge," said the warrior. "It has fallen away."

"What did he say?" Ferrar demanded.

Quinto repeated what the warrior had said.

"What is that?" asked Abdullah.

"Appears to be quicksand, old fellow," replied the Englishman dryly. "And we can't cross . . . wait! There is one hope."

"What?" snapped Ferrar.

The cleft was particularly wide at this point, and Tennington pointed toward the wall on the right of the rift. There, clinging with tenacious, gnarled roots to the very brink of the rift, was a dead tree — the only vegetation, apparently, that existed here, having once somehow found nourishment in this now sterile gulf. It was very tall, and it had been dead for a long time. The outermost roots overlapped the edge of the rift and thrust out into space. Due to the lack of support on that

235

side, the tree inclined outward, leaning far over the gorge of quicksand.

"That's our only chance, Ferrar," Tennington said. "The other choice is to stand and fight with the quicksand at our backs."

They looked back. The warriors were coming forward now, shouting triumphantly, as they must have known that those they pursued would be stymied by the quicksand. They were not coming slowly, either, for this terrain was native to them, and they were fresh and carried no burdensome packs or rifles — only their long, stone-bladed spears and knives. Instead of clamoring laboriously over obstructions, they were leaping from one rock to the other, like mountain goats, and were closing up the intervening distance with astonishing rapidity. The meaning of Tennington's words struck all of them at once. In a second Tennington had taken over command to which Ferrar voiced no objection.

"There's only room for one to fell the tree," Tennington snapped. "Abdullah, you're the only one who can do it. Put your whole weight into it, but, when it falls, get ready to jump back fast, or, when it goes, it may take you with it."

Abdullah, accustomed to obeying only Ferrar's commands, hesitated a moment and then, putting down his rifle, took his place against the great tree. There he braced his huge body, thrusting against the bole of the giant tree with his hands and shoulder. The muscles rolled and tensed beneath his skin. His forearms swelled until it seemed that the titanic power of his effort must burst his arteries. His face was contorted. His teeth were set tightly. Sweat began to pour down his rugged face.

Ferrar, facing the rear now, fired at the pursuing Quivaris. The shot went true. The foremost warrior collapsed. The others slowed, while Ferrar aimed and fired again.

A little earth crumbled away at the edge of the rift and sifted downward in a thin stream, fraying into yellow dust as it fell. Then about the roots of the tree the ground proceeded to break and rise in little mounds. The wood creaked agonizingly under the efforts of the big Negro. There were several sharp, dry snaps and cracks, then, with a slow yet gathering impetus the once-proud forest giant toppled, majestic even in its collapse. With a terrific crash and splintering of dead branches, it fell across the gulf, spanning it neatly, the top resting securely on the opposite side.

Ferrar had felled another of their pursuers and for the moment had stopped the onward rush.

"Hurry across," called Tennington. "And don't look down. Keep your feet balanced but your eyes before you."

Abdullah had fallen forward with the tree when it toppled. Now he lay on top of the trunk. He rose, picked up his rifle, and staggered across slowly, stepping safely off on the other side.

"One at a time!" exclaimed Tennington. "An extra ten pounds of weight may cave it in. Don't forget, the base is just resting on this side."

Quinto went next, then the warrior, prodded by Ferrar's rifle, then Tennington. As Tennington leaped off safely on the other side, Ferrar set his feet on the log. The tree had easily sustained their weight this far. Would it bear the final weight? Now that the shooting had stopped, the Quivaris had resumed their pursuit and had almost caught up to them.

As Ferrar was moving across, the earth around where the trunk rested suddenly crumbled. Ferrar halted uncertainly, balancing himself with his rifle. Tennington beckoned frantically for him to come on. Ferrar did. Then the whole section of the bank where the trunk rested collapsed, and the trunk slipped. The Spaniard was halfway across by this time. Had he remained on the tree, he might have been able to get to the other side safely, but instead of doing that he flung himself forward, hoping by means of this desperate leap to reach the opposite bank. In his panic, however, he misjudged the distance he had yet to reach and struck the quicksand. The force with which he landed immersed him immediately up to his hips. In terror now, he saw that it had been a mistake to let go of the trunk, for the end that fell had only rolled against an outjutting rock on the embankment and the other end still rested safely on the opposite side where the others were waiting for him.

Ferrar frantically dropped his rifle and extended his hands upward, clutching for the trunk. In vain. His fingers barely brushed its smooth bark, and inexorably he was being pulled down in the oozing mire.

The others stared down at Ferrar's predicament in hopeless consternation with the exception of the wounded Quivari warrior who now dashed up the cleft. The Quivaris in pursuit saw Ferrar had lost his thunderstick and a vengeful fury spurred them on. By the time they had reached the brink of the rift they could clearly see Ferrar's predicament. Abdullah lifted his rifle, but Tennington grasped his arm.

"Not unless they try to harm him," he cautioned. "A shot may set the whole mob off." He turned and called: "Don't struggle, Ferrar! You'll sink all the more swiftly!"

The incensed Quivaris, seeing that the other thunderstick was not shooting at them, began now to launch missiles both at those on the opposite side of the gulf and at the helpless Ferrar in the quicksand. The spears hurled at Ferrar were deflected to one side by the tree trunk which was lodged very near to him. He was screaming impotently while Tennington urged Quinto to move ahead up the cleft where their captive had disappeared in order to escape the deadly missiles.

Only Abdullah made no attempt to retreat. He would not abandon Ferrar. He knelt now at the edge of the pit and pumped lead from his automatic rifle into the Quivaris.

Frenzied by the heat of battle, even as some of them fell, others were able to fling spears viciously across at the great Negro. One quartz-tipped missile tore away his fez. Another ripped through the sleeve of his shirt, drawing a little blood as it scratched him in passing, yet by a miracle he was unhurt while he methodically killed three of them and wounded another who staggered blindly forward and pitched off the brink of the trail, joining Ferrar in the quicksand below. Then all their spears were exhausted, and they turned in retreat from this black giant who apparently could not be killed and yet himself had killed with a terrible vengeance. As they pressed backward to escape the fire from his thunderstick, Abdullah brought down another of their number.

As soon as the remaining Quivaris were no longer an immediate threat, Abdullah, without a moment of wasted effort, dropped the rifle and sprang onto the top of the log on his side and ran down the trunk nimbly. The root section on the other side then slid down a little more as the buttress of rock and earth upon which it rested crumbled a little under his great weight, but it did not collapse. In a moment he was poised on the trunk over Ferrar. By this time, however, the Spaniard had sunk down so far he could only gasp for breath, and he had to thrust his face up to keep the mud from getting into his mouth. Yet his arms still flailed wildly, only making his situation worse, as every movement immersed him more deeply in the tugging gumbo.

Abdullah bent down, extending one hand to grasp one of the Spaniard's wrists, and now again the giant black man's tremendous strength manifested itself, for with one Herculean thrust he drew the much smaller man up from the sucking quicksand and safely onto the trunk at his side.

Ferrar was gasping, covered with muddy ooze. It had been a most remarkable feat of strength given the meager leverage

239

Abdullah could obtain from his position, but Ferrar was too shaken at first to say anything and only his dark eyes gleamed his gratitude.

Abdullah then proceeded to lift the Spaniard again, his hands under Ferrar's armpits, and carried him swiftly and securely to the far side. The trunk continued to remain in position, although a sharp cracking sound was heard.

"Where are the others?" Ferrar gasped as soon as he was standing again on firm ground.

"Ahead," said Abdullah, picking up his air rifle.

Ferrar carried his Enfield .38 automatic in a holster with a flap. The surface of the holster and what showed of the gun butt were covered with viscid mud, but the Spaniard unsnapped the flap and took the automatic in his hand.

Still shaken, but obsessed with those who had fled, Ferrar with Abdullah now behind him began stumbling after them up the cleft.

Tennington and Quinto, in the meantime, having taken advantage of this opportunity to elude Abdullah and Ferrar, continued at a rapid pace up the cleft. Tennington expected that they would see the Quivari warrior who had preceded them, but he appeared to have lost no time in outdistancing his captors. Although goaded by urgent fear, both Quinto and the Englishman were finally forced to slow their pace due to their increasing exhaustion and the rugged passage through the cleft.

They stumbled on for perhaps half a mile in silence when it occurred to Tennington that this route they were taking seemed much longer than it should be, if, indeed, it reached the top of the plateau at all. Then he realized from the innumerable twistings of the passage only dimly lit from the narrow opening of the walls at the very top, that this might actually be a very long circuitous route extending the length of the plateau and that they might well emerge at the other side of the plateau it-self.

It was then that suddenly the cleft passage broke out onto a ledge — and below, down a rocky and precarious slope, lay a great basin, an acreage of swamp. It looked very marshy with heavy vegetation, and Tennington realized to his astonishment that this jungle basin — for it did not approach the size or dignity of a valley — was a bowl, perhaps a former volcanic crater, enclosed within the plateau itself. All around it they could see the plateau walls.

Quinto had an anguished expression as he looked at the Englishman. "I am too old now and too weak, *señor*. I cannot endure much more of thees escapeeng."

"It isn't only a matter of escaping from Ferrar or the Quivaris, Quinto," Sir Wilbur replied, somewhat breathlessly. "There is Ramón and the others."

"Let the *muchacho* look after heemself. I tell you . . . I am ver' tired."

"I don't wonder. But you didn't quit the last time you were here. You cannot quit now."

"But, *señor,* I truly want to queet."

"Quinto, we must descend to the bottom of this escarpment and make it across to the far side of this swamp. It is our only hope to regain the top of this plateau."

The man was reluctant, but he did not argue further and followed Tennington begrudgingly down the escarpment. There was an ancient trail of sorts here, used long ago and now barely perceptible. They could only follow it and hope it might be the trail leading across the swamp and back up onto the top of the plateau. At least, Tennington wanted to believe it was, for it was only on the vast and rugged plateau that they stood a chance of losing Ferrar if, indeed, he had survived the quicksand and was now in pursuit of them.

The trail, once they had descended, continued forward beneath towering swamp vegetation, gigantic trees and ferns, and networks of lianas. The terrain was spongy and yielding beneath their feet. They went on, then, the jungle becoming more dense. The ground was soggier beneath their feet, and Tennington now reckoned that the swamp was actually lower as they neared the middle. This was confirmed once they emerged onto the bank of a small lake within the marshland jungle of the basin. The trail wound around this lake, bordering the shore line, and around it they found a profusion of animal and bird life.

There was a large number of tapirs, iguanas, peccaries, and Tennington felt more acutely than ever the hunger pangs in his belly. He was surprised to see a gigantic species of capybara, the largest rodent in the world, an aquatic creature peculiar to the rivers of South America. He soon sighted other mammals, reptiles, and birds unfamiliar to him, and perhaps to Quinto as well, and he began to realize that in this remote arm of the Andes sierra evolution might have been a delayed process for the lower animals while it seemed to have accelerated with human beings, if the puissant race of the Incas had really sprung from a tribe of mountain natives in this region as had been suggested by Cadika. The very landscape seemed one of a bygone age.

Suddenly a bellow ahead apprised them of a new unknown danger, and in an instant they saw a huge creature rear itself up from a thicket scarcely a dozen feet from them. They both recoiled, and, as the animal wheeled about, they saw that it held the twisting, groaning body of the warrior who had guided them to the cleft. In the warrior's hand was a golden knife with which he was striking viciously, but futilely, at his antagonist. Then the monster whirled again and, with a great crashing of underbrush, disappeared with the warrior amid the primeval vegetation.

"What was it?" Tennington asked the exhausted Quechuan.

"I do not know, *señor*."

Tennington thought of the close, full, terrifying view they had gotten of the creature — the long, reddish-brown hair, the tremendous height and size, the bear-like appearance, the very long, curving claws that armed the massive paws, the long, narrow snout like an anteater's — and could think of only one creature in the world that might answer its weird appearance — a creature that hadn't been readily seen since the Spanish explorations of the New World.

"A giant ground sloth," he said slowly to Quinto, responding to his own inquiry. "It is very rare, although I recall now that natives of Patagonia have reported recently that they saw a huge monster answering its description. It wrecked several villages in the sector. They are dangerous and fearless."

Quinto thought with wonder of the little tree-sloths he had seen. Those small, greenish-brown, ineffectual creatures who lived their lives out hanging upside down by long curving claws from the boughs of jungle trees. He shuddered. Truly the world itself seemed to him to be upside down. "But eet was so quiet," he said, "and then that sloth reared up weeth the warrior. How did they both get een front of us?"

Tennington drew a breath. "Unless I'm much mistaken, our erstwhile guide was waiting in that thicket to attack us as we went past. Did you see that knife in his hand? Ferrar or I should have disarmed him. But the sloth must have crept up on him and seized him before we passed. That sloth probably saved our lives."

"*Quizá* the Quivari saved our lives."

"*Quizá*," Sir Wilbur conceded, "perhaps."

Chapter Twenty-Two

From where she had been concealed Marcelina O'Day ran out to join Luis Valera as he and Ramón left the village of the Quivaris in advance of Sir Wilbur Tennington and Chris Fallon. Valera grasped her shoulders.

"Thank God, you're all right, Marcie," he said hurriedly. "Chris wants us to run ahead and hide. They'll join us later."

"But shouldn't we wait?" Marcelina asked.

"They're armed, Marcie. Please, we must go!"

Marcelina fell in behind the archeologist, Ramón bringing up the rear. The moonlight helped light the way, and they actually ran all out until, winded, Valera slowed them down to a rapid walk.

"If we get too far ahead," Marcelina said, breathing heavily through her mouth, "Chris and Sir Wilbur will never find us. Hadn't we best find some place to hide and wait for them?"

"You may be right," Valera agreed.

Presently they stepped off the trail behind the cover of some boulders. Unwittingly, however, they had forked off the main trail and onto another, and, pausing here, it was, indeed, unlikely that their companions would be able to locate them in the darkness.

And wait they did, for a very long time, and any noises from the pursuing Quivaris eventually ceased and only the sounds made by nocturnal creatures could occasionally be heard. It was Ramón who finally suggested that they must be lost.

"In that case," Valera responded, "we have no choice but to wait until daybreak. In this moonlight, we might see well enough, but all the trails look alike."

"I have my pistol," Marcelina said, trying to be reassuring. "I do hope nothing has happened to Chris . . . and Sir Wilbur."

"It is best if we remain silent, Marcie," Valera said, "and listen."

Accordingly, they tried to rest, although rest came hard to all of them. Ramón was the first to doze off, then Valera, and finally Marcelina. But it was Marcelina who awoke early, rather suddenly as the sun topped the great plateau. She crept away to seclusion where she could attend to herself, and, when she returned, she awoke Valera and Ramón.

Cautiously they stole out from where they had been hiding with Marcelina in the lead. She backtracked for a distance, convinced that somehow they had lost the right trail, and she was not long in finding their way back to the trail from which they had deviated during the night. They found that, since the main trail continually ran along the foot of the plateau, they would not have lost it at all had they simply followed the cliff wall. Valera was chagrined at himself, but Marcelina affirmed that it was not a matter for blame. She did suggest, however, that they might now backtrack some distance along the main trail to see if they could find any trace there of Chris and Sir Wilbur. If they didn't, then they might best continue away from the Quivari village, which was certainly the direction Fallon and the Englishman would have logically taken.

Marcelina remained in the lead as they passed carefully down their back trail, and it was not long before they came upon the blood of the warrior Fallon had shot. It was spattered all over the ground where he had fallen. While Marcelina and Valera were studying the blood stains, Ramón came up and touched the *señorita*. Marcelina turned to him, and the boy pointed now into a deep, sheer pit at the bottom of which lay the corpse of another Quivari warrior, distended awkwardly.

Peering down into the pit, Marcelina said very softly:

"There appears to be an opening of some kind down there . . . could it possibly be a tunnel?"

Ramón was excited. "Do you not see it, *señorita?*" he asked in Spanish.

"See what?" Valera asked, also standing now at the edge of the pit, looking into it.

"Chris and Don Wilbur must have been overtaken by the Quivaris here," Ramón told them. "There was a fight . . . as seen from the blood. One of them probably wrestled with that Quivari, and they fell together into the pit. The Quivari must have been killed in the fall. Whoever was down there with him, *Señor* Chris or Don Wilbur, would not be able to scale the sides of this pit without help. Fearing capture, he must have crawled into that tunnel down there. It is the only way out of the pit."

"I think the boy is correct, Marcelina," said Valera.

"Do you think Chris is still in that tunnel?" she wondered. "We don't dare call down to find out."

"Perhaps the tunnel leads elsewhere, *señorita,*" Ramón suggested, "and, if so, we may find *Señor* Chris or Don Wilbur by following it."

"The boy may be correct, Marcelina," Valera agreed.

"If we lower ourselves down there, *Tío* Luis, we may not be able to climb out again."

"Let me go, *señorita,*" Ramón volunteered. "I am small and do not weigh very much. You and *Señor* Luis could help me get back up, if the tunnel leads nowhere."

"Just how do you propose we do that?" Valera asked.

"The same way I would get down," Ramón answered impetuously. "You, *Señor* Luis, must hold onto the *señorita*'s ankles as she lowers herself over the side. Then I shall climb down over you as if you were a rope."

Valera could not help laughing, but Marcelina was inclined to take the boy's suggestion seriously. In the event, however,

Ramón did not use the professor and Marcelina as a rope ladder, but, instead, was able to climb unassisted about half the distance down into the pit and then leap the rest of the way. Should he need to climb out, that would be soon enough for the means he had proposed.

Once on the floor of the pit, Ramón reported to the two standing above that, indeed, the Quivari was dead, and then that the tunnel did lead far inside and in an upward direction. Marcelina and Valera agreed that they should descend into the pit to see where the tunnel led. It was possible that both Fallon and Tennington had taken it. Valera lowered Marcelina over the side. She had weighed about a hundred and five pounds in San Francisco and probably less by now. As Valera, holding onto her wrists, let her down slowly, Ramón was able almost to touch the soles of her boots. Valera had to tell the boy to stand aside, after which he let go of Marcelina, and she landed agilely, able even to keep to her feet without falling over. Valera followed her somewhat more clumsily.

"He must've taken the dive head first," Valera said, examining the dead Quivari. "Neck's broken." He glanced toward the tunnel. "I suppose we'd best go."

Now with Ramón in the lead, they moved gingerly, crawling on their hands and knees into the dark tunnel. Glancing up, Ramón, as Chris Fallon before him, could see that, far above them, there was a speck of daylight, indicating an exit.

"*Señorita y señor,* I do believe this tunnel leads up onto the plateau," he said excitedly to the two behind him.

They were eventually able to move up the steps slowly, gropingly, and finally they emerged into the bright sunlight at the surface. Once they were all standing together, they could look around across the barren, irregular flats, but could see no sign of a human being or any other life.

"There is a rise toward the north, *señorita,*" suggested the boy. "Perhaps from there, we can see more . . . perhaps where the others have gone."

Marcelina and Valera agreed, so they scrambled over the rocks toward the summit of the mild hillock, in the opposite direction to that Chris Fallon had taken. Once on the rise, they were able to scrutinize intently the vast surrounding landscape. Below them the rise veered sharply down. It seemed to be a great, circular bowl in the center of which there was a jungle marsh and what, in the distance, seemed to be a tropical lake.

"Señorita!" said Ramón, looking directly down on the cliff wall below them. "I thought . . . something moved . . . down there." He pointed toward a visible ledge perhaps halfway between where they stood and the bottom of the bowl-like basin.

Valera shaded his eyes with his hands and peered below. "I don't see anything."

"I caught a fleeting glimpse," Ramón insisted.

"There seems to be a way down this side to the ledge," said Marcelina. "Perhaps we should go down to see if anyone is there."

Ramón once more led the way, followed by Marcelina and Valera. It took them several minutes to make the descent, but, as they neared the ledge, it did seem to be deserted. The ledge was narrow where they encountered it, and so they had to remain in single-file. As a result it was Ramón who saw Abdullah Simbel first, as the giant stepped out of the opening of a cleft and stood, blocking the trail.

"Come forward, *querida mía*," Marcelina heard Don Esteban's voice, and then she saw him, standing behind Abdullah, the Enfield in his right hand.

Ramón did move forward hesitantly, Marcelina behind him.

"My God, Ferrar!" exclaimed Luis Valera. "How did you get here?"

248

By this time they were all able to stand in the somewhat wide mouth of the cleft.

"My loving niece provided me with a map," Ferrar said.

The Spaniard was covered with drying mud; even his face was smudged with it. Abdullah stood back slightly, and he was still carrying his burdensome pack on his back. In one hand he held his air rifle.

"I don't believe you," Valera said.

"We are here, are we not?" the Spaniard countered suavely. "How else . . . were it not for my dear Marcelina?" He regarded his niece. "You certainly are a sight, my heart. I trust you haven't lost your virginity, traveling with these animals! A most touching scene." His tone was close to a sneer.

"I have not lost my honor, *tío mío*," she said softly.

"I dislike correcting you, my dear," said Ferrar, "but your clothes are as filthy as your honor." He was suddenly enraged. "You shall be whipped for what you have done . . . whipped as your parents never whipped you!"

Ramón did not know who these men were, but he had come to love the *señorita* and did not want anyone to whip her. There was, he thought, only one chance to protect her. Ferrar was now closer to him than Abdullah. If he could subdue Ferrar and disarm him before Abdullah reached them. . . . He lunged suddenly forward, and, catching the barrel of Ferrar's automatic, he wrenched it savagely out of line. The unexpectedness of this action, and Ferrar's proximity, made the maneuver momentarily successful. Ferrar shouted in surprise, but did not relinquish his grasp on the weapon. Abdullah, seeing Ferrar's predicament, in almost a single motion dropped his rifle and moved in. Younger, more wiry, if scarcely bigger or stronger, Ramón was able to take advantage of Ferrar's somewhat weakened condition and, because the man's foot slipped, was actually able to drive Ferrar to his knees. Abdullah, however, was

249

on the boy in a moment, and, seizing his lithe body with his big hands, he swung him aloft, intending to hurl him down the face of the precipice. It was then that Marcelina fired.

Chapter Twenty-Three

Sir Wilbur Tennington and Quinto were around the small crater lake and again into a marshy area, keeping as much in the open as they could to guard against being surprised by ambush as had happened to the Quivari warrior who had stalked them. The cliff wall was much closer to this side of the lake than was the cliff wall on the other side. They both heard what sounded like a distant gunshot. Tennington paused and listened, but there were no further gunshots.

"Ees eet Ferrar?" Quinto asked, looking back toward the cliff down which they had climbed into this jungle marsh. Only the very top of it was visible, and jungle foliage, to say nothing of the distance, prevented any clear view of the ledge onto which they had stepped at the end of the cleft.

Then the sound of three more shots in quick succession carried to them. Again there was a pause, followed by firing from a heavier caliber rifle.

"There's fighting back there, Quinto" Tennington said. "We simply have to push on now. If Ferrar escaped the quicksand, you may be assured he'll be in pursuit. That firing is far away. If it weren't for the stone walls of this cañon carrying the echo, we probably wouldn't even be hearing it."

"*Sí,*" agreed Quinto, "but eet came from back where we were."

"Let it go," insisted Tennington. "We sha'n't go back to find out about it."

They resumed their trek forward toward the cliff wall. Quinto was now stumbling, almost falling, repeatedly. The Englishman realized the Quechuan needed rest, and he, too,

251

before the two of them did collapse from exhaustion. But they didn't dare stop. If Ferrar and Abdullah had escaped the quicksand and the Quivaris, they would, as he had told Quinto, surely be in pursuit. If Ferrar had died in the quicksand, and Abdullah had been killed in battle with the Quivaris — perhaps that battle was the gunfire they'd heard — the make-shift bridge they had used in the cleft had certainly not been destroyed, and the Quivaris would be able to cross over as readily as they had.

The Quechuan was probably too weary to comment further. His pace was ragged, and yet, somehow, he was still able to move ahead.

Tennington, who was in the lead, could presently make out something very like a trail leading up the face of the cliff. It seemed to have been cut at an angle along the cliff wall, a rough jag on the perpendicular wall, like a continuous ledge leading from the bottom to the top. Unless he was mistaken and although it appeared badly eroded now, the Englishman reckoned it must have been laboriously hollowed out by primitive hands centuries ago, possibly by a race of cave-dwellers antedating the Incas, perhaps by the primordial progenitors of the Incas. When they attained the bottom of the cliff wall, the man-made trail actually turned out to be about five feet wide — quite a feat for antediluvian engineering.

As they began the ascent, Tennington found he had to support Quinto, which he did by taking an arm. Despite the Englishman's assistance, however, the Quechuan finally collapsed on the trail.

Quinto looked with a wan smile at Tennington who was bending over him.

"You must go on," he gasped softly. "Alone you may escape."

Tennington didn't trouble to answer him. Grimly he

stooped, lifted the Quechuan in his arms, and, staggering himself now, continued up the trail. Not once did he look down at Quinto, but only ahead. Yet Tennington, too, was very near exhaustion, and carrying Quinto's weight on the rough upgrade forced him to stop frequently to rest. He would look off then, across the jungle marsh, trying to make out anything to be seen on the opposite wall, but it was too far away, and no movement attracted his eyes. Quinto remained silent until, following the final pause, he insisted on trying himself to make the last several yards to the top.

When they reached the end of the trail at the top, Quinto sprawled heavily. Tennington looked out again across the landscape to the other side, his face glistening with sweat. The noonday sun, at its zenith, streamed down in torrid heat on their bared heads.

"We'll stay here for now and rest," Tennington said, sitting down beside Quinto, his back against a boulder. "We'll keep a lookout. If Ferrar comes, we'll see him in plenty of time to push on."

It was just as he leaned his head back that the earth began to tremble. He didn't move, nor did Quinto. They sat, their hands pressed onto the ground on either side of them, as if they were in suspension. There was no thinking, no urge to escape. Instead, they were very nearly holding their breaths, waiting until the awful tremors would cease.

Marcelina O'Day did not aim the bullet to hit her uncle, but it ricocheted off the rock surface very close to his right hand which held his Enfield. She turned swiftly to Abdullah, aiming her pistol toward him.

"Stop!" she said sharply. "Put that boy down. He hasn't hurt Don Esteban!"

The gunshot was so unexpected that Abdullah hesitated,

even as he held Ramón aloft, ready to hurl him over the side.

"Abdullah!" Don Esteban shouted frantically. "Savages! They're in the cleft! I just saw one!"

Abdullah acted quickly then, ignoring the stern Marcelina's revolver. He set Ramón down hastily, and at once the boy struggled away. Don Esteban had rolled over onto his stomach now, his automatic aimed at the interior of the cleft. He fired three snap shots.

Abdullah retrieved his rifle.

"Marcelina!" shouted Don Esteban "Leave here at once!"

It was, under the circumstances, an act of extraordinary generosity, but Marcelina did not think of it at all . . . then.

"Ramón," she called, and turned.

Luis Valera had been watching in some amazement all that had been happening. His first inclination was to stay and fight, so he hesitated.

"*Tío* Luis . . . move!" Marcelina's blue-gray eyes flashed.

Valera turned and began making his way swiftly up the ledge pathway. Marcelina was right behind him. Ramón came quickly behind her.

Abdullah now fired a shot down into the cleft.

Ferrar got to his feet.

"We have to drive them back!" he shouted. "We have to drive them back down and across that tree, and then seal them off. That bridge must be destroyed!"

The Spaniard was frantic, but Abdullah could see the necessity quite clearly in what he had said. Ferrar dashed into the cleft and Abdullah, leaving his pack behind but carrying his rifle, followed.

The Quivaris, realizing they were being pursued by men with thundersticks, turned tail and ran as quickly as they could downward into the cleft. They had reached the trunk spanning the quicksand before they stopped, congregating before it. The warriors had taken time to retrieve their spears where they could. Slowly, cautiously Ferrar and Abdullah pressed down the cleft after them.

The sun was nearly overhead now, and enough of it did shine down into the cleft so there was even better visibility than there had been earlier. Ferrar stopped in his tracks as he saw the Quivaris grouped on this side of the tree trunk. He fired a shot down into them, and it unnerved the warriors again. They began crossing over the trunk to the other side of the quicksand.

"Kill them!" Ferrar screamed, and fired his automatic again.

One of the warriors who had not yet leaped onto the tree trunk swung back his arm and hurled his spear at Ferrar. It was a well-aimed cast, and the spear hit Ferrar in his right thigh. He went down in pain, firing his automatic for the last time. There were no more bullets left in his clip. He dragged himself again to his feet, reaching down and yanking out the spear. Then he turned to flee. Abdullah had not been able to get a clear range, being hindered by Ferrar in front of him, and so he had to try now to step backward quickly.

Encouraged by Ferrar's sudden flight, the few warriors who remained on this side of the tree trunk decided to give chase. Two had only golden knives but felt the time to use them had come. Abdullah had made an about-face and was hastening back up the cleft. Ferrar, completely panicked, was stumbling and screaming, but the two Quivaris with the knives were on him in moments.

The other warriors, seeing the turn the battle had taken, began crossing back over the tree trunk. Again the rooted side of the trunk slipped, and one of the warriors with a howl fell off into the quicksand.

Abdullah saw the two warriors swarm over Ferrar and with a

deep, booming bellow he sought to fight his way to the Spaniard's side. But now a Quivari with a spear rammed it forward, and the Negro received the thrust in his left side. His bellow ended in a cough, but that was all. Apparently unfazed, he clubbed his rifle and knocked sprawling the warrior who had speared him. Then, dropping his rifle, he picked the warrior up by his feet and swung him up into the narrow cavity of the cleft above them so that his brains were dashed out against the rock walls.

More spears were being hurled at Abdullah then as he turned his attention to the warriors with knives who had lunged at Ferrar. He plunged into their midst with a stentorian roar, carrying them and several warriors behind them across the fallen body of Don Esteban. It was too close for a rifle or for the casting of spears. Abdullah drew the great machete from his belt and brought it down against the two warriors with drawn knives. One man's head was lopped off by the blow, and the blade, not slowed in the least in its lethal path, went on to cleave the other man from his left collarbone clear down to the center of his chest.

Then another warrior lunged in as Abdullah withdrew the machete with a terrific yank and stabbed the giant before he split his skull open. All of them were after him now, but Abdullah slaughtered them like sheep swarming to the block. Although he was covered with blood from the innumerable wounds they inflicted, his gigantic form still stood erect among the mashed and bloody corpses of his enemies.

Those who did not fall at last turned and fled. Ferrar, by what must have seemed a miracle, was still alive, although mortally wounded. He called for Abdullah to come to him. One Quivari had got up sufficient courage in the face of the rout to come back and lunge at the black man with a drawn knife, but Abdullah brushed the weapon aside, dropped his machete, seized the man, and broke his neck with a single twist of his hands.

Abdullah then stooped over where Ferrar lay, but his bloody eyes were rolling almost blankly, his great form being jerked by tremors, his great hands reaching out, as if in supplication, toward Ferrar.

"Abdullah," gasped the Spaniard. "At least . . . Marcelina . . . is . . . safe."

But Abdullah was no longer standing firmly. He would never stand firmly again. That first spear thrust had found his lungs, and now the inevitable result had come to pass. He swayed. A gobbet of bloody foam spouted from his mouth before he fell like a downed oak.

It did not matter any longer to Ferrar. His eyes had closed.

Chapter Twenty-Four

It was with unrestrained eagerness that Marcelina O'Day, Luis Valera, and Ramón set off at a rapid pace toward the top of the cliff wall, stumbling occasionally over steep and jagged stones. They had heard the gunfire behind them and were sure there was a pitched battle between Ferrar and Abdullah and the Quivaris. When they attained the top of the rim of the basin once more, it was Valera who suggested that they had best head south by southeast. The plateau undulated in that direction, but they could scarcely return by means of the tunnel through which they had come, and they had no desire to remain with Ferrar and Abdullah.

Ramón took the lead, feeling proud of the way he had come to the *señorita*'s aid. Marcelina and Valera walked abreast behind him. Their pace was brisk, but they were not jogging.

"Tell me, Marcelina," Valera asked in Spanish, looking sideways at her, concern in his eyes, "do you really believe your uncle will try to hurt you for what happened . . . should he overtake us again?"

"My grandfather was a very stern man. My mother told me that he often whipped both of his children . . . to the bone, she said . . . even after they had entered adolescence. Yes, I believe he meant what he said . . . but that is not why I fired that shot near him."

"No, I do not think so."

"I did not want Abdullah to murder Ramón who has harmed no one, least of all my uncle. I probably have a whipping coming for what I did to him."

"Marcelina, you aren't being fair to yourself. Your uncle had no right to ask of you what he did. Do you remember what it was Cortés said? . . . 'the Spaniards are troubled with a disease of the heart for which gold is the specific remedy'."

"Yes, *Tío* Luis, I remember he said that . . . but it is more with *Tío* Don Esteban. He regards Sir Wilbur as an interloper . . . and, I fear, you and Chris as well."

"And you?"

The question brought a smile to her face — the first one Valera had seen in days with this girl who had always seemed so fundamentally blessed with the joy of life.

"Perhaps not," she replied, "but what he has in mind to give me . . . as you well know . . . is something other than a share in any gold he finds."

"Perhaps Don Esteban is in great danger back there."

"I am not certain. I think Abdullah could probably defeat the entire tribe of the Quivaris without much help from anyone. You saw how strong he is. And he loves my uncle. I am sure he would give his life for him."

"Then you do not think there is a chance the Quivaris will get past them and continue their pursuit?"

"I do not know. But should *Tío* Don Esteban overtake us again . . . no matter what he does to me in anger over the way I betrayed him . . . for he is of my family, and what I did to him *was* wrong and deceitful . . . I shall never forget that this day he saved my life . . . perhaps the lives of all of us."

They fell silent then and doggedly proceeded ahead, becoming weary from the ardors of the crossing in the thin air. It took what seemed to them a very long time before they approached the far end of the plateau, but it had not been actually so long.

Back in the cleft the Quivari warriors were trying to lift Abdullah's massive body to transport it across the fallen tree trunk that passed over the rift of quicksand. Ferrar's body had already been carried across. Sir Wilbur Tennington and Quinto had just reached the top of the far rim of the basin.

It was Ramón who saw it first, across a great gorge, the massive stone buildings appearing gray-green in the sunlight.

"Is that Haucha?" he asked, pausing. Marcelina and Valera stopped, looking ahead across the gorge.

"*Sí*, Ramón," Valera said, relieved and excited by the sight of the lost city of the Incas. "I am certain it is."

"Oh . . . ," breathed Marcelina, "after so many centuries . . . !"

And then they clambered over a huge boulder. The gorge now yawned before them, and the sight that met their eyes made them hesitate.

A black jaguar of unheard-of proportions with great tusk-like fangs was prowling about at the bottom of the gorge, growling horribly as it stared upward. Another jaguar, its skull crushed, sprawled nearby. On a ledge not many yards above the baleful beast crouched Chris Fallon. For a moment, Valera had the illusion the figure in Inca ceremonial garb was a Quivari warrior, but Marcelina recognized him at once and cried out his name.

The giant cat was in the very act of springing toward the ledge where Fallon prepared helplessly to repulse the attack. Marcelina's cry did not halt the beast, but it was then that the terrible tremors in the earth began. Marcelina and Valera were knocked from their feet by the powerful, chaotic vibration, while Ramón fell forward, grasping a boulder to steady himself. The giant cat froze and then let out a scream, clinging to the ground. The force of the tremor was too much for Fallon's precarious footing on the ledge. He was flung flat on his belly on the ledge. As soon as the long tremor passed, the saber-tooth wheeled and raced away, bolting in fright, clearing great boulders before him like a scared rabbit.

Back in the cleft the warriors carrying Abdullah's corpse across the trunk, two on each end, being balanced precariously as it was, were shaken off, the root end of the trunk crashing down after them into the quicksand.

"Chris . . . are you all right?" Marcelina called over the gorge, having picked herself up from where she had been thrown.

"Yes!" Fallon shouted back. "Are you all right?"

"Yes!" Marcelina called back. "What was it?"

"The volcano most probably," said Valera, also having recovered himself.

"We are steel alive," Ramón informed Fallon, calling across to him.

Ramón, Marcelina, and Valera worked themselves down their side of the gorge. Fallon abandoned the ledge he had been on and arrived at the bottom of the gorge more quickly than the others.

Ramón ran up to Fallon where he stood. He was smiling. Marcelina followed him. Quickly and spontaneously she clasped Fallon in a welcome embrace. Valera was smiling as he came up.

"Ferrar's here," he said, somewhat out of breath.

"Where?" Fallon asked, still holding Marcelina to him.

"He very nearly caught all of us when we got to the top of the plateau," Valera said.

"I theek we got up the same way you deed, *Señor* Chris," Ramón said.

For a time, then, they stood together at the bottom of the gorge, telling each other of their various experiences.

"Have any of you seen Tenny?" Fallon asked.

Marcelina said: "I hope the Quivaris haven't captured him again. We thought you would be together."

Fallon explained how he and Tennington had become separated, and added his fear that perhaps by this time the Englishman might be dead.

"Never!" cried Ramón. "I weel find heem. I do not beelieve he ees dead."

Chris shook his head. "We can't be sure of that, Ramón." He thought it almost strange, the loyalty the boy seemed to feel for the Englishman despite the way Tennington had sometimes treated him.

Ramón said fiercely: "Don Weelbur had good reason for all he say to me. Upon heem ees great responsibility. I failed to drop the rope when the great birds attacked you, *Señor* Chris. I know now I put the extra burden on Don Weelbur with my unwanted company . . . on all of you. Eef few words of kindness have passed hees lips, there ees no greater among us than Don Weelbur. I am proud to be with heem."

Fallon did not wish to argue the point. "We've got to know, anyway," he said. "If Tenny *is* alive, the place to find out is the Quivari village. First, we have to get back our rifles and packs. Then we'll be in a position to bargain. And this may help us." He walked over and picked up his Colt from where it had fallen.

Valera and Marcelina went over to examine the dead sabertooth.

"What kind of jaguar do you suppose this is?" Valera asked.

Fallon briefly gave his impression of the beast's origin. Then he glanced up toward the city on the cliff above them. "There's the end of our trip."

"Rather a costly success," Valera commented, "when Sir Wilbur may be. . . ."

"We'd best be going," Fallon interrupted. "Marcelina . . . do you think you'll be up to going back?"

"Chris . . . ," she began quietly, and her blue-gray eyes

flashed what was left unsaid.

In a few minutes, Ramón in the lead, they had again topped the near side of the plateau, and at the edge they hesitated momentarily, looking about, again wary of danger that could come from so many directions. The air had become pungent — an unpleasant pungency — and the sky was actually darkening. Fallon thought at once of volcanic smoke and looked off in the direction of Pahatahala.

It was Ramón who cried: "Look! Do you not see a movement . . . there? No, directly to the north . . . there." He pointed to the near rim of the basin.

Fallon glanced in the direction Ramón indicated. "What is it you saw? . . . exactly?"

The boy could not restrain his excitement now. "Let us go see. Eet ees . . . perhaps . . . Don Weelbur."

Fallon looked at Marcelina and then at Valera.

"He was right before . . . this morning," Valera recalled.

Fallon nodded. "Then let's do as he suggests."

They swerved due north, plodding tiredly along beneath the darkening sky, Ramón still in the lead, Fallon and Marcelina walking almost abreast, and Valera bringing up the rear. No one had said anything, but their insides pained from hunger, and all of them were increasingly dry from the lack of water even though they had previously drunk from the contents of Marcelina's canteen. Fallon had left his canteen behind when he had exchanged clothing with the Quivari warrior whose ceremonial costume he still wore.

"Just a leettle farther," said Ramón.

"There seems to be some kind of drop-off ahead," Fallon said.

"There is," Marcelina replied. She told him of the jungle marsh they had first seen when they had encountered her uncle and Abdullah and which they had skirted, as probably Chris had, when they had come across the plateau.

"If there's a marsh, Marcelina," Fallon said, "then we'll find water at least, and perhaps something to eat." Fallon's eyes moved up and beyond to one side. "Ramón . . . down! Flat!" he demanded, as he drew Marcelina down with him into a crouch. Ramón ducked, and Valera behind them also dropped down.

"Quivaris?" Marcelina asked in a whisper.

"Possibly," said Fallon. "I'll go ahead and make sure."

But before he could move, the impetuous Ramón, although crouching all the way, went forward the short distance to the brink of the basin. Fallon, angry at the boy's foolhardiness, crept forward after him.

"*Señor* Fallon . . . eet cannot be!" said Ramón, standing up now. "Eet ees my uncle . . . and Don Weelbur . . . I am esure of eet."

He was pointing off to the right now where the two men were still sitting near the rim of the basin.

"Tenny!" called Chris Fallon, standing beside the boy.

The Englishman looked over, his haggard, strained face peering intently at them. Then he was on his feet. "Chris!" he called, his face brightening. "Ramón!"

Marcelina and Valera, having heard what had been said, joined Fallon in following Ramón, as the boy ran hastily across the expanse that separated them.

Fallon shook hands with the Englishman.

"I'm certainly happy to see you again, Sir Wilbur," said Valera, "although I may not be as demonstrative about it as Marcie was when we met up with Chris."

"Oh . . . *Tío* Luis," Marcelina said, flushing beneath her sombrero.

Tennington smiled rather formally, acknowledging Marcelina's and Valera's presence.

Ramón had rushed forward enthusiastically, and then

paused to stare at Quinto, who was still sitting on the ground, before hurrying over to him.

A good deal of talking ensued, comparing experiences. Quinto got shakily to his feet and joined in the conversation.

Some concern was raised about the earth tremors they had all experienced, as well as the darkening of the sky, although it did seem now to be clearing somewhat.

Tennington nodded grimly. "Have you noticed how rocky and barren this section is? That is lava . . . all of it under our feet. Centuries ago, that volcano must have erupted, and the entire flow of lava was somehow diverted onto the plateau here, and onto the sector down near the caves of the Quivaris. I'm sure these tremors are commonplace."

"You do not think there will be an eruption, do you?" Marcelina asked.

"There might be," the Englishman replied. "We'll see how it goes tonight and in the morning. What we felt may just have been dome-building. It's just one more thing we must worry about."

"The Cordillera Azul has long been known as an area subject to earthquakes, such as we've felt," Valera put in. "The Incas believed that there was a great serpent beneath the ground throughout this entire area. They did not leave behind great monuments to their civilization, as did the Egyptians or the Greeks, but they did leave another kind of imperishable monument. To this day, at places like Pisac and Chincheru, tier upon tier of massive stone terraces built by Incan masons to afford agriculture on mountainsides have survived. Behind these walls the soils were carefully laid in layers to ensure drainage and aeration, and the walls themselves are interlocked by ashlars that are connected in such a way that the walls flex and cohere during an earthquake. In all these centuries, those stone terraces have endured. I'm not saying that this volcano won't erupt, only that earthquakes are commonplace in this region."

Fallon nodded and then suggested, notwithstanding the presence of Ferrar and Abdullah in such proximity to them and the continuing threat from the Quivaris, that they should make camp nearby in a hollow protected by some boulders. Tennington said he would descend again into the basin and bring back water in Marcelina's canteen. It was Fallon's proposal that he backtrack to the floor of the gorge where he had killed the big cat and that he should butcher it on the site, bringing back the meat for a meal. Valera volunteered to accompany him. Marcelina and Ramón would gather combustibles for a fire. Quinto, who was still recovering from exhaustion, would remain in camp until they all returned. Marcelina left her back pack with him. She gave her revolver to Sir Wilbur for what protection it might provide as he descended into the basin.

None of them had ever eaten jaguar meat, but they were all too famished to be particular, and actually, thanks to the condiments Marcelina still carried in her pack, the reactions were generally positive. As evening approached, the sky cleared some more, which, Tennington declared, was a good sign.

The next morning at dawn, pausing only for breakfast (consisting of more tiger meat and some wild fruit Tennington had brought back with him from down in the basin the previous day), Chris Fallon set out across the plateau with Ramón. Fallon planned to go back down the tunnel by which he, and later Ramón and the others, had come up to the plateau, take the body of the dead Quivari warrior, if it was still there, and conceal it in the tunnel, and then they would do their best to close off the entrance from discovery. It was possible that, although the Quivaris may have known about that tunnel at one time, it might have been forgotten. The way it had been sealed certainly seemed to have been done several generations in the past.

Sir Wilbur and Luis Valera would accompany them part of the way back across the plateau. They would then split up. It was Tennington's intention to reconnoiter the passage through which he and Quinto had passed with Ferrar and Abdullah and at the mouth of which Ferrar and Abdullah had met Marcelina and the others before the combat had erupted with the Quivaris. Tennington was determined to negotiate a peace with Ferrar, something, he reasoned, that would be very much to the Spaniard's advantage, given the fierce hostility of the Quivaris and the other dangers in this wilderness terrain. Tennington also intended to make it quite clear to Ferrar that he would not countenance any attempt at reprisal against his niece. He respected Marcelina's feeling that in a sense Ferrar and Abdullah may have saved her life, but he fully intended to let the Spaniard know that Marcelina was, indeed, family and that she must be spared any violence.

Marcelina's revolver had been returned to her by Tennington the previous evening, and, even though it meant that the Englishman would be unarmed when he encountered her uncle, he felt it preferable under the circumstances that Marcelina be able to protect herself at the camp. Quinto, who was feeling better, would accompany the girl back down into the basin to get more drinking water and to collect what edibles they could find. Tennington was careful to warn Marcelina of the dangers from snakes and sloths like the one he and Quinto had seen. Marcelina assured the Englishman that she could run really fast, if she had to. Fallon wasn't pleased with leaving her behind, but less did he want her to accompany Ramón and him, and he certainly did not want another confrontation between her and her uncle until Tennington had had a chance to settle the matters at issue with the Spaniard.

Tennington and Valera returned to camp in the mid-afternoon. Marcelina and Quinto were already back from the basin. The sky was clear, and there had been no new tremors. That was on the positive side. Far less so was what Tennington had to report. On the Englishman's back was the gigantic pack that Abdullah had carried and under one arm he carried the black man's air rifle. The clip in it had still been half loaded and more ammunition for it had been in the pack along with numerous other necessaries and several boxes of the Egyptian cigarettes Ferrar had been accustomed to smoke. The path up the cleft had been found to be empty, and half the tree trunk was submerged in the quicksand. The blood on the floor of the cleft indicated a terrific and deadly struggle had been waged, and Tennington and Valera had concluded that probably both Ferrar and Abdullah had been killed in the course of it. Valera had brought back Abdullah's machete, a golden knife, and a stone-bladed spear that had been found in the cleft. It was Tennington's surmise that the tremor had somehow interrupted the Quivaris in clearing the area and taking back to the village what had been left behind. He did not mention to Marcelina the probable disposition of the heads of the fallen had the Quivaris been successful.

As it was, Marcelina did not weep, but she was visibly shaken, and a sadness came over her that was not wholly dispelled when even Fallon and Ramón returned. They had sequestered the dead warrior — obviously the Quivaris had not known what had become of him — and had sealed up the entrance to the tunnel as best they could. Ramón had claimed the dead warrior's golden dagger as his trophy.

A much bigger canteen had been attached to Abdullah's pack, and Quinto again descended into the basin to replenish their water supply. There was also a half pound of ground coffee and a pot in which to make it. Marcelina and Quinto had been able to find some berries and roots which they had brought back, and these things were added to make the evening meal.

Marcelina remained despondent and quiet that night after they had eaten. Fallon walked with her beyond the camp all the way to the brink of the gorge where, in the clear moonlight and star shine, even from this vantage point they could see the ghostly and silent brick edifices of Haucha. The next day they all planned to venture into the gorge and then up the cliff side to the secret Inca city.

They stood alongside a great boulder. They were both smoking.

"I didn't get to know the man very well," Fallon said, breaking the silence that had stolen between them, "but I am sorry if your uncle was killed by the Quivaris . . . and, although we cannot be sure, it really does seem that he is dead."

Marcelina said nothing for a moment before she replied. "My country has long been so beautiful and so sad. The Incas, you know, called gold the tears of the Sun." She looked up into the sky. "Have you ever seen so many stars?"

"In remote places like this, yes. They are dimmed by the lights of our cities. But here, in addition, we are at a greater elevation . . . closer to them, somehow."

"They all change their positions," she said softly. "Every night a little bit . . . so you can't see it with your eyes one night to the next, perhaps, but you can over time. The Incas did not measure time by the word ages the way we do, but rather by Suns. They called their time that of the Fifth Sun. And they did not want it to pass away as had the Suns of other times in the past. In their most secret teachings they believed it might be possible to stop the flow of Time. To make the Sun remain fixed where it was. To stop the movement of the stars and the planets. It was at the time of the winter solstice that they held a great festival in Cuzco. It was during this festival they believed they could commune with the spirits of the dead. It was during those three days of the solstice, what they called the Capac Raimi, that they brought forth the mummies of past Incas and dined and celebrated with them, as if they were alive again. New warriors were recognized in the military. And . . ." — she hesitated for a moment, as if it were a struggle to go on — "it was then that the priests offered sacrifices to the Sun and to the stars."

"What kind of sacrifices?" Fallon asked.

"You know, Chris, in a way it is possible to judge the sincerity of a people . . . of any people . . . by what they are willing to sacrifice for that in which they believe."

"Yes, I imagine that's true."

"And the Incas wanted to stop Time, to hold it captive, to keep the Fifth Sun in place. Because they so fervently believed they might, they sacrificed llamas, a sacred animal to them, by the hundreds, and made offerings of wheat . . . and . . . finally . . . of children."

"Children?" Fallon inquired, astonished. "I know that the Aztecs wanted to propitiate the Sun and so practiced human sacrifice, but I didn't know that about the Incas. It isn't in Prescott's history."

"No," Marcelina admitted, "it isn't . . . and I'm not sure why it isn't. But at winter solstice, every year, about five hundred children, boys and girls, were buried alive at Cuzco. Nor was that all of it. Emissaries then went forward in the forty directions from Cuzco, representing the forty rays of the Sun, and the many *huacas*, or local gods, of the tribes of the Incan empire. When each emissary reached the end of his path, at the central city or tribe in whose direction he had gone, there was a festival, and a boy or girl of ten would be sacrificed there, by having their living, beating heart torn from their chest, or being

270

strangled to death, and their blood was painted on the faces of the priests and on the walls of the temple and on the faces of the lineage *huacas* of the tribe."

"My God, Marcelina, to what purpose?"

"Those children, Chris, were themselves to be emissaries. Each *huaca* represented a star in the heavens, and it was believed that to those *huacas* . . . to those stars . . . the souls of the children would return and, once there, plead for the Incas and for their own tribe . . . to plead that the stars should become fixed in the sky and that the Fifth Sun should also remain fixed . . . that Time should stop."

Fallon extinguished his cigarette, and his voice involuntarily trembled when he spoke. "I thought the Spaniards deceitful when they garroted the captive Inca. Now I am not sure it wasn't all for the best."

"For the best, Chris?" Marcelina turned toward him, a tone of accusation in her voice. "To melt down Incan gold to send to Spain to fight the Ottoman Empire? And what of the civilization that has come after them? The civilization that expended thousands . . . perhaps a million lives . . . in the Great War? Those were mostly young lives, too, Chris, young men from all over the world."

"I was in that war, Marcelina, a volunteer in the British Army."

"And you can say something good came from it?"

"I can only hope, Marcelina, as we all hope . . . that it was so terrible this time it will never, never happen again."

"Do you honestly believe it will not?"

"I honestly hope it will not." Fallon paused as Marcelina inhaled one last time on her cigarette before casting it to the ground and extinguishing it. "This whole journey has been one of sadness and death," he said to her then. "I did not tell you . . . Valera and I agreed we would tell no one . . . but you know that big cat I killed and we butchered?"

"Yes?"

"It was a female. And she still had her young inside of her."

Chapter Twenty-Five

Several days passed for them quickly up there on the cliff in the ruins of Haucha. These were days spent in feverish exploration and discovery. Several times Chris Fallon went out hunting with Ramón who, alone, had a distaste for the dead city. The second morning they were in Haucha, in fact, Fallon had walked out beyond the city to glance across ancient fields where Quechuan herdsmen had grazed their llamas and alpacas which they raised for food and later for clothing. A herd of wild llamas was discovered during one of these outings, and wild fruit was brought back from the jungle marsh. Early on they had found an ancient reservoir of cold mountain water, which still flowed, and this they could drink. The sky was never overcast, and they experienced no more earth tremors. They also had no further sight of the Quivaris, but they all knew what to expect should they try to leave the plateau by either of the two ways by which they had ascended.

There was a high state of excitement among them all. Marcelina seemed to recover from her despondency over her uncle's death in her enthusiasm for being able actually to step back in time across four centuries. The Inca ruins were actually a vast sprawling catacomb of mystery to tempt any explorer. They marveled at the huge stone aqueducts. Luis Valera had seen Machu Picchu, and he was well beginning to believe that this ruin might add far more to modern man's conception of Incan culture if only from the outer vestiges of it, for Haucha had been unviolated by man since a plague had wiped out the last of the original inhabitants.

They had found an entrance in the high stone walls sur-

273

rounding the city, and it had been by this means they had entered. They marveled at how perfectly and exactingly the monstrous smooth stone slabs constituting all structures were fitted together. Though they were unjoined by mortar, it was impossible to thrust a hunting knife into an interstice where they were joined.

The very existence of this city, Valera knew and Tennington agreed, would shatter many theories regarding the origins of Inca culture, while it would substantiate others. Within the fortress, they found one-story and two-story gray stone buildings in excellent preservation. Entering some of these, they found a few clay pottery pieces and vessels for water and cooking, and a few lumps of white dusty stuff like lime which were all that remained of human bones, the bones of those who had perished in the plague, dying so rapidly that the Incas had not troubled to bury them. Occasionally they found skulls and whole skeletons in more protected places, still wearing a few small gold trinkets. Marcelina was horrified anew, however, when they uncovered the mass grave of children who had been sacrificed to the Sun, and found their blood stains still discoloring *huacas* even after all this time had passed. More children had perhaps been sacrificed here because of what had happened to these people all that long ago.

They found weapons, corroded knives and swords made of a very tough alloy of copper and tin that the Incas had known how to make. In a metal box in the floor of a deserted building, particularly large and palatial, Tennington found the ancient and rotted remnant of a message card, or *quipu*. The Incas had possessed no written language. Their only means of conveying an unspoken message had been in knotted cords consisting of varied colors — red, white, blue, and brown. Yet by this means they could convey as irrevocable a picture in the mind of the reader of a *quipu* as did a printed page in a book from Europe.

This particular cord, to Tennington's amazement, Valera was able to decipher. The Englishman, having learned how well Valera knew Quechuan and its dialects, was still miffed over his silence when they were captives of the Quivaris, having seemingly to depend on Ramón's inadequate ability to translate what Cadika had been saying. Valera insisted that, since they were going to die anyway, he had not thought it necessary for him to engage in conversation with the chief, especially since Tennington seemed far more adept in dealing with him through Ramón. In any case, he claimed that he was able to read this *quipu* only because he had once had its duplicate translated by the curator of the museum in Lima. It comprised part of an ancient Incan motto, or prayer, to the Sun. Most of this one was rotted away, but the remaining segment began: **Thou who vouchsafest that man shall live in health and peace. . . .**

At the time Tennington had slowly put down the remnant of a *quipu*, after thinking to himself of the vain dreams of men which men themselves destroy. **Health . . .** yet this city had been wiped out by a plague. **Peace . . .** yet the warring Spaniards had wrecked the Incan empire in great part because of its weakening from internal strife.

They explored the silent city, walking between buildings that had once known human voices and had for centuries since known only the silence of the tomb — down avenues that had once known the human foot, now only the byways for scurrying rodents — a city of death and decay and a decadent, vanished splendor. They found the convent of the Virgins of the Sun, and not far from it the Great Plaza.

Although Tennington had long insisted, including in his dealings with Don Esteban de Ferrar, that he was not going to Haucha to find gold, he was somewhat disappointed by the entire absence of any outward wealth. Where were the gold and silver and jewels of Inca legend? Valera explained that the citizens of Haucha, as Incas all over the empire, must have taken what the Europeans considered their "wealth" — save for a few trinkets — and hidden it. He reminded Tennington that it was recorded that the Incas threw their gold and precious stones into lakes, pits, any natural receptacle, when the invading Spaniards had taken to sacking the homes and temples of the People of the Sun, with the result that many of the great hoards of Incan wealth have remained hidden, but he did suggest the possibility that perhaps one such hiding place might be discovered outside of Haucha. It was possible still to see how the great blocks of solid gold that had once lined the main plaza had been torn out, leaving only the stone base, and where the golden cornices on the houses had been ripped off.

"The Incas," Luis Valera concluded in a reconstruction of what must have happened, "anticipated an invasion of Haucha before the plague that finally finished them. Fearing that the Quivaris, ferocious but few, could not stand against an overwhelming onslaught by the Spanish, they tore out all the gold furnishings, all decorative emblems, all valuable jewelry, and undoubtedly hid it in places where we might never find it . . . in a lost cañon, buried under a landslide, or perhaps in some subterranean cavern."

Whatever his disappointment, Tennington could assure himself that the mere existence of this city would be a vast boon to men of research and that his name would forever be associated with its discovery.

It was not too long before they located the palace occupied by the Inca when he came to Haucha. Its great, echoing halls were bare and stripped of ornamentation like the other buildings in the city, and its great gardens were overgrown in tangled jungles, but withal there was a quiet magnificence about it. Tennington found himself musing about how the heart of the

Incan Empire had been so serene, but, of course, Chris Fallon could have told him, had Sir Wilbur only observed it aloud, that this seeming placidity had resembled nothing so much as a natural pool in a wilderness savannah where the surface is perfectly calm and pure, but where in its depths you can see an enormous crocodile that somehow is able to find nourishment in those waters.

When they came to the Temple of the Sun, they found it to be an imposing structure, two stories in height, but with its golden ornamentation and its golden shingle-plates torn off. Yet, once, it must have been the supreme edifice of Haucha, for it was easy to perceive how it had been entirely coated with precious metal where now only the bare, gray stones remained. But it was first when they entered that they had to stop in the doorway, for here was a sight that each one of them would surely carry to the grave. The great interior was golden-walled, golden-roofed, golden-floored, with solid plates of the metal, and lining the walls were golden replicas of Inca royalty. At the far opposite end, imposing over all else, was a gigantic golden disk representing the Sun, with its forty rays of gold radiating out from the circumference. Mentally, Chris Fallon followed along each one of those rays as they stretched out so far, because, as Marcelina who was beside him and who now caught his arm, he knew what had rested at the end of each one of the roads they represented.

All the interior was covered with beautiful engravings of native plants and animals, infinitely adding to the soft metal's burnished beauty. But in the center, basking in the refulgence of the Sun's image was the great climax — the amassed wealth of Haucha.

It lay there in a tremendous heap: vases of gold and silver; unworked bars of silver; golden clothing of flexible beads of the metal; golden dishes and silverware; images of the vicuña, the alpaca, the llama, all worked in solid gold with golden fleece; a gigantic image of the moon in silver; flowers of gold set with emeralds and turquoise and diamonds; ceremonial vessels of gold and silver; golden ewers and jars; golden birds, and countless other works of precious metal and precious stones, and, accumulated there, all the ornamentation they had seen torn from the outer buildings. It hadn't been hidden in the earth, after all.

To see it, to advance to it, to touch it would have been the fulfillment of many a person's wildest dreams. The quantity was unbelievable, especially of gold, gold, gold!

"But how?" Tennington demanded. "Luis, you said they had probably hidden it. Why would they leave it here . . . in plain sight?"

"I think I see now," replied the archeologist. "The people . . . perishing rapidly from the plague . . . had had no time . . . they had run out of time . . . to hide all this wealth in places of total concealment. So the remaining Incas must have hauled all their wealth here to the temple . . . you'll notice that it's open to the sky above the treasure . . . and so they left it to bask in the all-seeing eye of the Giver of Life. It was the best they could do . . . hoping that the Lord of the Heavens would safeguard his own treasure."

Behind all the gold they found a stone altar and the remains of two children who had probably been suffocated in the light of the Sun.

"*Los tesoros del sol,*" Marcelina said in a hushed voice, and then tears of salt came into her blue-gray eyes, and for a long time she could not see.

They also found the skeleton of some mammal — apparently a gigantic cat — off to one side, shackled by a golden collar with a golden chain to the wall. From the upper jaw of the flat skull projected two long, curving fangs, so that Fallon could identify the creature as being of the same species of saber-tooth cat that had attacked him in the gorge.

It was Valera, then, who recalled how Cadika of the Quivaris had told them of the Ones with Teeth Like Knives who had once been the guardians of the Temple of the Sun.

It was in the afternoon several days later when Chris Fallon and Ramón returned to Haucha after a day of hunting, after a big meal that morning of roast wild peccary meat, that they were startled by the sight of a larger group of people than usual about the campfire that was kept burning even during the day. They quickened their pace. Fallon found himself wondering if some of the Quivaris might have found their way up here, but, as they neared the group, he saw the strangers were two white men. A slender, bespectacled gentleman in a sun helmet was talking to Tennington, Marcelina, and Valera. Another wore a leather jacket and the leather cap and goggles pushed up onto his forehead marked him as an aeroplane pilot. But could it be possible? This plateau had hitherto been so isolated from any exploration.

In a few moments Fallon was shaking hands with Dr. Paul Ramsey and Mark Dworski, the pilot. Ramsey, a spritely, tanned individual, was the head of a geological exploration party from the United States. Fallon learned that Ramsey and his associates, who were not here, had been farther inland to examine mountain strata, when they had seen the volcano, Pahatahala, giving off a plume of smoke. Wishing to obtain data, Ramsey and the pilot had taken the aeroplane to fly here, landing on one of the great level pampas a mile to the west.

"We thought we had made a great and new discovery in that volcano," Dr. Ramsey stated. "It would appear that we have made an even greater discovery in this Inca ruin."

"The Tennington party made *this* discovery," Sir Wilbur

corrected him mildly. "It would also appear that you arrived propitiously, as many of our supplies and weapons were taken by the Quivaris, a tribe of local hostiles, and it might just be we couldn't get back to civilization without some help."

Marcelina glanced at Chris Fallon, and tears glistened in her large blue-gray eyes, before turning to the Englishman. "How far do you think, Sir Wilbur," she asked, "we are really away from it?"

Ramsey and Dworski flew out the next day. In another two days Dworski would be flying a Blériot-SPAD S.33 from the Lima airfield, an aeroplane that could accommodate six passengers in the interior of the ship, four actually seated in wicker chairs, while the fifth and sixth would be somewhat more cramped in the rear. Such a seat, however, would be ideal for a boy of Ramón's stature, and Ramón was thrilled at the prospect, whereas Quinto didn't like the idea of going aloft in any kind of aeroplane. The two Quechuans were to be set down near Tacho Alto. Sir Wilbur Tennington, who was financing the chartering of this aeroplane, Luis Valera, Chris Fallon, and Marcelina O'Day were all to be flown on to Lima. Tennington was most anxious to make the announcement of their discovery himself to the world at large from Lima, and Dr. Ramsey had promised him nothing would certainly be said to the press prior to Sir Wilbur's arrival.

Chris Fallon and Marcelina O'Day knew in their hearts that for them the journey would be over when the passenger aeroplane arrived, although Tennington and Valera both intended to return with an augmented expeditionary force, possibly this time by aeroplane, to sort through and catalogue the many treasures of this find. For the present Tennington chose to take with him only the fragmented *quipu* and a single small piece of Incan gold engraved with the face Haucha. The night before the exodus would take place Chris Fallon and Marcelina O'Day realized that not only would these be their last moments in Haucha but more importantly for both of them the last time for many days, and perhaps even weeks, that they could be alone together. It was well after midnight that they stole away from camp. Only Ramón awoke and was aware of their passing, but he said nothing to either of them or to any of the others. Marcelina took with her the blankets she had been using and her pack which was somewhat depleted without them. She did have in her pack her tooth brush, her wash cloth, and soap, and in relative darkness the two of them paused at the cistern long enough for each, sharing these things, to take a partial body bath before venturing out onto the pampas west of the city where Ramsey and his pilot had landed their aeroplane earlier and from which they had taken off again.

What neither had gauged accurately was the depth of their passion or how, once they had cleaved, they would want to remain close to each other and share the pleasure they both experienced, and cleave again, and again. Marcelina's time had passed days before, but, in truth, it would not have mattered greatly to either of them if it had not.

They also smoked and conversed softly about their future together, and for both of them the sense of inner loneliness was gone, replaced now by this most intimate touching of their souls, and the talking — for, truly, they could talk and talk and talk, and never be exhausted in each other.

Fallon could tell from the heliacal rise that dawn was very nearly breaking and that the winter solstice in this latitude had drawn much closer and, somewhat in suppressed embarrassment, they knew they must return to the lost city, or their absence would surely be noticed. They rose from the blankets, seemingly of one mind, but Chris paused, as he looked back toward Haucha.

"Marcelina," he said suddenly, his voice hushed, "I still have trouble understanding it . . . why the children?"

"I was brought up Roman Catholic," she replied, standing beside him. "My parents, as I told you, shall insist I be married in the Church. And I have known since I was very young that there is no greater fear that any man or any woman or any child can have than the fear that God shall turn His face from them . . . that God shall abandon them. Did not even Jesus, who was God become man, feel that fear on the cross when he asked God why He had forsaken him? The Incas feared God would turn His face from them, that the Fifth Sun would vanish in a deluge as had the Suns before it. And God *did* turn his face from them, Chris. They could not stop Time. The pleas . . . even of the children . . . could not stop Time. And God *did* punish them. He sent the Spaniards."

Chris Fallon's dark eyes had formed tears. "And you, Marcelina? Do you believe what that old satyr told King Midas about the best fate for man?"

"Zenophon tells that story, Chris. It is not my story. I believe King Midas should not have asked, and the satyr only answered because he was drunk . . . and, remember, he was a *satyr*." She shook her head ever so slightly. They could see each other more clearly now in the early dawn. "We should not ask. You once told me that life is something where we can know only half the tale . . . or even less . . . ever."

"Marcelina . . . I love you so." He reached out for her where they were standing.

"And I love you, Chris. So there just isn't any more." She did come closer, smiling up at him with her large blue-gray eyes, and her reddish-brown hair in the dawning light seemed to form an aureole about her gentle, beautiful, angular face. She did not embrace him, however, but, instead, raised her index finger and held it before her lips as she spoke very softly, her expression edged with humor. "Scheherezade, too, was a storyteller, but she was wise enough to know the importance of silence . . . when first she saw the early morning sun."

RATTLESNAKE

T. V. OLSEN

The Apache wars took almost everything from Indian Jim Izancho. Now Senator Warrender wants the one thing he has left—his land—and Warrender's Indian-hating son soon begins a reign of terror against the Izancho family. The only man who will try to save Jim is his boyhood friend, Sheriff Frank Tenney. Only Tenney can stop a deadly feud between a white man—who happens to be his father-in-law—and the Apache who once saved his life, a man who has been pushed too far and is now hell-bent on vengeance, a man as dangerous as a cornered rattlesnake.

___4620-2 $4.50 US/$5.50 CAN

Dorchester Publishing Co., Inc.
P.O. Box 6640
Wayne, PA 19087-8640

Please add $1.75 for shipping and handling for the first book and $.50 for each book thereafter. NY, NYC, and PA residents, please add appropriate sales tax. No cash, stamps, or C.O.D.s. All orders shipped within 6 weeks via postal service book rate. Canadian orders require $2.00 extra postage and must be paid in U.S. dollars through a U.S. banking facility.

Name_____
Address_____
City_____ State_____ Zip_____
I have enclosed $_____ in payment for the checked book(s).
Payment <u>must</u> accompany all orders. ❏ Please send a free catalog.
    CHECK OUT OUR WEBSITE! www.dorchesterpub.com

A KILLER IS WAITING

T. V. OLSEN

Will Parry lost an arm in the Civil War, but he finds the strength to carry on with his life, to build a future for himself and his family on a ranch in the Wyoming Rockies. But that bright future starts to turn dark when a shadowy gunman begins shooting at Parry's house. It isn't long before Parry learns the identity of an enemy he never knew he had, a man with a bitter grudge still festering from the war. A man with the cunning of an animal—and the cold-blooded patience of an executioner. Parry knows he'll die if he has to in order to protect his family, and when he looks out into the black night he also knows a killer is waiting.

___4549-4 $4.50 US/$5.50 CAN

Dorchester Publishing Co., Inc.
P.O. Box 6640
Wayne, PA 19087-8640

Please add $1.75 for shipping and handling for the first book and $.50 for each book thereafter. NY, NYC, and PA residents, please add appropriate sales tax. No cash, stamps, or C.O.D.s. All orders shipped within 6 weeks via postal service book rate. Canadian orders require $2.00 extra postage and must be paid in U.S. dollars through a U.S. banking facility.

Name_____
Address_____
City_____State_____Zip_____
I have enclosed $_____ in payment for the checked book(s).
Payment <u>must</u> accompany all orders. ❏ Please send a free catalog.
CHECK OUT OUR WEBSITE! www.dorchesterpub.com

BLOOD RAGE

T. V. OLSEN

Mike Rhiannon's Irish temper rarely slips, but when it does, Alec Dragoman—Rhiannon's oldest enemy—is almost always the cause. Now Comanches have kidnapped Dragoman's daughter, and he will go to any lengths to get Melissa back, even if that means forcing Rhiannon to help him. Against his will—and his better judgment—Rhiannon leads a ragged band against the Comanches to rescue young Melissa. But will Dragoman keep his end of the bargain?

___4500-1 $3.99 US/$4.99 CAN

Dorchester Publishing Co., Inc.
P.O. Box 6640
Wayne, PA 19087-8640

Please add $1.75 for shipping and handling for the first book and $.50 for each book thereafter. NY, NYC, and PA residents, please add appropriate sales tax. No cash, stamps, or C.O.D.s. All orders shipped within 6 weeks via postal service book rate. Canadian orders require $2.00 extra postage and must be paid in U.S. dollars through a U.S. banking facility.

Name_____
Address_____
City_____ State_____ Zip_____
I have enclosed $_____ in payment for the checked book(s).
Payment <u>must</u> accompany all orders. ❑ Please send a free catalog.
        CHECK OUT OUR WEBSITE! www.dorchesterpub.com

DEADLY PURSUIT

T. V. OLSEN

Silas Pine is about to turn fifty. What he wants more than anything is one last chance to make peace with his son, who is marshal in the isolated town of Grafton, Wyoming. But arriving in the middle of a bank robbery isn't quite the way Silas has pictured the reunion. Neither is leading a posse in a pursuit more deadly than bullets.

__4463-3 $4.50 US/$5.50 CAN

Dorchester Publishing Co., Inc.
P.O. Box 6640
Wayne, PA 19087-8640

Please add $1.75 for shipping and handling for the first book and $.50 for each book thereafter. NY, NYC, and PA residents, please add appropriate sales tax. No cash, stamps, or C.O.D.s. All orders shipped within 6 weeks via postal service book rate. Canadian orders require $2.00 extra postage and must be paid in U.S. dollars through a U.S. banking facility.

Name_____
Address_____
City_____ State_____ Zip_____
I have enclosed $_____ in payment for the checked book(s).
Payment <u>must</u> accompany all orders. ❑ Please send a free catalog.

ATTENTION BOOK LOVERS!

CAN'T GET ENOUGH
OF YOUR FAVORITE WESTERNS?

CALL 1-800-481-9191 TO:

- ORDER BOOKS,
- RECEIVE A **FREE** CATALOG,
- JOIN OUR BOOK CLUBS TO **SAVE 20%**!

OPEN MON.-FRI. 10 AM-9 PM EST

VISIT
WWW.DORCHESTERPUB.COM
FOR SPECIAL OFFERS AND INSIDE
INFORMATION ON THE AUTHORS
YOU LOVE.

LEISURE BOOKS
We accept Visa, MasterCard or Discover®.